THE SEA WITCH'S REDEMPTION

SEVEN KINGDOMS TALE 4

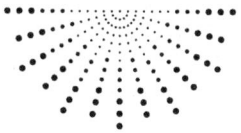

S.E. SMITH

ACKNOWLEDGMENTS

I would like to thank my husband Steve for believing in me and being proud enough of me to give me the courage to follow my dream. I would also like to give a special thank you to my sister and best friend, Linda, who not only encouraged me to write, but who also read the manuscript. Also to my other friends who believe in me: Julie, Jackie, Christel, Sally, Jolanda, Lisa, Laurelle, Debbie, and Narelle. The girls that keep me going!

And a special thanks to Paul Heitsch, David Brenin, Samantha Cook, Suzanne Elise Freeman, and PJ Ochlan—the awesome voices behind my audiobooks!

—S.E. Smith

The Sea Witch's Redemption: A Seven Kingdoms Tale 4
Copyright © 2018 by S. E. Smith
First E-Book Published May 2018
Cover Design by Melody Simmons
ALL RIGHTS RESERVED: This literary work may not be reproduced or transmitted in any form or by any means, including electronic or photographic reproduction, in whole or in part, without express written permission from the author.
All characters and events in this book are fictitious or have been used fictitiously, and are not to be construed as real. Any resemblance to actual persons living or dead, actual events, or organizations are strictly coincidental and not intended by the author.

Summary: She expected to die saving her world—instead, Magna wakes in a strange, new realm. When Gabe finds a wounded woman off the coast of Oregon and brings her home to his best friend, Dr. Kane Field, he has no idea what's in store for them…

ISBN (kdp paperback) 9781717309969
ISBN (BN paperback) 9781078746915
ISBN (eBook) 978-1-944125-34-9

Romance (love, explicit sexual content, ménage) | Action/Adventure | Fantasy (Urban) | Fantasy Dragons & Mythical Creatures | Contemporary | Paranormal

Published by Montana Publishing, LLC
& SE Smith of Florida Inc. www.sesmithfl.com

CONTENTS

Prologue	1
Chapter 1	9
Chapter 2	20
Chapter 3	28
Chapter 4	39
Chapter 5	47
Chapter 6	59
Chapter 7	66
Chapter 8	80
Chapter 9	94
Chapter 10	100
Chapter 11	110
Chapter 12	117
Chapter 13	123
Chapter 14	129
Chapter 15	142
Chapter 16	151
Chapter 17	165
Chapter 18	177
Chapter 19	185
Chapter 20	197
Epilogue	211
Additional Books	228
About the Author	231

SEVEN KINGDOMS/CAST OF CHARACTERS

The Seven Kingdoms:

Isle of the Elementals – created first
King Ruger and Queen Adrina
- Can control earth, wind, fire, water, and sky. Their power diminishes slightly when they are off their isle.
- Goddess' Gift: The Gem of Power.

Isle of the Dragons – created second
King Drago
- Controls the dragons.
- Goddess' Gift: Dragon's Heart.

Isle of the Sea Serpent – created third
King Orion
- Can control the Oceans and Sea Creatures.
- Goddess' Gift: Eyes of the Sea Serpent.

Isle of Magic – created fourth
King Oray and Queen Magika
- Their magic is extremely powerful but diminishes slightly when they are off their island.
- Goddess' Gift: The Orb of Eternal Light.

Isle of the Monsters – created fifth for those too dangerous or rare to stay on the other Isles
Empress Nali can see the future.
- Goddess' Gift: The Goddess' Mirror.

Isle of the Giants – created sixth
King Koorgan

- Giants can grow to massive sizes when threatened – but only if they are off their isle.
- Goddess' Gift: The Tree of Life.

Isle of the Pirates – created last for outcasts from the other Isles
The Pirate King Ashure Waves, Keeper of Lost Souls
- Collectors of all things fine. Fierce and smart, pirates roam the Isles trading, bargaining, and occasionally helping themselves to items of interest.
- Goddess' Gift: The Cauldron of Spirits.

Characters:
Magna: half witch/half sea people. She is Orion's distant cousin on his father's side
Gabe Lightfoot – human – works for the U.S. Fish and Wildlife collecting data.
Dr. Kane Field – human – doctor.
Drago: King of the Dragons.
Carly Tate: Banking Associate from Yachats, Oregon
Orion: King of the Sea People
Jenny Ackerly: School Teacher and Carly's best friend
Dolph: Orion's 8 year-old son from his first marriage
Kapian: Orion's Captain of the Guard and best friend
Coralus: Royal guard & mentor to Orion and Kapian
Kell: Magna's father
Seline: Magna's mother
Ross Galloway: Fisherman from Yachats, Oregon
Mike Hallbrook: Detective for Yachats, Oregon Police Department
Ruth Hallbrook: Accountant and sister of Mike
Oray: King of the Isle of Magic
Asahi Tanaka – CIA Agent investigating the disappearances in Yachats, Oregon
Tonya Maitland – Undercover news reporter pretending to be an FBI agent investigating the disappearances in Yachats, Oregon.

SYNOPSIS

She expected to die saving her world.

Magna's existence was once filled with laughter, love and joy, until a mysterious object fell from the sky into the ocean and she woke to find herself held captive in her own body. As the centuries passed, she became known as the Sea Witch—a creature who is feared and reviled. Her efforts to save the Seven Kingdoms and destroy the alien creature living inside her should have ended both their lives—instead, Magna wakes to find herself in a strange, new realm.

Gabe Lightfoot and his best friend, Kane Field, have stood side by side through thick and thin. Brothers by circumstance, they have seen the darker side of life and lived to remember it. When Gabe rescues a wounded woman in the waters off the coast of Oregon, they have no idea what's in store for them.

PROLOGUE

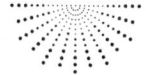

Centuries Ago:

Magna lay on the soft sand in the secluded cove that she, along with her cousin, and their best friend had found and claimed as their private fortress when they were younger. She released a contented sigh and stared up at the stars. It was truly a magical night. A warm breeze swirled around her, and she dug her fingers into the sand.

"Do you ever wonder if there is anyone else in the world besides us, Orion?" she asked, letting the sand trickle through her fingers

"I don't know. I suppose so," he murmured.

Orion gazed morosely out over the water. She turned her head to look at his frowning face.

"Lighten up, cousin. You are thinking too hard about the future again," she teased, tossing a handful of sand onto his leg. "Accept that you'll be king of all of this and be done with it. There is nothing else you can do," she advised with a wave of her hands.

"I hope it is not for a very long time," he said with a grimace.

Magna sat up. "What, is there more going on in that head of yours? Are you upset because Kapian couldn't join us tonight?" she asked.

Orion shook his head and looked down at the sand. He picked up a handful and let it filter through his fingers before doing it again. She waited, barely containing a huff of impatience.

Finally, he sighed and spoke. "Kapian went with his father to the Isle of the Monsters," he said in a distracted voice.

"The Isle of the Monsters! Oh, I would love to go there. We should have followed them. I heard the Empress has these wonderful birds that are made of lightning, and beasts so huge that they make even the Giants appear tiny in comparison. I think we should go there tonight," she breathed, thinking of all the amazing creatures she had heard about while growing up.

Orion chuckled and shook his head. "Why am I not surprised you'd say that?" he retorted before he sobered.

Magna twisted and scowled at her cousin. "Why not? If we left now we could be there by tomorrow night. Our stags are the fastest in the ocean! I bet we could beat Kapian there. Can you imagine his expression when he sees us?" she said in excitement.

She stood and twirled around to look at Orion. Biting her lip, she gazed at him with a pleading expression that usually worked. Her smile faded when she saw the glum look on his face.

"I can't go," he said, rising to his feet to stand next to her.

"What's wrong? You've been all moody tonight," she complained.

Orion was silent for a moment before he shrugged. "Father and Mother have chosen my bride. I'm to be married," he said.

"Married! But...," she started to protest before her voice faded as the realization of what he had said sunk in. "Can't you tell them you aren't ready? There are so many things we planned to do still," she murmured, gazing up at him in dismay.

"Those were childish dreams. It is time to grow up. We each have our responsibilities. Kapian told me yesterday that his father reminded him that I would one day be king. Servants and guards are not the friends of a king. They are there to serve him," Orion stated in a tight voice.

Magna snorted. "Kapian's father has a seaworm stuck up his butt. Just because you are a king does not mean you are no longer a person! Even a king needs friends. Besides, Kapian and I know too much about you to act like we never saw you covered in Sea Hares or helped you escape from Coralus when he insisted on extra training lessons, but you wanted to ride Sea Fire instead. Your father and mother are great rulers, Orion, but you will be an even better one because you have a genuine connection with your people," she declared with a wave of her hands.

Personally, she wanted more from life than being tied down with the weighty expectations of others. She loved exploring the vast world they lived in. Her plans were to visit every kingdom and meet the people who lived there. She wanted to learn everything that she could about the wonders of their world until she felt like her brain would explode from all the knowledge.

Then, I will find new worlds to explore, she thought with excitement.

She wanted to fly like the dragons, do magic like her mother's people, live in the clouds with the Elementals, and swim to the bottom of the oceans as free as the sea dragons. She was in love with the independence, the differences between the people, and the unexpected treasures that she found when she visited each place.

Orion chuckled. "How did you get to be so smart?" he teased, bringing her back to the present.

She tossed her long black braid over her shoulder, looked up at him, and grinned. "Why from my cousin, the future King of the Sea People, of course," she retorted just before a light in the sky caught her attention.

She parted her lips in awe. Orion took his cue from her and looked up.

A bright flash of light was cutting across the dark sky. They both turned, following the path it made across the sky until it disappeared into the sea with a tremendous splash, not far from the cove.

"I call it! It's mine," she yelled, playfully pushing him down onto the soft sand before she laughingly raced for the water.

"Not if I find it first," Orion yelled after her, rising to his feet as he was overcome by her excitement and the challenge of finding the meteorite first.

Magna raced him to the water. With a loud whistle, she called to her sea dragon, Raine. Diving into the waves, she swam as fast as she could out into the water. Raine swam up under her once the water was deep enough. She grabbed the reins and glanced over her shoulder. Orion was a good two hundred feet behind her.

"Go, Raine!" she encouraged, clinging like a second skin to her sea dragon.

Magna loved the heady feel of the race. She really didn't care who found the meteorite first – or even if they found it. It was the thrill of the adventure, the fun of riding as fast as they could through the ocean, and the joy of not worrying about things like getting married or becoming a warrior like Orion and Kapian.

Several miles out to sea, the ocean floor dropped from a sheer cliff into a deep canyon. Orion, Kapian, and she had explored the long narrow canyon a few times out of curiosity. Raine swept down along the cliff, turning in a tight spiral that left Magna laughing and slightly dizzy. Orion charged after her, swiftly closing the distance between them.

"Magna, wait up!" Orion called.

She glanced over her shoulder when she heard him. "I called it, Orion!" Magna replied. "This is my treasure."

She turned back and focused on guiding Raine through the long, narrow crevices that ran along the ocean floor. They weaved through tall ghostly lava vents left over from the volcanoes that had risen up out of the sea to create the islands that would become the Seven Kingdoms. She swayed from side to side in unison with Raine as the sea dragon rounded the columns.

Up ahead, Magna could see a red glow illuminating the darkness. She knew that the canyon dropped again into an even deeper ravine. She had explored the deeper sections once before, but had found them dull and boring. There was not much down there except dark gray sand and volcanic rock.

"Magna, wait!" Orion demanded behind her.

Magna turned to see Orion reining in his sea dragon. She slowed Raine and patted the side of the young sea dragon's elegant neck when it fought against her hold. She turned on her saddle and grinned at Orion. If he thought that she was going to be tricked into letting him race ahead of her, she and the young sea dragon would show him.

"It isn't much farther," Magna replied with a smile. "I can feel it, Orion."

Orion shook his head and frowned. "I don't like this, Magna. Something is wrong," he said, glancing around at the tall, rugged cliffs not far from the drop-off. "The water doesn't feel right."

Magna shook her head and chuckled. Her eyes danced with merriment. She waved her hand through the water surrounding them. It felt the same to her.

"You aren't afraid, are you?" she teased. "The water hasn't changed."

Orion shook his head again and pulled back on the reins of his sea dragon. "No, there is something very different about it," he said in a slow measured voice. "We should go back."

Magna's face crumpled with disappointment, and she glanced back over her shoulder toward the dark crevice with a look of longing. While she wanted to see if they could find the meteorite, she knew that if Orion said the water felt different, then there was something wrong. Pushing aside her disappointment, she reluctantly nodded.

"Okay," she muttered with a sigh of regret. "But, I still call it, even if we never found it."

Orion laughed. "I'll give you this one," he agreed with a grin. "I'm still ahead though."

Magna rolled her eyes. She was about to argue with Orion when a dark shadow rose up from the depths beneath him. Her eyes widened when she saw the mass of dark tentacles reaching for him. Without thinking, she kicked Raine's sides and rushed toward him in a race to get to Orion before the black mass did.

"Orion, look out!" Magna cried in horror.

Orion yanked the reins in surprise to avoid colliding with Magna's mount. The move startled his stag, and it bucked. Magna watched in horror as Orion flew over the neck of his sea dragon. His head struck a section of the rock face, and his body went limp. Terrified, she moved on instinct. She grabbed Orion around the waist as he began to sink and pulled him over the saddle in front of her.

"Go, Raine, go!" Magna urged as the tentacles began to close in around them. "Go!"

The young sea dragon, weighted down by two riders, fought in vain to rise above the reach of the creature coming up out of the abyss. Raine cried out in pain when one of the black tentacles grazed her hindquarters, leaving behind a long welt. The frightened sea dragon kicked back, but the ugly tentacles continued to reach for her.

Magna realized that if she didn't immediately do something, they would all be lost. Sliding off of Raine, she slapped the sea dragon on her hindquarters. The sea dragon bolted upward and away.

A strangled scream of pain and terror slipped from her lips when a tentacle wrapped around her slender ankle. Searing pain exploded through her and began spreading up her leg. She struggled to break free, but more of the creature's tentacles wrapped around her, pulling her struggling body down into the abyss.

She reached up, grappling for a hold on the rock wall of one of the lava vents. Her palms were shredded by the sharp rocks. Blood from her torn flesh mixed with the water. Anguish filled her when she realized that there was no way she would be able to break free. The grasp around the lower half of her body was slowly moving upward, consuming her.

"No!" she choked.

Despair filled her as she watched Raine disappear with Orion, still unconscious, on her back. The black sludge was rising higher and higher. She felt like she was on fire instead of surrounded by water. Fear gave way to a certain knowledge that all her dreams would never be realized, because she was about to die.

"Help me," she whispered, stretching her lacerated hands upward in a silent plea even as her vision began to blur.

Magna twisted and was pulled deeper into the abyss. Shivers wracked her body. The water had never sent a chill through her before. As one of the sea people on her father's side, the oceans were her home. Now, the frigid temperature of the water seeped into her bones. Whatever held her in its grasp was sliding beneath her skin, scorching the very core of her bones with a fiery cold. The pain burning through her was overwhelming. Her heart thudded violently as she desperately tried one last time to break free.

Please, do not let me die like this, she silently begged as her mind became cloudy and disoriented.

You will not die, a hollow voice whispered through her mind. *We need you. We need your world and you will give it to us.*

For a moment, Magna saw what the creature was and what it wanted. It would use her to take over not only the sea people but all of the kingdoms. It would spread like a deadly virus; taking, using, and destroying everything in its path until there was nothing left. The alien creature would feed on the misery of every species here. Only when it had used up all of its resources would it move on to other worlds.

"Never," Magna whispered. "I will… stop you. I bind you to me.

Neither you nor any of your kind may live inside another. Let this spell unite us and give only me the power to set you free."

The spell she wove was powerful, born from fear and the determination to protect those who she loved. If the creature thought to destroy her, it would also destroy itself. She bound the alien to herself, trapping it inside her own body. She could feel the creature's shock and rage at the unfamiliar magic that slid through her and wrapped around it.

Magna's lips parted as agony ripped through her. As the spell continued to wrap around the creature, it tried to withdraw from her. Rage poured through the alien when the spell prevented it from leaving her body.

The creature's tentacles shot outward in an effort to catch up with Raine when it realized what Magna had done. It thought to seek out Orion, to use his body as well. Barely conscious, she felt the recoil as it was jerked back toward her. The spell had held.

A sense of relief swept through her even as she felt the cold surround her heart. With one last effort at self-preservation, she tucked a small part of herself away. To protect that part of herself in a place where the creature could not find her, she used a touch of the ancient magic she had learned from her mother. She would bide her time, and when the creature was least expecting it, she would kill it.

Even if it means destroying myself, she vowed before she slipped away, and the creature took control.

CHAPTER ONE

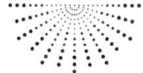

Present day – Isle of Magic:

Relief filled Magna. It was a feeling she had not felt in so long that she almost didn't recognize the emotion at first. Relief and a sense of peace – another sensation that she had not felt in over a century. Today, she – and the Seven Kingdoms – would finally be free. She had to believe that they would be, because this last shred of hope was all that was keeping her sane. The Goddess would give her the strength she needed, and they would all be free.

Her failures and successes – some new, some old, and some previously forgotten – flooded her until she felt like she was reliving them over and over again. Her heart ached when she thought of how Orion's father had been forced to banish her to the depths of the ocean over a century ago, but it had gotten the alien entity isolated.

She had hoped that given enough time, it would die, and she would be free of its evil grasp, but that wasn't what had happened. Instead, the creature had tirelessly plotted the destruction of her world.

When the Isle of the Sea Serpent was no longer easily accessible, the creature had searched her memories until it discovered her fascination with her mother's home, the Isle of Magic. Tapping into her magical skills, it had forced her to return to the beautiful isle and betray her mother's people.

The creature had wanted her to kill everyone who resisted. Instead, she had turned them to stone, convincing the creature this was a crueler punishment than death.

When the creature had used her to weave a spell that took the magic from the Isle of Magic's residents every night, intending to harvest their magic for its own use, she had twisted the words at the last second to include herself – and by extension the alien – among those who would be powerless at night. Enraged by her blunder, the creature had come close to killing her. The only thing that saved her life was the alien's need for her body.

Over and over again throughout the years, she had tried to take her own life or give others an opportunity to kill her. Each time, the creature had prevented her from destroying them both. Their lives were melded – it could not leave this world, nor could it exist without her.

But finally, her diligence and patience would pay off. Outside of the throne room, she could hear the battle raging. A malicious smile curved her black lips. She ran a trembling hand down her white gown. Deep inside, she could feel the alien's growing frustration and rage.

The creature, in its thirst for power, had spread itself too thin, just as she had hoped it would. The attacks by the combined forces of Drago, Orion, and the other rulers of the Seven Kingdoms were weakening it, and the alien was beginning to realize that it was in mortal danger.

Magna took a deep breath. She would know when the time was right to strike the final, deadly blow. Almost a century of imprisonment had passed before she'd conceived of a way to defeat the parasitic creature possessing her body. The planning had taken time, and she'd had to wait in the shadows of her mind, carefully manipulating the creature until the pieces fell into place.

She had lost count of the times she had been forced to commit atrocities against the peoples of her world. Her acts of defiance had to be subtle, but they had preserved a small amount of hope that one day she could reverse her spells and free those she had turned to stone.

As the years passed, though, harboring the creature's dark essence had drained her. Now, her body was frail from the constant stress of fighting the creature, but she fought to retain enough strength to ensure that her spell would be powerful enough to succeed. This would be her one and only chance to destroy the creature. If she failed, the Seven Kingdoms would be doomed.

Taking another deep breath, she mentally considered her plan. In order for everything to work, four things had to occur. The first three had been the most difficult to set up, but it was the last one that was the most important.

The first thing she needed was the magic of dragon-fire. Guilt-ridden grief struck her at the high cost to the Kingdom of the Dragons. The alien inside her had rightly feared that the dragons had the most potential to destroy it, and so a whole species was taken out of the war, all except one dragon.

Dragon-fire burned hotter than a normal flame, and none was more intense than that of Drago, the Dragon King – especially now, fueled by his all-consuming need for revenge. That was why she had refused to turn him to stone so many years ago.

The creature had railed against her, inflicting excruciating pain on her after she had briefly taken control and escaped into the sea. During it all, Magna had desperately tried to convince the alien entity that leaving Drago alone was the smart choice. She had told the creature that only the natural death of Drago would void the spells and wards protecting the famed power of the dragons – the Dragon's Heart. She'd told it the King of the Dragons would suffer greater pain if they did not turn him to stone. He would retreat into his unbearably empty kingdom and die of loneliness and grief. When the spells lifted, she reasoned, she would safely be able to retrieve the Goddess's gift to the dragons.

The creature had finally relented, but only because it could sense the tremendous pain and the piercing silence that had followed when Drago had retreated to his lair. She'd gotten lucky that Drago really hadn't died of loneliness and grief.

She needed Drago's aid to weaken and destroy the tentacles the alien had posted along the surrounding wall and huge portions of the palace itself, while she focused on the parasitic host that was her master. Only a fire created by a dragon's magic could injure the alien creature.

Second, she needed the power of Orion's trident. The electrical energy contained within the trident would disrupt the creature's ability to communicate with, not only her, but also with the unnatural creatures it had created from itself with the help of her magic, like the Hellhounds and the living vines.

The third element she needed was a weapon not of her world. This had been the trickiest part of her plan. She had opened a portal between the Seven Kingdoms and another world using a spell she had discovered in King Oray's library. The portal had allowed the arrival of Carly Tate which had resulted in a series of events that had led to today's final battle.

The final element was the spell she had carefully crafted. The alien had to have a host to thrive. The only way to kill it was to release the bonds she had crafted so long ago, allowing the creature to leave her body. Currently it was incapable of leaving her body – unless she died, and then, she feared, the creature would merely find another host.

Timing was everything. She needed to release her bond on the creature inside her and utter the spell to kill it while the alien was still within a few feet of herself. At the same time, she needed the others to attack the alien, disrupting its powers and distracting it, while continuing to prevent the creature from finding another host. She had to do this while giving everyone else in the room enough time to escape. Anyone remaining with her and the alien would perish from the power of the spell.

There were so many factors which could go wrong that she was beginning to have serious doubts about being successful. She ruthlessly pushed them away. Each horrible thing she had been forced to do, each day of torture she had endured since that night so long ago, and each desperate ploy had led to today. She refused to give up and concede defeat.

She didn't wince when the doors to the throne room exploded inward, the burning body of a Hellhound collapsing under the scorching heat. From where she stood in the shadows behind the throne, she saw two figures cautiously enter the room. She recognized the woman as a witch from the Isle of Magic, but it was the man with her who drew her attention. He was from the other world, the one that Carly Tate had come from, and the one who would unwittingly help her machinations succeed.

She lifted her chin and breathed deeply in an effort to quiet her eagerness. Orion and Drago were not far behind the man and witch. Inside her, she could feel the creature trying to command its minions to coalesce in the throne room. There were few remaining. Vast sections of its vines stationed outside and most of the Hellhounds had already been destroyed. The creature's extensions who persisted inside the palace came closer to the throne room, covering the ceiling with a thin film of black ooze.

Prepare to attack, the malicious voice whispered in her head.

I am ready, she dutifully replied.

You will unleash all of your power on them. Our combined strength will not be defeated, the alien vowed. *Without their leaders, the Kingdoms will be ours. It is time to destroy them all!*

Yes, Magna agreed.

Do not fail me this time or the pain you feel will be unlike any I have given you before, the alien warned.

I will not fail, Magna quietly vowed.

The creature sensed the resolve inside her, unaware of the true reason behind it. The alien's arrogance was a tumor, rapidly growing out of its own control, much like its tentacles. Keeping a tight grip on her own emotions, she patiently watched and waited for her opportunity. Her eyes drifted to the throne where King Oray, the King of the Isle of Magic, sat. His body was unnaturally stiff and frail; the spell he had cast to protect himself and the kingdom was slowly draining the life from him. Once again, a shaft of remorse swept through her at the pain and suffering she had been forced to cause.

Taking a deep breath, she waited until the witch and man neared the throne before she stepped out from behind it. She inwardly grimaced at the high-pitched laugh that escaped her and echoed throughout the room. Sliding one hand along the back of the throne, she drew a long, curved dagger from the sheath strapped to her waist.

The witch was the first to straighten when she saw her. Magna caught and held the woman's intense gaze.

"Release him, Sea Witch," the female demanded, her face and voice filled with fury. Magna's head tilted to the side and a sardonic smile twisted her lips in a silent reply. "We are not alone. The Sea King and Drago have joined with my people to stop you."

"I tremble at the mere thought," Magna drawled sarcastically, looking at the woman with utter disdain.

She turned her head slightly to the side so that the witch couldn't see the flash of grief in her eyes. She focused her attention on the bent form of King Oray. He looked ashen and listless. His continued fight against the alien had drained him of most of his power. It was time to free him and the others as well.

It shouldn't be too difficult to convince the others to attack me, she thought with morbid self-loathing.

Taking a deep breath, she returned her gaze to the woman and raised the curved dagger. With a quick motion of her hand, she cut a thin, shallow line across the king's throat. The alien inside her grew excited by her bold move. A soft hiss slipped from her parted lips when the creature surged forward for the next action.

Not yet, she murmured.

Kill him! He will be the first to die. I no longer need him, the alien entity ordered.

If I kill him, the others will have no reason to come closer. We must wait until they are all close enough before we strike, she insisted, keeping the swirling mass along the ceiling in her peripheral vision.

Magna released another shrill laugh before she addressed the witch. "The Sea King is bound by the laws of his people. He is weak and unable to harm me," she goaded with a shrug of one slender shoulder.

"He might be, but I'm not," a loud voice retorted from the entrance to the throne room.

Her eyes shifted to the doorway. Inside, she felt the alien recoil. She could almost taste the creature's fear and craving for the overwhelming power of the dragon. She took in Drago's massive form with a surge of satisfaction and anticipation.

Drago stood in the center of the now destroyed door frame, his face and body taut with rage. Magna bit her lip. The alien inside her was still too strong for her to release her bonds. Before Drago's fire could be effective enough, she needed the last element of her plan – Orion and his trident.

"It is time to die, Sea Witch! I have waited far too long for this moment. You should be thankful that I will make it swift. I would love nothing more than to make you feel a measure of the agony that you have caused others," Drago sneered as he stepped into the room.

His eyes blazed with a ghost of his dragon-fire. Vengeance burned so brightly within him that his chest glowed a dark, blood red through the fabric of his shirt. His features were hard, and his long black hair flowed around him as he strode toward her. The intent was clear in his eyes – death.

Out of the corner of her eye, she saw the movement of long threads of the black, thorny tentacles reaching downward to wrap around Drago. Her hand reached out in warning, and a cry slipped from her lips.

"Watch out!" she cried.

You defy me! the creature hissed inside her.

It was time. She could not wait any longer.

"Goddess, please… give me the strength I need to finish this," she whispered.

Her eyes teared with the sudden intense pain that swept through her. Fire burned through her veins. Her lips parted in a scream of agony when another intense wave hit her, but she swallowed it. She had to do what she could to distract the alien so that Drago or one of the others could strike at her.

A shuddering breath hissed from her. "Yesssss! You will never be able to defeat Drago and Orion," she whispered to the being inside her as she fought for control.

I will destroy them all. Then, I will take care of you, the creature inside her hissed in fury.

"I… will not… allow you to harm… them," she vowed.

She fought, but the creature forced the hand holding the knife to rise. She knew exactly what it was intending to do – kill King Oray. She wrapped her other hand around the wrist of the hand holding the knife, pushing against the movement with both hands.

"No!" she screamed, her body twisting away from the King.

The alien creature sent shards of electrical charges through her body, and her body bowed, her heart stuttering. She straightened like a puppet on a string and the knife again headed for the king's throat. At the same time, the sound of an explosion resonated throughout the chamber. Magna felt a mind-shattering pain rip through her left shoulder. The knife fell to the floor as the force of the blow violently jerked her body backward, forced to turn from the impact on her shoulder, and she collapsed onto the floor.

She lay dazed on the cold stone near the throne. She could feel the warmth of her blood seeping through her clothing and beginning to pool under her. As she panted, the alien strained to free itself from her body, and she instinctively tightened her hold on the spell binding it close to her, but the alien surged through the spell-less path which had been created with the weapon's gaping wound.

She issued a long, pain-filled gasp and her body arched as the dark entity poured out of her body through the wound in her shoulder. A shudder ran through her and she watched as the black cloud rose above her in a swirling mass. She sank back to the floor as the last of the entity vacated her body. A strange feeling, as if there were a huge, cavernous void inside of her, left her feeling momentarily confused and weak.

The feeling was quickly replaced with one that was all too familiar – fear. It burned through her, leaving her fingers and toes numb with it and her lungs constricted when she realized that the alien was now searching for a new host. It was too soon for it to be unbound; Orion hadn't yet hit her with the Trident's power. The alien was still fully in control of all of its own power.

The creature turned its attention to King Oray. Lifting her right hand, she whispered the spell that had bound them. Her body jerked when the spell hooked the entity, compelling it away from the frail King.

On the other side of the throne, she heard her cousin's voice. Tears filled her eyes at the sound of it. There was so much she wanted to tell him. She would give anything to be able to beg for his forgiveness for everything that she had been unwillingly forced to do.

"Fire on it," Orion shouted.

Release me, the alien hissed, wrathfully twisting and turning as Orion and Drago attacked it. *I will destroy you!*

Magna ignored the threat, knowing that she would be the one doing the destroying. She held the slender thread of connection between herself and the alien that had controlled her for the last two centuries with an iron will born of hope, desperation, and grief.

Closing her eyes, she focused on that link, slowly wrapping a second spell around it. The spells would hold the alien suspended in place above the throne, preventing it from moving away from her while also stopping it from returning to her body. A shudder ran through her when she felt the touch of a warm hand under her chin. She opened her eyes and stared up at the man who had injured her with his strange weapon. Tears slowly trailed down from the corners of her eyes at his look of concern.

"Go!" she ordered, licking her dry lips. "You have to… go," she repeated, forcing the whispered words past the tight lump in her throat.

The man shook his head. "Not without you," he replied in a grim tone.

He started to slide his arm around her shoulder and lift her. Her face contorted at the intense pain threatening to drown her in its fierce waves. Her right hand reached up to push against the man's shoulder. She shook her head in regret.

"What is your name?" she asked, needing to know.

The man gave her a startled look. "Mike Hallbrook. I have to get you out of here," he replied with a frown.

Her gaze moved to the ceiling above them again. He turned his head to see what she was looking at. Now was the time to strike. The creature was being torn apart by Drago's dragon-fire and the disrupting bolts of power from the tridents of Orion and his men. She would kill the alien creature once and for all.

"No," she said with a slight shake of her head when he started to lift her again. "No, I know how to… how to kill it now. Go! What I have to do will kill you all if you don't. Go, Mike Hallbrook. Save my king and the Isles. Take the others with you. There is no hope for me. I would be sentenced to death anyway. Let me at least have some purpose to my life," she pleaded in a tired voice.

She watched Mike's eyes darken with indecision. Fear and determination gave her the strength she needed to push him to the side. She unsteadily rose to her feet. Taking a deep breath, she pulled on the last dwindling ounce of her strength and lifted her head. She ignored the agonizing pain in her shoulder as she raised her arms above her head and began chanting in a clear voice filled with determination.

Magic flooded her body, and she could feel the energy from the Isle of Magic seep into her, giving her the added strength she needed to cast the final blow that would free them all. Bright red blood ran down from her shoulder, staining the front of her white gown. She ignored everything but the magic of the spell building inside her and the black swarm of the alien near the ceiling.

I will not fail, she vowed to herself.

In the background, she could hear the urgent sound of Mike yelling for Drago and Orion to retreat. Mike had King Oray over his shoulder and was hurrying toward the burnt-out entrance of the throne room. Drago and Orion stopped their attacks to leave with him, and the alien refocused all its remaining strength to fighting against her hold.

"Let the light of truth guide me and be my sword," she chanted.

Bright light flared out from around her as the spell she cast ignited the air in the room. Surging waves of power rolled through the room like a thick fog, sucking the air out of it. She could hear the sizzle of the alien's body as the power swept over it, igniting its body with the bright light.

The creature struck out at her, but the blinding power of the light radiating from her prevented it from reaching her. Magna felt her body rising above the stone floor. Closing her eyes, she thought of the vast ocean that was her home and wished its cool liquid was surrounding her, extinguishing the flames that were scorching her tired body. As the air around her blazed with power, she felt her body being ripped apart until the void of blackness finally gave her relief.

It is over, she thought. *I am free.*

CHAPTER TWO

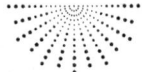

Off the coast of Yachats, Oregon:

Gabe Lightcloud powered his thirty-two-foot trawler along the rocky coast. He took a deep breath of the crisp salty air. Today had been a good day.

He glanced at the time on the depth finder. *No wonder my stomach is protesting,* he thought. It was nearly seven o'clock in the evening. Turning the wheel, he started the long trip back to the docks. He had left the house just before sunrise and had spent most of the day doing catch and release for the U.S. Fish and Wildlife Service. A new program at the University of Oregon had given him an opportunity to combine work with research. The University of Oregon's grant was part of an on-going research program backed by the USFWS to study the migratory patterns of Chinook Salmon.

As far as Gabe was concerned, he'd been assigned the fun part of the research – tagging, releasing, and not having to deal with people. He enjoyed the peace and quiet of working offshore. The sound of the motor, the waves slapping against the hull of his boat, and the high-pitched cries of seagulls hoping for an easy meal were his companions. He preferred them above anything else. He rolled his shoulders, glad he had finished his last catch for the day.

He hadn't had anything to eat except an egg sandwich and a thermos of coffee this morning. He grinned as he stared out at the water. A nice shrimp dinner sounded pretty good right about now. If he couldn't snag any, he'd settle for a nice grilled halibut. His mouth started watering at the thought of them cooking on the grill. Either one would be a welcome treat and was just what he needed to quiet his rebelling stomach. Hell, he might even be nice and see if Kane wanted to come over to watch the football game.

He turned the wheel when he saw a school of fish on the depth finder and pushed the throttle to neutral. Stepping out of the wheelhouse, he released the lock on the winch and lowered the net into the water. He made sure it wasn't tangled before he turned back to the helm. Checking the settings on the depth finder, he searched the bottom for any structures that might be an issue before he pushed the throttle forward. He decided he'd troll for half an hour before pulling everything in and heading back home.

The time was almost up when he felt a slight drag on the boat. He turned in time to see the buoy attached to the net violently dip below the surface. He quickly pushed the throttle back into neutral. He muttered a curse and sighed in frustration. He should have quit while he was ahead. If the net was caught on the bottom or worse, tangled around some floating garbage, it could mean a long night, which meant it would be even longer before he had anything to eat.

Gabe grabbed the net and began pulling it in. The one thing that bugged him more than anything else was when people decided to use the ocean as their own private garbage dump. He was always finding shit that someone had thrown out.

He frowned when he felt the net shift. Afraid it might have caught on something, he looked over the side, but didn't see any sign that it was snagged. He hoped it wasn't, because the net was a pain in the ass to patch. Shifting the winch into gear again, he continued reeling in the net. Then he heard a moan.

"What the hell?" he muttered, pressing the stop button on the winch control. "Shit!"

Muttering under his breath, he decided he must have snagged some unsuspecting seal pup. He grabbed the net and continued pulling it in by hand. His eyes widened in shock when he saw a person caught in the net. Moving swiftly, he finished pulling the net in. He lowered it and his unexpected catch to the deck of the rocking boat. Grabbing the side of the net, he released it from the rigging and knelt next to the still, cold body.

"Damn it," Gabe muttered under his breath. "I don't need a dead body on my boat."

He gently rolled the body over, pulled away the netting tangled around it, and gasped when he saw that it belonged to a woman. Yanking off his gloves, he carefully brushed the long tangle of midnight hair back from her pale face. He touched the icy skin of her neck, feeling for a pulse, and pulled back in surprise when she shuddered and moaned.

He gently touched her cheek again, smoothing back a long strand of hair. She was deathly pale with dark shadows under her eyes. His shocked brain also noted that she was beautiful in a weird, exotic way.

"Hey, lady," Gabe said in a rough voice. "Can you hear me?"

He watched in fascination as her lush, black eyelashes fluttered for a moment before she opened her eyes. He gazed down into crystal-clear green eyes. He couldn't help but wonder who in the hell she was and why she was miles off the Pacific Coast in freezing water. He was just about to ask her when she rolled to her side and threw up all over his rubber boots.

"Ah, hell," he muttered, looking down at the heaving figure.

Half an Hour Earlier:

Magna softly moaned as the pain from her shoulder pulled her to consciousness for a brief moment. The pain was the first thing telling her that she hadn't died from her Starburst spell. The gentle sway of her body surrounded by water and the feeling of weightlessness was the second thing.

For a brief moment, she wondered if the Goddess had granted her a measure of compassion. That thought quickly fled when she tried to move and was in too much pain and too exhausted to do it. The current flowed around her, sweeping her along the rocky bottom, and she was powerless to prevent herself from bumping against the rocks, causing even more excruciating pain to radiate through her. The spell had taken every ounce of energy she had left.

Eventually, an upwelling current caused her to rise, mercifully giving her a measure of relief. As she floated along, Magna didn't bother opening her eyes. She preferred not knowing where she was for fear of waking up and discovering it was all an illusion and she was once more a captive inside her own body. She wanted to hold onto the feel of the water surrounding her, even if it came with pain.

She listlessly floated for what seemed like an eternity before something wrapped around her. The weight of the coarse threads pushed her back down to the bottom. She tried to lift her hand and push it away, but it was useless. She was too weak. She gave up, and let it take her. Deciding that her dream was coming to another agonizing end, she gave in to the darkness.

She awoke again when she was lifted out of the soothing comfort of the water. She wanted to scream in protest, but the scream came out as a soft moan. As she was lowered onto a hard surface, a stray tear slipped from the corner of her eye and grief filled her. All hope was gone. She couldn't fight the creature any longer. The only way she could still be alive was if she had failed. Nausea rose in her throat when the cold air connected with the wound in her shoulder. A protest formed on her lips when she was suddenly rolled onto her back.

A shudder swept through her when a warm hand pressed against her neck. Her eyes fluttered open and she found herself staring up into a pair of unfamiliar brown eyes. The combination of pain and the movement of her body was too much for her rebellious stomach. Rolling to the side, she ejected the last remnants of the dead creature from her stomach all over the man's scuffed up white boots.

She dropped her head to the side when she was done. She was too weak and tired to bother lifting it. Instead, she closed her eyes and shuddered again as the darkness rose up to claim her. She hoped this time it was for good. She really was too tired to fight any longer.

Gabe contemplated the woman lying on the deck of his boat as he knelt next to her limp body. There was a little more color in her face now that she'd thrown up. Muttering a series of expletives under his breath, he gently scooped her up in his arms and rose to his feet. He squinted, and carefully searched the water nearby before looking up to scan the horizon. There wasn't another boat in sight. He looked toward the rocky coast. Hell, he was at least a mile offshore. There was no way the woman swam that distance, especially wearing an evening gown.

He looked down at her again and froze. The gown on her left shoulder was bright red with fresh blood. He tightened his lips into a firm line and he walked toward the lower galley and cabin area.

Awkwardly navigating the stairs, he breathed a sigh of relief when the woman didn't react as he shifted her around to fit through the doorway. He walked over to his bunk and gently laid her down, then turned on the light above his bed. He gripped the material on her shoulder and ripped it open. His eyes widened, and he paled when he saw the evidence hidden beneath the silky material.

"Shot?" he hissed, glancing back up at her pale face. "Lady, what the hell happened to you? Why would anyone shoot you and dump your ass in the Pacific?"

He gently lifted her enough to see the other side of her shoulder. There was no exit wound. Gabe stood up and pulled open the cabinet above the bed. He pulled out the first aid kit and sat back down. Setting the kit down on the bed, he opened it and pulled out some gauze bandage and tape. There wasn't much he could do for her on the boat. It wasn't the cleanest place in the world and he didn't have the medical expertise to remove a bullet. He would patch her up as best he could and radio for assistance.

He quickly dried the area, covered the wound with the clean gauze, and taped it down. He looked at the relaxed lines of the woman's face. She hadn't moved an inch during his clumsy patch job. Unable to resist, he reached out and turned her face toward him. Her features were arresting. She didn't look like she was of European descent, but she didn't look like she had any Asian ancestry either. His fingers ran down her pale cheek.

A slight, rusty smile curved his lips before a frown creased his brow when he noticed a thin line along the right side of her pale neck. It started just behind her ear and curved down about two inches. Another line of faint but colorful tattoos ran down beside it. He reached out to touch the marks but quickly pulled back when he felt the smooth, glossy texture of each design. They reminded him of…

"Scales?" he muttered with a disbelieving shake of his head. "What the hell is going on?"

Standing, he quickly deposited the scraps from the bandage into the trash. He returned the first aid kit to the cabinet before he grabbed a thin blanket and covered her with it. He frowned and ran a hand through his hair, trying to think if there was anything else he should do before he returned to the upper deck.

He decided he had done the best he could for the moment. Glancing down one last time to make sure the woman was still unconscious, he turned on his heel and strode back up the stairs. It looked like it was going to be a long night. He grimaced when his stomach growled in protest again. Dinner would have to be pushed back until his unexpected guest was safely delivered into the hands of the proper authorities.

Gabe quickly secured the net and made sure the deck, and his boots, were cleared and cleaned before he stepped through the passage to the bridge. He pushed the throttle forward, slowly picking up speed, and headed for home again. He reached for the mic on his radio, then paused. With a low growl of frustration, he pulled his hand back and ran it through his disheveled hair before he reached for his cell phone instead.

His gaze flickered from the sea in front of him to the phone. He released the breath he hadn't realized he'd been holding. He had three bars. Pressing the phone icon, he punched in the number he knew by heart.

"This is Kane," a distracted voice said on the other end.

"I need help," Gabe bit out in a sharp voice.

There was a slight pause before Kane spoke again. "How bad?" Kane asked.

"Gunshot to the left shoulder," Gabe replied.

This time the pause was filled with a low hiss. "Who'd you piss off this time?" Kane asked sharply. "You know I'm supposed to report anything like this."

"Yeah, I know," Gabe said in a low voice. "It's not me this time. Just be at my house in an hour. I'll be coming in from the dock."

"I'll be there," Kane responded in a tense voice. "You sure you don't want to come to the clinic?"

Gabe's lips twisted in a sardonic grin. "Naw," he said. "Then you'd really feel like you had to report it."

The sound of a frustrated sigh made Gabe thankful he wasn't onshore yet. Kane wasn't above bending the rules or looking the other way when he felt it was necessary, but Gabe wouldn't ask his friend to jeopardize his practice or his medical license by having to cover for him there. Now, coming to his house... What happened there, stayed there.

"One of these days I'm going to ignore it when you call," Kane threatened. "I'll be at the dock."

"Thanks, man," Gabe replied in a soft voice. "Something tells me that this should be kept quiet."

"You can explain when we're together," Kane retorted.

"Right now, there's not much to explain," Gabe admitted. "I'll be coming around the point in about forty minutes."

Gabe clicked the phone off and slid it back into his pocket. Exactly forty minutes later, he automatically swung wide into the mouth of the narrow inlet and slowly pulled back on the throttle so he wouldn't create a wake. Frustration ate at him, and his fingers twitched in impatience on the throttle. He knew the feeling of restlessness and unease was due to his unexpected passenger.

"I hope to hell this doesn't become more complicated," he grunted as he navigated the narrow, winding passage to the dock below his house.

CHAPTER THREE

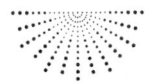

A low rumble and change in motion woke Magna from her restless slumber. She blinked several times and frowned when she tried to remember where she was. Her body, while still wracked with pain, felt lighter – almost empty. For a moment, fear choked her as she did an internal inventory of herself. She did not feel the pressure that had plagued her since the alien took over her body.

Tears blurred her vision, then slowly trailed down from the corners of her eyes. It was gone. The creature was finally gone.

Rolling onto her side, she let the sobs of relief wash through her, cleansing away the pain of her long imprisonment. She held her left arm close to her body as she buried her face in the pillow. After several minutes, she finally felt more in control, of herself and she took a deep, shuddering breath.

A startled hiccup escaped her when she caught the musky scent of a man. Carefully pushing herself into a sitting position, she blinked several times to clear her vision when the world suddenly tilted. She stared blindly down at the pillow for several seconds before everything came back into focus.

Turning her head, she carefully surveyed her surroundings. A frown furrowed her brow as she scanned the strange room. It was different from any ship's room that she had ever seen before. For one thing, it was cramped and noisy.

Her breath caught when the sound level decreased before disappearing altogether. Tilting her head to the side, she waited until she felt a gentle bump. When she didn't feel any more movement except the gentle rocking of the boat on the water, she decided it was time to plan her escape. She would slip over the side while the crew was busy. She could return to the deep abyss that had become her home and live out her days in its darkness.

She pushed aside the coarse blanket covering her and slid her legs over the side of the bed. Grabbing a long railing attached to the wall, she struggled to a standing position. Her knees trembled, threatening to give out. She leaned against the wall, sliding her right hand along the surface to stay upright while she cradled her left arm against her body. A soft whimper slipped out when she accidentally jarred her injured arm. She closed her eyes as a wave of pain washed through her.

"What the hell do you think you're doing?" a deep voice demanded.

Her eyes snapped open to stare at the man. She gasped when her trembling legs gave out beneath her. A low, painful cry burst from her lips when she instinctively reached out with her left hand to steady herself. She felt the edge of darkness threatening to swallow her again.

"Aw, shit," the man exclaimed, wrapping one arm around her waist and the other under her knees. "Stupid woman. You've got no business standing up. What the hell were you thinking?"

Magna let her head fall back against his shoulder as he tenderly cradled her in his arms. A scowl creased her brow at his words and she glared at him through the tears in her eyes. Her lips were tightly pinched together to keep any more sounds from escaping, but his comment had rubbed her the wrong way.

She raised her head. "I am NOT stupid," she declared, blinking rapidly to dispel her tears before she warily laid her head against his shoulder again.

Clamping her lips together, she refused to say anything else. It wouldn't matter anyway. The man would probably call her things much worse than stupid once it dawned on him who she was. If he was from the Isle of Pirates, she'd be lucky if he only left her in a cage hanging above the water to die a slow death.

That would indeed be a cruel way to die, so close to her beloved water, yet unable to touch it. Once again, waves of grief and despair flooded her. If only she could slip beneath the surface of the water. She would find a place no other creature would ever venture and claim it for herself.

∾

A Few Minutes Ago:

Gabe shut off the engines to the trawler. Glancing upward, he saw Kane watching from the deck of his house. He quickly tied off the bow and stern lines before turning back to the lower galley. It would take Kane a few minutes to get down to the dock.

Impatient to see how his 'catch' was doing, he descended the steps two at a time. He hoped the woman hadn't bled out all over his bunk. A movement in the shadows took him by surprise. The last thing he would have expected was to find the half-dead woman not only standing up but, from the looks of it, trying to escape.

A loud curse burst from his lips when he saw her startle. He didn't mean to scare her, but he was so alarmed to see her up that the curse slipped out. He reached out, barely catching her as she collapsed. He carefully lifted her in his arms, trying not to hurt her unnecessarily. Any movement was likely to be painful, which was why she should have stayed in bed as long as she could.

"I am NOT stupid," she defiantly mumbled, laying her head against his shoulder.

He grunted, not wanting to debate their differences of opinion until Kane at least took a look at her. Still, he couldn't quite keep from smiling in amusement at her defiance. Shaking his head, he turned on his heel and gingerly retraced his steps back up to the top deck.

He was almost to the stern of the main deck when he saw Kane stepping onto the dock and heading toward them with a sour expression on his face. Gabe stepped from the boat onto the dock. He glanced down when he felt the woman in his arms stiffen, but she didn't complain. Her face was paler than before, and her eyes were now closed. His jaw tightened when he saw the lines of pain etched around her mouth.

"Sorry," he muttered, before turning his attention to Kane. "She's got a bullet hole in her left shoulder. I didn't see an exit wound, so I think it's still in there. She's in a hell of a lot of pain."

"I thought you were out on the boat all day. Where the hell did you find a woman with a bullet in her?" Kane demanded, taking in the situation in one glance.

"I was. I fished her out of the ocean," Gabe retorted, pushing past Kane and heading toward the trail that led up to his house.

He could feel Kane's eyes burning a hole between his shoulder blades as he walked up the path. It was quite a hike up the side of the cliff, but he was used to it. Climbing the staircase, he silently made his way up to the back deck. He strode across the stained faux-wood decking and pulled open the sliding glass door.

"Stay!" he ordered, glaring at the two Huskies that raced into the family room. "Damn it, Buck! Will you move your big ass?" Gabe snapped. "Wilson! Kane, grab that damn hairball."

"Wilson, stay!" Kane demanded as he slipped through the door and closed it before the hundred-pound Husky pup could dart out. "Get your nose out of my crotch, dog. Damn, Gabe, why can't you get a normal pet?"

A soft, strained chuckle escaped the woman in his arms. Gabe glanced down and almost tripped on the hall rug when he saw amusement mixed with pain in her vivid green eyes. He grunted an apology when she hissed at the sudden movement.

He turned into the guest bedroom and crossed to the bed, stepping over and ignoring the prancing dogs who kept darting in his path and brushing against his legs. He gently lowered her to the soft covers. It was impossible to ignore how thin she was as he placed her on the bedspread. She felt like she was about to fade away in his arms. When he saw the bright red blood seeping through the bandage he had taped to her shoulder, concern about the bullet wound made his voice sound harsher than he meant.

"Kane!" Gabe barked out, starting to turn.

"I'm here," Kane said with a raised eyebrow. "Go fix some food for us, I haven't eaten all day. I'll take care of her."

Gabe opened his mouth to protest, but the look on Kane's face warned him that now wasn't the time to argue. With a grunt, he looked at the woman's pale face before he nodded. Walking past Kane, he paused to look at his friend.

"Thanks," he muttered.

Kane returned his intense stare with a crooked smile. "I want salmon, grilled, with shrimp, and a salad," Kane replied with an easy grin. "Soup for our patient. I'll see if she is allergic to anything and let you know."

Gabe nodded, glancing over his shoulder one last time before he ushered the dogs out of the bedroom and closed the door. He leaned back against the polished wood paneling and listened to Kane quickly asking the woman if she was allergic to anything. Her softly spoken 'no' barely carried through the door. Pushing away, he decided he would make her a bowl of cream of chicken soup.

"Come on, boys," Gabe ordered in a soft voice. "I'm starving. Let's go make some dinner."

Buck and Wilson gave low rumbles of approval and wagged their tails. He followed the two gray and white Huskies as they hurried into the kitchen, then pulled out the pans he would need, and reached into the freezer to pull out some fish. He would have preferred fresh, but beggars couldn't be choosers.

~

Magna stared up at the male named Kane. Her gaze flickered to the black bag he carried in his right hand. He sat down on the bed next to her and placed the bag beside him. He studied her for a moment before he opened the bag.

"What will you do to me?" she asked in a barely audible voice.

"I'm going to take a look at that wound in your shoulder," he responded in an easy voice, giving her a reassuring smile.

She watched as he pulled items out of the bag and carefully laid them on the small bedside table. She waited in tense silence as he worked. Clearing her throat, she pushed past her fear and asked the question that had been brewing as she'd taken in the details of the unusual dwelling.

"What kingdom is this? I have been to all of them but the home of the giants. Is this it?" she asked.

Kane paused for a moment before he shook his head. "The only giants that I know of live in New York. Are you allergic to any medications or have any medical issues that I should know about other than a gunshot wound to your shoulder?" he asked.

Magna grimaced as she glanced down at her shoulder. "No." If they weren't in the Isle of Giants, where was she? And where was New York?

Kane nodded and tapped on a clear vial. Magna watched as he

inserted a small, metal needle into the vial. Panic gripped her when he pulled some of the clear liquid into the narrow tube.

"What are you going to do?" she whispered in a tight voice. "I... This... liquid, do you plan to strike me dead with it?"

Kane looked at Magna in surprise. "Of course not," he said with a scowl. "I'm going to numb the area around the wound so that it doesn't hurt. You really should be at the hospital for this. Do you know who shot you?"

Magna frowned. "It was the first time I had seen a male of his species. I'd only seen the woman who married my cousin. He came to my world because I brought Carly Tate to Drago, but you and the other male, Gabe, are of the same species as they are..." she said in a quivering voice as he picked up a pair of scissors. "Why do you help me? It is dangerous for your kingdom. Surely your king knows of my misdeeds and would order you to destroy me." She took in a hiccupping breath. "I will not fight you. I hoped...." She wearily shook her head. "Drago should have finished the deed that Orion could not."

Kane paused and looked down at her with a frown. "So...it wasn't Drago or Orion...?" he asked.

She blinked in confusion. "Of course not. Drago and Orion have no need for such weapons as the one Mike Hallbrook used on me," she said.

Kane froze. "Mike Hallbrook? As in Detective Mike Hallbrook of the police department? The one who disappeared?" he asked with a stunned expression.

Magna frowned. "I do not know. He said his name was Mike Hallbrook before I warned him to escape. The spell... it would have killed them," she whispered, growing silent at the memory.

Kane shook his head and focused on her wound.

She kept her gaze on his face while he carefully cut off the blood-soaked bandage covering her wound. An unexpected rush of feelings washed through her that had nothing to do with the questions he had asked her and everything to do with the two men.

This one seemed to be the exact opposite of the other one in both coloring and mannerisms. Gabe was darker, harder, and rougher. Kane, on the other hand, was lighter in color with dark-blond hair that reminded her of the sun-kissed sand along one of the beaches off the coast of the Isle of Monsters. Although Gabe had been surprisingly gentle with her, his touch was far different from that of the man touching her now. Kane's touch was light and efficient, though his fingers lingered against the flesh near her shoulder.

She winced when he pulled the bandage back. He frowned as he studied the damaged skin, then gently pulled the bandage off and set it and the scissors on the table before he picked up the long, thin needle again.

"Spells? Species? Kingdom? That's a new one. Sounds like something out of a fairytale. I haven't been spoken of like that before. By the way, what is your name?" Kane asked as he numbed the skin around the hole in her shoulder.

Magna's eyes widened. "You do not know who I am? Surely you have heard of me?" she whispered in shock, wincing with each sting of the sharp needle.

He studied her face intently for several seconds before he shook his head. "Nope," he replied with an apologetic smile. "Now lay still while I see where this bullet is. If I can't get to it easily, I'm afraid I'll have to insist that you go to the hospital."

Magna's eyes widened even further when she saw him reach for a long, metal device with teeth. Realizing what he intended to do, she shuddered. She could heal the wound much better without the barbaric methods of torture this man intended to inflict on her.

"Wait," she whispered, closing her eyes and licking her lips as she drew on the small amount of energy she had regained. She opened her eyes and stared up at him. "I will remove the metal from my body, but

I will not have the strength to close the wound. You will have to use your skills to do that."

"You'll... Listen," Kane began. He lifted his hand to prevent her from harming herself, then paused when he saw the center of her palm begin to glow with a supernatural light. His mouth dropped open when she raised her right hand, held it over her left shoulder, and wispy silver threads emanated from her palm into the wound "What the....?"

She whispered the incantation for a binding spell and concentrated on the silvery threads forming in the palm of her right hand. Sweat beaded on her brow as she focused on the image in her head. The silver threads flew down into the wound in her shoulder and grasped the metal bullet. Her fingers shook as the energy it took to cast the spell drained her limited strength. She panted as the strands wrapped around the metal. Even with the numbness from Kane's injection, she could still feel the slide of the metal against her torn flesh as it moved upward.

She raggedly cried out and arched her back as it pulled free. She could feel fresh warm blood pour from the wound. Grasping the bloody metal in her right hand, she held it out to the pale man sitting beside her.

"I... must... sleep," she whispered, her eyelids fluttering as she released the metal into his upturned palm.

"Who the hell are you? What the hell are you?" Kane asked in a hoarse voice.

For a moment, Magna fought against the sleep threatening to overwhelm her. Opening her eyes, she looked up at Kane with a sad look of resignation. Once he knew who she was, perhaps he would be merciful and take her life while she slept.

"I am... Magna," she forced out as her eyelids lowered again. "I am... the Sea Witch."

Kane studied the woman's face. It was thin, and dark shadows made the areas under her eyes look almost bruised. Although she looked very young, the faint lines near the corner of her eyes and mouth showed that she was older than he had first thought.

He softly cursed when he saw the red stain spreading across the remnants of her white gown. The physician in him kicked into high gear, efficiently depositing the bullet on the sterilized disposable instrument tray he'd brought with him. He picked up some gauze and staunched the flow of her blood. Rinsing the area with a saline solution, he made sure there was no foreign debris in the wound, and then he sutured it.

Once he was finished, he cleaned up the supplies. His mind raced through what he knew about Magna – the Sea Witch. If he were honest with himself, he would admit that he was still shaken by what she'd done to remove the bullet. His eyes moved to the lead bullet on the tray, to her shoulder, then to her hand. Reaching down, he picked up her right hand and turned it over. He ran his thumb across her palm and froze, his eyes locked on the thin webbing between each of her fingers.

He replaced her hand at her side and began a thorough examination, mentally noting each detail and storing it in his memory. Her hair was long, black, and thick, but there was something about it that was bothering his sensibilities. Picking up a handful, he was surprised at how soft it was. Normally, if someone had been in the saltwater as long as she had been, their hair would feel stiff and grainy.

Her skin was soft as well, devoid of any salt crystals. He traced a path down her neck and then paused. Bending closer, he tilted his head and studied a two-inch vertical line on the left side of her neck. Blue markings in the shape of scales were clustered along the line.

Fascinated, he ran his fingers over the scales. They were smooth and warm. He quickly pulled his fingers away when they changed colors, rippling a darker blue with black and silver threads. The combination reminded him of the ocean.

He didn't know what was going on, but Gabe – and this woman – had a lot of explaining to do. After all, it was the least they could do, considering he'd just put his medical license on the line. He continued his examination, trying to keep his touch as impersonal as possible, despite the heat warming his blood every time he touched Magna. With any other patient, he wouldn't have thought twice about it. However, his blood and body were literally growing warmer and it had nothing to do with the room temperature or his clothing.

Kane frowned when he touched Magna's side and felt her ribs. She was extremely thin, as if she had been starved. He added that information to his mental list of observations along with the dark shadows under her eyes, the lines of exhaustion around her mouth, and the gunshot wound. Memories of his own time in a war zone came back to him. He had seen his share of men who went through hell and returned as only a shell of who they had been when they first arrived.

He finished his exam and pulled up the duvet from the foot of the bed to cover her. A soft sigh slipped from her at the added warmth. He silently cursed himself. Between the chill in the room and her injuries, he should have realized she would be cold.

"Some doctor I am," he muttered in self-disgust.

Compelled to touch her once more, he tenderly ran his fingers along her pale cheek. His breath caught when she turned her head and rubbed her cheek against his palm. Muttering a curse, he pulled his hand away and stood up. It was time that he and Gabe had a very serious talk.

CHAPTER FOUR

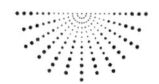

Gabe glanced over his shoulder when he heard Kane walking down the hall. He grabbed a potholder and opened the oven, then pulled out the salmon and shrimp combo. Sniffing the delicious aroma, he turned just as Kane came into the kitchen. He frowned at his friend's pale complexion.

"How is she?" Gabe asked, looking toward the hallway behind Kane with a concerned expression. "Were you able to patch her up?"

Kane nodded distractedly as he walked over to the small wine refrigerator built into the wall. Opening it, he scanned the selection before picking out a dry white wine. Gabe raised an eyebrow when Kane hesitated a moment, and then pulled out a second bottle. A two-bottle night for Kane didn't bode well for their upcoming discussion.

He placed the pan on the mango trivet on the table and tossed the potholder on the counter behind him, then leaned back against the polished granite countertop and folded his arms across his chest.

"What is it?" he asked in a blunt tone.

"Where did you find her?" Kane prompted, pulling the corkscrew out of the drawer next to the wine fridge and quickly removing the cork from the bottle. Gabe raised an eyebrow when his friend lifted the bottle of wine to his lips and greedily drank straight from the bottle. The way Kane was chugging the alcohol was more suited for a bottle of beer than the Sauvignon blanc. He waited with a sense of growing apprehension.

"Aw, shit! She's not… dead, is she?" he muttered, raising his hand and running it over his face.

His throat felt constricted and his voice sounded slightly strangled. He looked back toward the hallway. An intense and unexpected ache formed in his chest. He unconsciously slid his hand down to rub his chest over his heart at the thought of the woman's death.

"No!" Kane replied in a sharp tone. "No, she – her name is Magna, by the way – is not dead."

He blew out a loud, relieved breath. "Thank you," he replied and glanced toward the ceiling as the feeling in his chest eased a bit. He turned back to shoot Kane an accusing glare. "Then what the hell is wrong with you? I haven't seen you down a bottle of wine like that in… ever! You had me thinking she had keeled over dead!"

Kane walked over to one of the kitchen chairs, pulled it out, and sank down onto it, then glanced forlornly back at the second bottle of wine on the counter. Worried that Kane would get drunk and pass out before he shared what he'd found out, Gabe walked over and set a wine glass down in front of his friend, then pulled the half empty bottle out of Kane's hand and filled the glass before retrieving another and pouring one for himself.

He picked up the glass, looked at it, and downed it with a shrug before he poured himself another one. Only then did he slide onto the chair across from Kane with a fierce look of determination. He opened his mouth to ask, but Kane beat him to the punch.

"Tell me where you found her. I want to know everything," Kane said, looking intently at Gabe.

Gabe frowned as he stared at the food he had placed on the table minutes earlier. He picked up the spatula and slid a piece of salmon and several shrimp onto a plate before he passed it across to Kane. He thought about the question as he prepared another plate for himself.

"I was a mile or so off the coast of Yachats State Park. I had just finished my last run and was going to see if I could catch something for dinner. I dropped the net and trolled for a half mile. I was about to call it a night when there was a tug. I thought the net had snagged on something, or worse, caught a sea lion pup, when I heard a moan. When I pulled the net up, she was in it," he explained. He picked up his fork and moved the shrimp around on his plate, suddenly not as hungry as he had been.

"She said her name is Magna," Kane murmured as he picked up his glass of wine and took a sip before he continued. "She also said she was called the Sea Witch."

Gabe raised an eyebrow. "I'm not sure I'd call her a witch, more of a mermaid dressed in an evening gown. Anyway, Magna was in the net. I thought she was dead when I first pulled her in. Hell, I honestly don't know how she survived. She must have been in the water for a while since there wasn't another boat in sight. At the very least, she should have been suffering from severe hypothermia. When I turned her over, she moaned, then threw up all over my boots. I took her below to the cabin. That's when I realized that she had a bullet hole in her shoulder. I was going to call the authorities but figured if someone was willing to shoot her and dump her off the coast, maybe it was better if they didn't know she was alive… yet," he reasoned.

∽

Kane leaned back in his chair, his dinner forgotten for the moment as he stared across the table at Gabe. He thought of the slits along Magna's neck, the blue markings along it that heated and changed color when he had touched them, and the webbing between her fingers and delicate toes.

He shook his head and stared down into his wine glass. At the moment, nothing was making sense to him. There were two things that he was positive about, though. The first one was that Gabe did the right thing by not notifying the authorities. The second was that he was positive that Magna was very different than anyone he or Gabe had ever met before. He looked up when he heard the impatience in Gabe's voice.

"What?" Kane asked with a frown.

Gabe scowled at him. "I asked what else did she tell you? Is she hiding from some drug dealer, a possessive husband or boyfriend, or was she kidnapped and jumped ship?" Gabe asked irritably.

"She said Mike Hallbrook shot her and she told me her name – both of them – right before she pulled the slug out of her shoulder with some glowing silver threads flowing out of the palm of her right hand," he replied with a terse snort.

Shaking his head at the memory, he looked down at the plate in front of him and released a deep sigh. He picked up his fork and began eating the delicious meal Gabe had prepared for them. Maybe having food in his stomach would help him figure out what was going on. His mind spun. He kept thinking about what he'd seen and what his mind kept saying couldn't be real.

"Silver threads? How much wine did you drink before you arrived?" Gabe demanded, stabbing the fish on his plate and taking a bite.

Kane chuckled. He could understand Gabe's disbelief. If he hadn't seen what Magna had done with his own eyes, he wouldn't have believed him either! The problem was – he *had* seen what she'd done, and it still shook the hell out of him. He continued eating, deciding he might as well take the time to process all the information before he tried to explain it to Gabe.

They had been friends since their days in the army. That was over ten years ago. It was strange how they could be so different, yet so in tune with each other. He had seen the same type of relationships in twins and some siblings over the years, but never really between two people who came from such diverse backgrounds.

They saw the world and what they wanted from it in a slightly different way than most people did. Anyone looking at them would see two men who were the polar opposite of the other. Kane came from a wealthy family, had gone to exclusive private schools, received the best education money could buy, and was orphaned at a young age. He had enlisted in the Army after he achieved his medical degree at the tender age of twenty-four, searching for the one thing money couldn't buy – a family.

Gabe came from a low-income family. He'd been told his mother died when he was young, but he later learned that she just couldn't deal with his father anymore, so she'd left. Supposedly she planned on returning for him once she was financially able. His father hadn't believed her, and he'd gained full custody based on abandonment.

In the end, he was raised by a father who believed hard work and religion were the answers to all of life's problems. At eighteen, Gabe married and joined the Army to get away from home and to support his new wife with a better life. A year after he left, his dad died from a heart attack.

Gabe and Kane met when Gabe came into the infirmary. Kane had been relatively new to the Army while Gabe was nearly six years in by that time. Kane had discovered two things the first day they met. First, Gabe had an intense reaction to painkillers. They made him loopy and very talkative, which was uncharacteristic for the huge man. The second was what had connected them in a strange and serendipitous way. Gabe shared that he'd come home early one day to find his wife in bed with the Colonel in charge of his unit. When he had offered to join the two of them, his wife became outraged and kicked him to the curb. It was alright for her to screw around behind her husband's back, but by damn, he'd better not expect to join her in bed while she was with the bastard she was screwing.

Blackballed, Gabe had been transferred to another base while his soon-to-be ex-wife did everything she could to take what little inheritance he had received from his father. The Colonel didn't fair quite as well. His ex-wife had gone for blood. Gabe's ex had finally roped the

Colonel into getting married and having a kid. The marriage lasted less than two years before she was calling Gabe to complain.

Kane would never forget Gabe's unexpected comment. "Hell, if she had said yes, I'd have tried to forget, you know? Go for it, despite the fact that I couldn't stand the bastard," Gabe had said in a slightly slurred voice. "Maybe there's something wrong with me. I just want...."

Kane had waited, but Gabe had become quiet and somber. A week later, Kane ran into Gabe again while they were on temporary duty between reassignments. A few beers while playing pool, and they discovered they had a lot more in common than they'd thought, and after a lot more alcohol, they found a hot brunette who liked having two men at the same time. She had given them both a wild night that started a lifestyle they both enjoyed.

Since that night, their friendship had grown until they were more like family, which was something neither of them would ever admit they wanted or needed. Kane didn't mind. He didn't expect to ever find a woman who would complete him. Almost immediately, the dark-haired sea nymph lying asleep in Gabe's spare bedroom flashed through his mind. No matter how hard he tried to push the vision of her face away, it kept coming back.

He grunted and drained his wine glass again. Personally, he had never found a woman who attracted him enough to risk everything he had worked for and the wealth he had inherited. Most women, including the nurses at the hospital, were only interested in his money and the lifestyle he could give them. Once again, Magna's haunted eyes flashed through his mind.

"She's not like us, Gabe," Kane suddenly said, breaking the silence.

Gabe frowned and set his fork down on his empty plate. "Explain," he demanded.

Kane groaned and pushed his plate away. He ran his hands through his tousled hair, then finally looked at Gabe with determination. Rising out of his seat, he pursed his lips before he jerked his head. It would be better to show Gabe than try to explain it.

"Come on," Kane ordered. "I need to show you something."

Gabe was surprised enough that it took a moment for his friend to rise up out of his seat, but Kane finally heard the scrape of the chair as Gabe pushed away from the table, then, as usual, he heard no footsteps as Gabe followed him. For such a big bastard, Gabe was light on his feet. That was one reason he'd done well in the army, not to mention how he was able to catch his ex-wife in the act with the Colonel.

He walked down the hallway and back to the bedroom where Magna was resting. Opening the bedroom door, he stepped inside and quietly walked over to the bed.

Kane silently gazed down at Magna's thick black hair. The strands were spread out around her, creating a halo effect against the pristine white sheets.

Taking a deep breath, he waved his hand at Magna. "Look at her neck," Kane quietly instructed, moving aside so Gabe could step closer.

Gabe looked down at Magna before he glanced at Kane. "I already did. She's got a scar along her throat and… tattoos that look like real scales along her neck," he replied.

"They aren't scars or tattoos," Kane replied with a firm shake of his head. "They are slits and she has them on each side of her neck."

"Slits?" Gabe asked in surprise, glancing at Magna's peaceful face. "Did someone try to cut her throat as well? I don't see Mike Hallbrook as the kind of guy who would carve up a woman – and what do you mean those aren't tattoos?"

"They look real because they are. I observed reactive scales along her neck… and elsewhere," Kane stated.

"Where else does she have them?" Gabe asked.

Kane took a step closer to the bed and carefully pulled back the covers. The long slits that ran down the gown's skirt on each side had been torn further at some point in her misadventure and her sides were now bare from just above her waist down to her feet. There were faint lines of scales running down and around her legs. He pulled aside a torn section of the dress near her waist so that Gabe could see the pattern along her flat stomach as well.

Gabe softly whistled. "What the hell? Who is she? What is she?" he asked, repeating the same question Kane asked earlier.

They looked closer and noticed small patches of blue, silver, and black scales along both of her arms. Kane watched Gabe bend over and run his fingers over a part of her stomach that was peeking out from the torn gown. Magna moaned and restlessly moved against the soft, cotton sheets.

Gabe carefully pulled the covers over her before he stepped back. Kane gave his friend a strained smile when he noticed that Gabe's tanned face was paler than normal. It was obvious from the way Gabe was rubbing his fingers that his friend had felt the same slight shock and warmth that he had when he had touched the colorful scales on Magna's skin.

"I need a drink," Gabe said bluntly as he turned on his heel.

"You're going to need more than wine when I tell you what else happened," Kane muttered, turning to follow his friend. "You'd better break out the good stuff."

CHAPTER FIVE

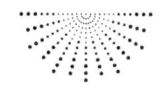

Magna yawned and slowly opened her eyes. She blinked in surprise at the bright light coming in through the window. For a moment, she lay there stunned. She was afraid that if she moved, the dream would disappear, and she would wake up locked in terror of the creature inhabiting her body again.

"If you don't close your mouth, it might get stuck that way," a deep voice drawled.

Magna snapped her mouth shut and carefully turned her head, dragging her gaze away from the lush vegetation outside the window. She looked into a pair of vaguely familiar brown eyes. A flush heated her cheeks when she realized that there were actually two sets of eyes glued to her. She brushed back a strand of her long hair.

A confused frown creased her brow. "You did not take my life. Why? Why did you not kill me whilst you had the chance? Your king will not be happy that you have kept me alive, unless…" Her voice faded as the fear she thought was gone rose once again to choke her.

She clenched the soft covers in her fists. Tears burned her eyes, but she blinked them away. She deserved no pity and no mercy for her actions.

No one would believe that she had been forced to do such heinous things. No one could understand the power of the alien creature unless they experienced it first-hand.

Just the thought of the creature impelled her to search her body once again to see if any of the creature remained inside her to fester and grow. Her heart beat with such ferocity at the thought that she couldn't breathe. Her hand shook when she laid it against her chest. She could feel nothing but the empty void and a choking fear. There was nothing inside her that reminded her of the alien creature.

Out of the corner of her eye, she saw both men rise from the two chairs near the door and walk toward the bed. She tried to slow her panting with a deep, calming breath. She pushed away the choking panic. She would never live in fear again.

She followed Gabe with her eyes. She held herself rigid when he sat down on the left side of the bed while Kane walked around the bed to sit on her right, effectively caging her between them.

Her mind swirled with confusion and suspicion. Her eyes narrowed, and she pursed her lips, glancing back and forth between them, wondering which one would strike out first.

A soft growl of indignation slipped out before she could stop it. She didn't know what game they were playing or what magic they must be using on her, but whatever it was, it was driving her crazy. Her body suddenly felt like it was alive in a way she had never experienced before. The burning in her shoulder suddenly moved down between her legs. She wiggled under the covers at the uncomfortable sensations. She snapped her head to the left when Gabe spoke.

"Why do you think we should have killed you?" Gabe asked in a deep, deceptively calm voice.

Magna's chin trembled as she fought back the tears threatening to escape. "I am the Sea Witch," she confessed, raising her chin. "I have caused many horrors over the centuries. I stirred the Kingdoms to war. I… tried… I tried to take Orion's… the Sea King's son, Dolph, under my control. I… I turned the people of the Isle of Magic, including their beloved queen, to stone and threatened to kill their king. I deserve nothing less than death. I only beg that you do it swiftly and with mercy, for I had little control over my actions. If you don't kill me, Drago will, regardless of whether I was in control of my body or not."

"Who is Drago?" Kane asked, his tone matching Gabe's. He leaned forward and slid his hand along her chin, gently turning her face toward him.

It had been so long since she'd felt the comforting touch of another. Yesterday, the men had acted like they had no idea who she was. While she held the memory of their touch close to her heart, she'd also thought they would not have done it had they had known her identity.

The fact that Kane's touch was tender caused her chest to hurt. She didn't try to stop the single tear that fell from the corner of her eye and rolled down her cheek. Instead, she swallowed and forced the answer to his question past the ache in her chest.

"He is the Dragon King," she whispered, unable to look away from Kane's intense blue eyes. He moved his hand from her chin to lightly rest on her collarbone. "Drago's was the first Kingdom that I… that the creature inhabiting my body ordered me to attack. Most of the dragons were taken within the first few hours, caught in their nests along the cliffs. The beast… He knew dragon-fire was the most dangerous of all to his species. That is what gave me the idea for the Starburst spell. I needed a spell that would burn hotter than a dragon's fire. The only thing that does is a star. It took me over a century to develop a spell that would work. I had to be careful. If it went wrong, it could destroy all the worlds. Not even my father's people who live beneath the oceans would have survived."

She started in surprise when she felt a warm hand tenderly lift the fingers of her left hand off the bed. He didn't raise it far; she suspected he was being careful because of her wound. She gasped when something cold and wet suddenly pushed against their joined fingers.

"Damn it, Wilson," Gabe muttered in aggravation as he released her hand and started to push the pup away.

"No," Magna protested. She winced as she stretched out her hand until her fingers hung over the side of the bed. "What is he?" she asked in wonder when she was rewarded with a tongue across her fingers.

Gabe stroked the furry head of the beast with an affectionate touch that belied his gruff voice. "This is Wilson," he replied. "He's a six-month-old eating, pooping, chewing machine better known as a puppy."

Magna couldn't keep the delight out of her eyes as she moved her fingers along the puppy's jaw. Her gaze flickered to the bottom of the bed where another beast, slightly larger and obviously older, placed its paws up on the end of the bed and looked down at her. Its tail moved back and forth, and its large tongue hung out crookedly from the side of its mouth.

"That's Buck, Wilson's dad," Kane explained with a chuckle. "It would appear you've been adopted."

She looked back and forth between the two furry beasts and the two men. Her face flushed when she realized that all of them were looking at her. She wasn't used to being around others, at least those who were curious about her instead of filled with fear or the desire to kill her. The strange warmth she'd felt earlier spread inside her until she felt lightheaded.

She looked at Kane. "I would like to get up. And… I am hungry," she requested in a hesitant voice.

Kane looked at Gabe. She could almost hear the silent communication between them. She waited in silence. She would not beg. She had done enough of that over the centuries with the alien creature.

Kane rose to his feet. "I'll help you. I want to check your sutures. Gabe is a much better cook than I am. You'll be filling out in no time," he teased.

Her lips parted in surprise, turning to look at Gabe when he stood up. She saw an easy grin curve his lips, and he nodded. "I'll make some of my famous soup. She'll be eating out of my hand after she has a taste of it," he replied with a wink at her. "Come on, boys. You two probably need to go out as well."

Closing her mouth, she watched in dismay as Gabe and the two beasts left the room. She bit her lip to prevent an unexpected cry of protest from slipping out.

She wanted him to stay. Confused by the feelings coursing through her, she started in surprise when she felt the cool air of the room as the bedcover was pulled off. Kane moved closer to her, and as he carefully helped her sit up, she turned her face toward him, and looked up at him with uncertain, pleading eyes. "I do not understand all of this," Magna whispered in a barely audible voice.

Kane uttered a short, rough chuckle. "I can promise you, neither do we," Kane replied in a slightly hoarse voice before he cleared his throat. "Listen, you may be a little unsteady. You lost quite a bit of blood. I'll help you to the bathroom. It might be best if you wait before taking a shower. I'd like to check your sutures, make sure everything looks alright."

She nodded, thankful for Kane's strong arm around her waist as she rose to her feet. The feel of his rough clothing against the bare skin of her arm was strange, but it was the warmth of his hand against the material of her tattered gown that sent a wave of longing through her. She couldn't help but wonder what it would be like to feel his and Gabe's hands sliding over her.

"Why do I want this?" she whispered out loud.

Kane looked down at her as they walked slowly into the guest bathroom. "Why do you want what?" he asked in a strained voice.

Magna looked up at Kane in confusion. "I wish to feel your and Gabe's hands on my body," she replied. "I have never felt this need before. I do not understand why even the thought makes my body warm in places that I have never felt before."

She saw Kane swallow as he carefully turned her around. His gaze flickered over her shoulder for a moment before returning to look down at her. Magna started when she felt Gabe's warmth suddenly pressed against her back. Tilting her head, she looked over her right shoulder. Kane's hands were on her waist, while Gabe's hands cupped her hips.

"Gabe," Kane cautioned in a tight voice.

"I know," Gabe growled, even as he pulled Magna back against him. "I came to see what kind of soup she wanted and heard her. You aren't the only one feeling the heat, Magna. Just be thankful you are hurt, otherwise, my lovely mermaid, you'd have more than my hands on you."

Magna took in a swift breath, her body melting against Gabe as her hands tightened around Kane's arms and she pulled him toward her. Her lips parted as she stared up at Kane. A shiver of… desire ran through her body. She wanted these two unusual men.

"Shit," Kane muttered as he closed the distance between them, capturing her lips with his in a barely controlled kiss.

Gabe's grasp on her hips tightened, and he groaned. Magna was vaguely aware of the fingers caressing her skin. Her lips instinctively parted for Kane's heated kiss. She moaned when his hands moved up to her breasts. She strained against them, seeking more when he began to pull away.

"I want more," Magna whimpered before she winced when she moved her left arm too high.

"And that is why we can't," Kane muttered. He glanced up at Gabe who was pressing a hot kiss to Magna's neck. "Gabe…"

Magna giggled when she heard the sound of exasperation in Kane's voice. She tilted her head so that Gabe could continue pressing his lips against her skin. She sighed in regret when Gabe reluctantly pulled away.

"You started it," Gabe complained in a gruff voice.

"Yes, you did," Magna teased, surprising herself.

Kane scowled at both of them. "No, you did," he accused, the scowl on his face destroyed by the grin he was trying to hide. "Let me check your wound. Gabe will feed you, then we need to talk about a few things."

Magna nodded, fear beginning to replace the happiness and excitement that she'd felt just moments before. She waited until Kane and Gabe stepped away from her. A shiver ran through her as the cool air of the room replaced the warmth they had provided. She gave Gabe an uncertain smile when he wrapped a large, thick cloth around her shoulders.

"Very well," she murmured, lifting her chin.

Gabe started to turn away, but paused and looked at her with a frown. "I forgot to ask you what I came in here for. What do you like to eat? I mean, do you eat regular food or something special?" he asked with sudden concern.

Magna's eyes softened at his look. "I eat just about anything. It has been so long since I ate anything that actually tasted good, I'm not sure it would matter what you prepare," she admitted with an uncertain smile.

A frown creased his brow at her response. "I have some more salmon in the freezer. I'll make that and some eggs…. That is…." He stopped and looked at Kane standing behind her.

"She should be alright," Kane assured him. "I could eat some of that myself."

Gabe rolled his eyes. "You're lucky I like to cook," he growled and stepped out of the room.

Kane chuckled and winked at Magna. "He knows I'm a lousy cook. We'd be living on peanut butter and banana sandwiches if he didn't cook," he shared with a wry grin.

Magna nodded, though she had no idea what manner of creature peanut butter was. She walked over and sat down on a small bench seat against the wall near the bathing room. She bowed her head and listened to Kane as he examined her shoulder. He talked about Gabe with affection, telling her funny stories about when the they were in the military together. Her gaze roamed around the small room, pausing on the long bank of windows. They opened onto a large deck and would be easy to access the path down to the water should she need to escape.

She looked up, startled, when she felt his fingers on her chin. He was staring into her eyes with an inquiring look of concern. She gave him an uneven smile.

"All done. The wound is healing faster than I expected," he said in a quiet voice. "Do you need any help getting cleaned up?"

"No, I can care for myself," she replied with a shake of her head, not sharing the fact that her wound would be healed already if she could return to the water now that the metal was no longer in her.

She blinked when Kane didn't remove his hand. Instead, he cupped her cheek. Magna knew she shouldn't respond to the light caress, but she was starving for physical contact.

"Magna, everything will be alright," he promised. "Gabe and I, we'll help you."

Magna's eyes filled with tears and, though she tried to prevent it, one escaped to slide down her cheek. She didn't answer. All she could do was nod her head. She couldn't help but think that Gabe and Kane didn't understand the scope of all the horrible things that she had done, despite what she had told them. It was only a matter of time before they learned that what she'd said was true. When they did, she knew they would feel differently about her.

Keeping her gaze locked with his, she leaned forward and pressed her lips against his in a brief kiss. She pulled back and moved to the side as she stood, then turned her back, and stepped into the room. With a wave of her hand, the door closed behind her but not before she heard his startled hiss.

Leaning against the door, she closed her eyes. Her body was trembling, and a hint of a smile curved her lips. She lifted her hand to touch them.

She decided right then that it didn't matter whether she had died and the Goddess had given her mercy by casting her here or if she was alive and was allowed a brief reprieve. She would grasp every second she could with both hands and hug it close to her heart so that no matter what happened, she would have these memories to take with her.

Straightening, she stepped away from the door and gazed around the room. It wasn't large, but the room was made warm and comfortable by the light wooden cabinets etched with designs that looked almost like they were telling a story, and smooth, dark wood under her feet. She walked over to the sink and ran her hand along the polished marble.

She looked away when she saw her reflection in the mirror. Her long hair looked limp and lifeless. Her dress was torn and stained. Dark shadows under her eyes and a gaunt, pale face finished off the image. In the brief glance, she saw more than she wanted to – the ravages of the alien creature's mark upon her.

A startling feeling of rage intensified until she felt like screaming. Gripping the torn material around her injured shoulder, she ripped it away from her body. She released the ruined material, and the gown pooled around her ankles. She stepped out of the crumpled material.

A large enclosure revealed a shower. She pulled open the glass door and stepped inside. Despite Kane's caution about taking a shower, she needed to feel the water against her skin.

It took her a minute to understand the mechanics behind the faucet, but soon, warm water flowed over her weary body. She closed her eyes and tilted her head back. It felt so good. It wasn't the same as the ocean, but it still gave her comfort.

Ten minutes later, she felt refreshed. She had washed her body and hair, not an easy task with her injured shoulder and dried off – with a little help from her magic. Unfortunately, even the tiny bit she conjured to create a simple wind spell left her so weak she wasn't sure she would make it back into the bedroom.

"Magna...," Kane's voice faded when he saw her holding onto the door knob. "Damn it, I knew I should have gone in there with you, especially when I heard the shower."

The towel around her started to slip. It took her a second to realize it wasn't just the towel slipping, but herself as well. Strong hands carefully tucked the towel around her body before she was lifted off her feet. She would have protested, but that would have taken more energy than she had at the moment.

"I will be fine in a few minutes. I shouldn't have tried to cast a spell when I was already weak. I knew better," she said with a touch of self-disgust.

"You shouldn't.... What kind of spell?" Kane asked in a slightly uneasy voice.

She looked up at him when he gently set her down on the edge of the bed. She saw him direct a cautious glance toward the bathing room. Once again, that feeling of anger grew inside her, leaving a bitter taste.

"A simple one. It would not have harmed anyone. I needed to dry off. I cast a dry wind spell. The spell worked, but casting it left me weak," she said, her voice growing softer by the end as she wondered if it was smart to share that information.

"Oh, just a simple dry wind spell," he lightly replied, glancing at the bathing room door again before he looked down at her.

"Yes," she responded.

Looking down, she wrapped her fingers around the blue shirt lying on the bed. She looked up again when she heard Gabe utter a long string of heated curses from another room followed by excited barking. An expression of indecision crossed Kane's face.

"I need...," he started to say, returning his attention to her.

"I can…," she said at the same time.

"I'll be right back. Stay here," he instructed.

Magna lifted her chin. "Am I a prisoner?" she asked, glancing at the door before returning her attention to him.

"Are you a…? Where the hell did that come from? Of course you aren't a prisoner! I should go rescue Wilson before Gabe decides to give that damn pup to me!" Kane exclaimed with a crooked grin.

"Oh," Magna replied, her eyes widening when Gabe's exasperated voice echoed down the hall.

"Kane! I swear I'm dumping Wilson's ass at your place first thing in the morning! Wilson needs intervention and I need help. He's brought another damn rat into the house and turned it loose in the living room," Gabe growled.

"Damn! Not again," Kane muttered, turning and hurried from the bedroom. "Why do I always have to catch the rodents? He's your dog," Kane yelled as he exited the room.

Magna couldn't help uttering a soft giggle. The sounds of excited barking, Kane's sharp and frustrated yells, and Gabe's deep laughter filled her with curiosity and a strange warmth that was slowly filling the emptiness inside her.

Standing up, she pulled on the blue shirt. It swallowed her figure, falling almost to her knees. She didn't have any underclothes to wear and was afraid to conjure any.

The fragrant smells of food caused her stomach to rumble, making her realize that she was actually hungry for the first time in ages. She buttoned the shirt as best as she could and followed the sounds of chaos and the smell of food.

"If I'm going to take back my life, I have to learn to live," she whispered as she walked down the hallway. "I will not live in fear any longer. I will never fear the shadows again for I have owned them, and I know what lives in the darkness."

More confident, she walked down the hallway to the large kitchen. Pausing in the doorway, she watched the two men in silence for several minutes. Gabe was mixing something in a large bowl while Kane was washing his hands in the sink, muttering dire threats under his breath to Wilson. The two dogs lay on thick padded beds to one side. The younger one lifted his head when he saw her, wagged his tail, but didn't move as he cast a wary eye at Kane's back.

CHAPTER SIX

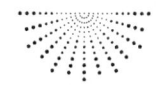

"You have to give Wilson credit, he doesn't harm the damn critters he brings home, he just wants to love on them," Kane said.

"Yeah, well, having the two dogs is enough company for… me," Gabe was saying before he realized that Magna was standing in the doorway.

A wave of uncertainty washed through her when both men turned to look at her. Of course, her stomach decided to rumble at that same moment. She drew in a deep, calming breath. A small moan of delight slipped from her lips when she breathed in the delicious scents filling the air.

She laid the palm of her right hand over her stomach and blushed. She nervously tugged at the hem of the oversized light blue shirt that she was wearing. It had been so long since she'd been around anyone, much less dined with them, that she was unsure of what she should do.

"I… It smells so good," she murmured with a weak smile. "I can't remember the last time I was actually hungry."

Gabe's eyes swept over her. Her skin tingled at the intense, assessing look. When his lips tightened, she turned her gaze away, looking to Kane. Her stomach flipped when Kane returned her gaze with a slightly reproving look that was mixed with concern as he stepped closer to her.

"I would have returned to help you. It took a little longer than I expected to rescue Wilson's latest acquisition," Kane quietly explained.

"What kind of acquisition?" she asked, curious.

"Rabbit this time," Gabe answered with an exasperated glare at the Husky who raised his head and wagged his tail. He lifted a pot off the stove and nodded at her. "Let's eat before the food gets cold. As Buck and Wilson will tell you, I'm the best cook in the house. Doc here can't even cook a boiled egg," he boasted.

Magna glanced over to where the two beasts were sleeping. "Are Buck and Wilson changelings?" she asked.

Both men stared at her in silence for a few seconds before they shook their heads. Unsure of what she had said wrong, she looked over at the stove.

"I've never boiled an egg before," she replied, moving to sit down in the chair that Kane pulled out for her.

Kane cleared his throat. "Boiling eggs is not as easy as it sounds," he said and nodded toward Gabe. "I'll take sewing up a cut any day over cooking. Don't ask him to suture a cut. He can't stitch worth a damn."

Gabe snorted. "Boiling eggs isn't that difficult, and I can stitch just fine – as long as it is a net. Besides, stitching up someone is highly overrated. That is why super glue was invented. Pull the skin together, pour a little of it along the cut, and voila! No holes and no gaps," Gabe defended, placing a plate of salmon, eggs, and toast in front of Magna.

Magna eagerly picked up her fork and began eating while the two men argued over the proper use of superglue. Her eyes flickered back and forth between the two of them. They were a beautiful contrast to each other: Gabe's short black hair, dark, serious brown eyes, deeply tanned face, and muscular frame, and Kane's light brown shaggy hair, dancing blue eyes, pale skin, and tall, lean build.

The conversation shifted when they finished their meal. She knew then that the men had kept up their running banter to keep her occupied while she ate. Magna swallowed and lowered her fork to the empty plate in front of her.

"So, tell us about yourself," Kane said in a soothing tone. "Where are you from? How did you get here?"

"Why did Mike shoot you and where is he?" Gabe added before he grunted and shot a glare at Kane. "What? I want to know!"

Magna bent her head to look at her plate for a moment before she drew in a deep breath. She thought about their questions, her mind running through all of the ways she could avoid confessing all of the horrendous atrocities that she had committed. She finally decided she had nothing left to lose if she told Kane and Gabe what had happened to her. It would only be a matter of time before someone told them.

She looked up to stare out of the sliding glass doors. Through the tall trees, she could see the ocean. Rising up out of her seat, she walked over to the glass doors and laid her palm against the cool surface.

"Two centuries ago, my cousin Orion and I were sitting on the beach of the Isle of the Sea Serpent. It is the home of my father's people. It was late, and the stars glowed brilliantly in the sky. We were talking about what we wanted to do when we grew older," she quietly explained, the scene before her fading as she remembered that night.

A soft smile curved her lips. She wasn't aware that both men could see every expression on her face in the reflection of the glass. In a way, she had forgotten they were even there as she became lost in her memories. She drew in a deep breath before she continued.

"Orion's life was already laid out before him. He would one day become king of our people, but me… I wanted to explore the world. I had always been too adventurous. My parents often cautioned me that my curiosity would lead me astray, but I didn't care. I had explored further and further away from the safety of the Isle of the Sea Serpent unbeknownst to them, and discovered many amazing new worlds. I went to the Isle of the Dragon and played with them in the surf. I loved the markets on the Isle of Magic where you could buy potions and spell books. I was planning to visit the Isle of Giants. I had learned an invisibility spell that I wanted to try, but everything changed after that night...." Her voice became heavy with sadness as it faded.

"What happened?" Kane asked in a quiet voice when she didn't go on.

Her eyes filled with tears, but she refused to let them fall. Crying would not change the course of history. Neither would it redeem her sins or wash away the pain she had inflicted on others.

"There was a meteor," she whispered, lost in the memories of that night. "I made a wish on it. Orion and I watched as it flew through the night and splashed in the ocean not far from the beach where we sat. I called for my sea dragon, Raine. If I found the meteorite, my wish would have to come true. We raced out to sea, searching for it."

Her fingers curled on the glass as she remembered the joy that had turned to terror. In a way, the young girl she had been had died that night. In her place a monster had risen – a monster known as the Sea Witch.

"Did you...? Find the meteorite, that is?" Gabe asked.

She turned her head slightly to the side and nodded, before looking back at the ocean again. "Yes, or rather I should say it found me," she replied after several long seconds. "Orion called for me to stop. He said the water did not feel right. I laughed at him. I thought he was just trying to distract me so he could find the meteorite first. We often teased each other, so I thought this was just another way for him to get ahead of me. He was right, though. I should have listened to him," she said, turning to look at Kane and Gabe and wrapping her arms around her waist. "We were about to leave when it came up out of the depths beneath us. Orion did not see it, but I did. I tried to warn him, but in my haste, I scared his mount. He was thrown from his sea dragon and struck his head on the side of the cliff. I was able to grab him before the creature could and I pulled him across Raine's back. I urged Raine to flee, but she was too young and small to handle the combined weight of both Orion and myself. I knew that Orion had to live. He was our future king. It was my responsibility to protect him when he could not protect himself."

She swallowed and absently wiped at the dampness on her cheek. She'd sworn she wouldn't cry, yet the tears came anyway. She angrily brushed them away.

"I tried to escape, but the creature had wrapped its tentacles around my legs and was pulling me down into the abyss. As it did... I could see what it wanted, what it would do to our world," she said in a tight, desperate voice. She waved her hand in the air as she remembered the horror she had witnessed. "There was nothing I could do. I struggled, but more of its limbs wrapped around me until I could barely breathe. The only thing I could do was try to protect a small part of myself. I hid deep inside my own mind, watching helplessly as the alien creature tried to destroy my world. I hoped that one day I would be able to find a way to kill it. The creature had unwittingly shown me what had happened to the others of its kind, but I was not sure how I could use that knowledge to defeat it."

A soft sob escaped her, and she shook her head as she tried to push the suffocating fear away. The memories were still so vivid, even after all this time. Locked in the memory of that darkness, she struggled to break free.

Both Kane and Gabe rose from their seats. The two dogs, sensing her distress, whined and padded over to her. Magna looked down at the light blue eyes of the Huskies. She reached down and curled her fingers in the thick hair at Buck's nape.

"What was it?" Kane asked in a somber tone.

She looked up at him, unaware of the tortured expression in her eyes. "Something that came from the stars," she replied. "Its own planet had been destroyed by a comet. In desperation, it and others of its kind melded with the debris that was thrown back into space. It stayed locked inside the metal, waiting until the time it could break free. It is a parasitic species. They take over the host."

"Couldn't this Orion or someone help you?" Gabe asked, running his hand over his nape. "I mean, you saved this guy's life, surely he could have figured out a way to kill the thing."

Magna shook her head and released a sigh. She turned to stare back out at the ocean. She could feel the tug of it on her body. She needed to go for a swim.

"I realized what the creature's plans were and I feared for my people. In desperation, I cast a binding spell, locking it to my body. As long as I lived, it did, but if I should die, it would as well. I would not give it a chance to overtake another. Later, I woke on the beach next to Orion," she said. "At first, I thought I had dreamed the entire episode until I saw the deep gash on Orion's head. I struggled up to the palace and notified the guards. Everything seemed strange and disorientated. I was hearing a voice in my head and the pressure… The pressure in my body made me feel as if I would explode. I returned to the water and disappeared beneath the waves, hoping that the soothing minerals in it would heal my body. Instead, I was pulled back down into the abyss. Over time, the creature became hungry to be set free. It grew stronger inside me until I could no longer separate it from myself. No one knew what had happened to me, including my parents, until I was forced to return as the creature tried to take over the Kingdoms."

"Shit! Didn't anyone suspect that something had happened to change you?" Gabe demanded.

"No," she replied with a shiver. She wrapped her hands around her waist again, ignoring the protest of her shoulder. "I spent years hiding and trying to figure out how to kill the thing inside me. I studied its memories. I even tried…" Her voice growing quiet at the dark despair.

"What did you try?" Kane urged.

Magna shook her head again. "I tried to kill myself," she said in an emotionless voice. "Several times, but the creature always stopped me before I could. That's when I knew I had to force my cousin to end my life. It took me years before I could finally combine several spells into one that I knew would be powerful enough to kill it, but I also knew I would need help to weaken the creature, to distract it, so that it could not stop me. That day came when Mike used his weapon against me. The timing had to be just right. I knew the spell would destroy any who remained, including myself."

"Damn. I heard that before Mike Hallbrook disappeared, he contacted his sister and said he was leaving, but it was all real strange," Gabe muttered behind her. "That answers my questions, but what about Kane's? Where did you come from and how did you get here?"

Magna turned around again and tilted her head as she studied the two men. A small, sad smile curved her lips. With a slight shrug, she gave them the answer to one and what she suspected for the other.

"My home is – was – part of the Seven Kingdoms. I lived on the Isle of the Sea Serpent, where our homes extend both above and below the waters surrounding our kingdom. I have never seen your kingdom before. As to how I came here, I suspect that when I cast the spell, I used a portion of it to take me away. I wanted to feel soothing waters once more before I died. I remember nothing else until you pulled me onto your vessel."

"Double damn," both men whispered at the same time, staring at her in stunned silence.

She returned their look with a steady gaze of her own. She wasn't sure what they had been expecting, but it clearly wasn't the explanation she had given them. She swallowed, her stomach knotting. She waited to see what they would say. Afraid to see their expressions turn to fear and disgust as they realized just how tainted and depraved she had been, she turned to gaze back out over the trees at the distant sea.

If I can make it to the water, she thought with a weary sigh. *I could disappear beneath the waves, even on this world.*

CHAPTER SEVEN

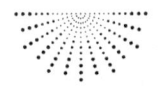

Another shiver ran through Magna as she continued to stare out the window, waiting for the two men behind her to decide what they would do. For so long, she had been the silent observer. Without the alien creature inside her, she felt hollow, disoriented, and clumsy. Still, she would rather feel that than the horrible darkness and loneliness that had filled her before.

"What are you going to do to me?" Magna finally forced out over the lump in her throat. Turning, she stared at Kane and Gabe. "If you let me go, I swear that neither you nor anyone else will ever see me again. I can hide in the depths of your oceans as well as I can in those on my world. I will never again raise my hand to harm another."

"No!" Gabe growled, taking a step toward her.

Kane's arm shot out and he stopped Gabe when she pressed back against the glass door. "I don't think that would be a good idea, Magna. You are still weak and need medical attention. Why don't we go into the living room? You've been through a very traumatic event and should still be resting," he commented in a soothing voice.

She stared with wide, uncertain eyes at the two men, then bowed her head to hide her feelings. Hadn't they listened to what she had just told them? Didn't they understand all the horrible things she had done, even if it was beyond her control? If she had been found in her world, she would have been lucky to have been killed the moment they realized who she was. At worst, she would have been imprisoned until she met a horrifying death.

She started when she felt a gentle hand on her uninjured arm. Glancing up, she stared into Kane's blue eyes. She bit her lip, wondering why she felt such an intense desire to step into his arms. She started to turn her head away, but Kane reached up and tenderly caressed her jaw.

"We aren't going to turn you away or condemn you for something that was out of your control, Magna," he said in a quiet voice. "You did what you could to stop the creature. That is what matters in the end… and, you have to remember, you were successful."

"Even if it almost cost you your life," Gabe added gruffly as he stepped closer to her.

She looked back and forth between the two men. "I do not understand either of you," she said with a self-conscious laugh. "I really don't understand any of this."

She waved her good arm outward, starting when Gabe grabbed her hand and gently tugged her against his hard frame. Her lips parted in surprise. The gasp on them was captured by his lips as he suddenly kissed her before he pulled back with a fierce look in his eyes.

"What's to understand? I found you, I get to keep you," he replied with a confident grin.

"We get to keep you," Kane said, wrapping an arm around her waist and turning her around until she was pressed against him. "That's if you want us. Give us a chance to help you heal. You'll be safe here. Gabe and I will make sure of that."

Pleasure and hope swept through her. Did they mean it? They weren't repulsed by her? Her eyes widened at the thought that she might be accepted.

She barely nodded, but it was enough for Kane. He bent forward, brushing his lips against hers before he deepened the kiss until she was so shaken, she would have fallen if not for his arms around her.

It was the soft expletive from Gabe that pulled them apart. She couldn't stop the delighted laugh that escaped her when she saw why he was cussing. Wilson, not to be left out, was standing on his hind legs with his paws on Gabe's chest, licking his face.

"Damn it, Wilson," Gabe muttered, tilting his head back. "I know you like to drink out of the toilet, you dumb mutt."

Kane's laughter mixed with hers as the Husky eagerly reached for Gabe's face. "Come on into the living room," Kane suggested, wrapping his arm around her to steady her when she swayed with fatigue. "You lost a lot of blood, and have been through a lot over the last few…." He broke off with a frown. "Listen, Gabe made a wicked dessert. Do you like chocolate?"

Magna gazed back at him with a puzzled expression on her face. "Chocolate?" she repeated before shaking her head. "I have never heard of it before."

"One hot fudge brownie coming up," Gabe replied with a wink, pushing Wilson down with a sharp command to behave. "I swear I need to send him to puppy school again."

"Come with me and give your master some peace, Wilson. I will give you attention," she murmured to the pup.

She leaned heavily against Kane and grinned at the mischievous pup that raced ahead of them into the living room. She murmured a soft thanks to Kane when he led her to the plush chair near the window. It was as if Kane knew she wished to look out at the ocean.

Her right hand slipped over the side of the chair and she scratched Wilson behind his ear. There was something very soothing and almost normal about what she was doing. She smiled her thanks when Kane draped a thick blanket across her lap and carefully tucked it around her. Resting her head back against the head-rest, she stared outside.

Dark clouds were beginning to form over the ocean. She loved it when the waves grew rough and wild. Orion, Kapian, and she used to ride the huge waves that would form, diving deep as they crashed.

After several minutes, Wilson released a contented sigh and trotted over to his bed where several thick chew bones lay. He circled several times before lying down on top of them. Buck followed Gabe back into the room and lay down on the rug in front of the large section of glass doors. She turned her head and watched as Gabe carefully placed a small tray in front of her, followed by a bowl filled with a strange mixture of warm brown cake and a white, creamy topping.

"There was one thing you said that has me confused," Kane said as he settled into the chair across from her.

"Only one?" Gabe asked with a raised eyebrow.

"I will tell you all I can. It is the least I can do for all your kindness. What would you like to know?" she asked, lifting a spoonful of the creamy concoction up so she could sniff it. It smelled delicious. She took a small bite, her eyes widening in delight at the mixture of warm chocolate and cold ice cream. "Oh! This is marvelous!"

Gabe gave her a slightly crooked smile as he sank down on the couch. "I'm glad you like it. Chocolate brownie and ice cream," he said, before looking at Kane. "So, what's your question?"

∼

Kane leaned forward, gazing at Magna as she eagerly scooped more of the dessert into her mouth.

"How old are you, Magna?" Kane asked in a quiet voice.

She paused and tilted her head as if she wasn't quite sure what he was asking. There was a slight frown that creased her brow. She slowly lowered the spoon back down to the bowl and licked her lips, making him want to groan again at his body's reaction to the innocent move. A thoughtful look came into her eyes as she stared at him.

"I'm almost two hundred and fifty years old," she said, biting her lower lip. "That may be very young by most standards, but I feel much older."

"Two hundred and…. Shit," Gabe muttered, sitting back in his seat and running his hand down his face.

Magna turned her gaze to him. "I really am mature for my age. After seeing and doing everything that I have, it forced me to grow up very quickly," she replied in a defensive tone. "Orion isn't much older than I am, and he rules the Isle of the Sea Serpent."

Gabe released a short, biting laugh. "That's nice to know," he responded with a shake of his head. "I'm going to get a beer. Do you want one?" he asked, standing up.

"Yeah, I don't have to do my rounds at the hospital until later this afternoon since it is Saturday," Kane replied, sitting back in his seat.

"May I have one?" Magna asked.

Kane bit back a chuckle when Magna looked up with a hopeful expression. He wasn't sure if she knew what one was or not, but she wasn't on any medication. He nodded his approval when Gabe raised an eyebrow at him.

"Go ahead. She isn't taking anything, so she should be alright, though it is a bit early for all of us to be drinking. I guess we can make an exception," he said.

∾

Gabe stepped back into the kitchen and walked over to the refrigerator. He opened one of the double doors and blankly stared at the shelves. His mind was swirling as he tried to wrap his head around everything that had happened since last night.

"How the fuck did life get so complicated?" he murmured, reaching into the fridge and pulling out three beers.

He twisted the tops off the bottles. Reaching for a glass from one of the cabinets, he poured Magna's beer into it. He and Kane would drink from the bottle.

"Two hundred and fifty years? Who the hell thought they were still young at that age?" he continued.

The only thing he could rationalize was that the time in Magna's world must go faster than time here. Maybe it was like dog years in reverse, he thought with a chuckle.

Grabbing the two bottles with one hand, he picked up the glass with the other. He walked back through the kitchen to the living room. Holding out the glass, he silently cursed when he felt Magna's chilled fingers brush against his.

He turned and handed one of the beers to Kane, but set his down on the end table next to the couch. Pulling the throw blanket off the back, he retraced his steps to Magna, gently eased her forward before draping the blanket around her shoulders. Between the blanket across her lap and the one on her shoulders, she should warm up. He moved the tray with her empty dessert dish to the side. He'd clean it and the kitchen later.

"Thank you, Gabe," she replied, smiling up at him.

"No problem," he responded with a shrug. "I can turn the heat on if you need it."

She shook her head. "No, it is actually very pleasant," she said.

He glanced at the clock on the wall near the corner fireplace and grimaced as he returned to his seat on the couch. It was a quarter to eleven. It was definitely a little early for beer, but close enough to lunch to justify it. The hard stuff would probably come later tonight, judging by all the things he was learning.

If everything she said was real, he reasoned.

"So, you said you come from the Isle of Sea Serpents?" Gabe asked, leaning back and picking up his bottle of beer.

Magna pulled her eyes away from the window to look at him. "The Isle of the Sea Serpent. It is my father's home isle. He often spoke of how he saw my mother along the beach one day and he rose from the water with plans of sweeping her away. My mother told me of an arrogant sea man who should have thought twice about trying to kidnap a witch." Gabe's fingers tightened when Magna chuckled and shook her head. "They fell in love," her voice faded and she bowed her head.

He cursed himself for upsetting her. He was about to apologize, something he didn't do often, when she looked up at him with a small, sad smile on her lips. Her eyes held a haunted look and she looked pale.

"Are they still alive?" Kane asked, sitting forward and resting his elbows on his knees.

Magna turned to look at Kane. "I don't know. I turned them to stone. I hoped that my death would break the spell. It should have, but since I did not die…." She shrugged, placing her untouched glass on the tray. "I would like to lie down if you do not mind," she murmured, pushing the blankets aside and rising unsteadily to her feet.

Gabe placed his bottle on the end table and swiftly rose to his feet. Kane was already by her side. As much as he wanted to be the one to escort her back to the bedroom, he knew that for the moment, Kane would be the best choice since he could make sure that Magna was alright.

"I'll clean up the kitchen," he said, stepping to the side when Kane swept Magna into his arms.

Kane nodded. "I'll be out to help in a few minutes," he replied.

Gabe watched as Kane carried Magna down the hall. She looked over Kane's shoulder at him. For a brief second, their gazes connected. He knew his was filled with curiosity. Hers was filled with grief.

He remained where he was for several seconds after they disappeared into the bedroom. His body was taut, and it wasn't until Buck nudged his hand that he realized that his fists were clenched. Today was going to be even longer than last night had been.

"Come on, boy. You and Wilson can have the leftovers," Gabe said.

He picked up his empty beer bottle before he picked up and gulped down Magna's untouched glass. Balancing the rest of the dishes in his hand, he returned to the kitchen, and quickly filled the two dog dishes with leftover salmon and eggs.

Ten minutes later, he looked up from where he was rinsing the last dish. His eyes locked on Kane's troubled expression.

"What is it?" Gabe demanded, turning off the water and placing the dish in the drainer before he turned to lean against the counter, and crossed his arms.

Kane glanced around, and spying his full bottle of beer, he walked over and snatched it off the counter. Kane drained the bottle in one long swig. Wiping a hand across his mouth, Kane pulled open the cabinet door where the recycling bin was and placed the bottle in the can before he closed it. Only then did he answer.

"I think she is the one. The one we've been looking for," Kane stated, his eyes glittering with determination.

Gabe returned Kane's steady look before his lips twitched. "You, doc, are just now figuring that out?" he dryly retorted.

"Well, shit," Kane groaned, running his hands over his shaggy hair. "What do we do now?"

Gabe thought about it for a moment. That was a good question – what did they do now? The fact that they had both arrived at the conclusion that Magna was The One at relatively the same time said something about how their two minds worked, he supposed. The issue was they really knew nothing about her but what she had told them. Was everything true? It was hard for him to wrap his head around the idea that Magna was from another world – a world where magic, mermaids, monsters, and aliens existed.

Kane had shared what Magna had done last night. He wasn't sure if Kane realized how crazy he had sounded. If it had been anyone else, he would have questioned either their sanity or asked what they were smoking. The fact that it was Kane made him have doubts. Hell, he was still trying to figure out a logical explanation for Magna turning up in his net and he couldn't find one, short of her escaping from a submarine.

Then, there was the mention of Mike Hallbrook. The Yachats Police Detective had disappeared a couple of months ago. Supposedly there had been a note from him and a call to his sister, but there had been nothing concrete, and from the Missing Person's posters stapled and posted all over town, Gabe had a feeling that Mike's sister didn't believe he'd just taken off either. Now, Magna was saying Hallbrook had shown up, shot her, and helped save a magical realm. The entire tale was straight out of a book or movie!

"Well, have you figured it out yet?" Kane asked with an impatient gesture.

Gabe scowled at his friend. "You're the one who is supposed to be so smart! What do you think?" he growled in retaliation.

Kane shrugged and shoved his hands into his front pockets. "I don't know," he admitted before releasing a soft curse when his phone buzzed. Pulling it out of his pocket, he frowned and lifted the phone to his ear. "Doctor Field speaking."

Gabe listened and knew that Kane was going to have to go in. His gaze moved to the window and he watched as the storm that had been darkening the horizon rolled closer. Even if today hadn't been a weekend, he would have been stuck ashore.

"I've got to go in. Stay with her," Kane muttered, sliding his phone into his shirt pocket.

"Of course," Gabe replied with a sardonic twist to his lips. "Anything else?"

Kane raised his hand and drew in a deep breath. Releasing it, he shook his head.

"I'd leave a long list, but you'd just ignore it," Kane chuckled, his worried gaze turning toward the door leading out of the kitchen. "She's been through hell."

Gabe's stomach clenched at the harsh words. The depth of emotion in her eyes, her body, and her words had been humbling. There had been no mistaking her fear, despair, acceptance, and her silent plea for understanding. The last is what tore him up.

"We'll just have to make sure that she never has to go back to it," he replied, watching Kane grab his jacket off the hook next to the side door.

Kane nodded. "I'll be back as soon as I can," he promised. He pulled the door open, and paused on his way through. "I'm staying here," he said abruptly, his voice laced with frustration.

He laughed. "You know the code to the door. Pick up some clothes for her before the shops close," he called as Kane started to close the door.

"I will," Kane replied.

Gabe stood in the kitchen for several minutes. He heard Kane's SUV pull out of the driveway. The soft hum of the dishwasher mixed with the muted sound of the gulls warning of the incoming storm. He needed to go check on his boat before it hit.

He'd check on Magna first, then his boat. The dogs could use the run up and down the stairs – especially Wilson. He muttered a curse under his breath when he saw both dogs were missing. Striding across the living room, he headed down the hall. He had a pretty good idea where they had disappeared to.

He noticed that Magna's bedroom door was slightly ajar. Gripping the edge of the door, he silently pushed it open. His gaze softened when he saw Buck curled up on one side of Magna while Wilson lay on her other side, his head resting across her stomach. Magna had the fingers of her right hand threaded through the pup's fur. He was a bit shocked when neither dog moved.

Magna lay sleeping. Her face was relaxed, and a small smile curved her lips. Every once in a while, her fingers moved along Wilson's nape. Her breathing was so shallow that if not for the tiny movement of her fingers, he would have thought she was a beautiful, frozen statue.

"Watch over her, boys," Gabe quietly ordered.

Buck thumped his tail twice before laying his head back down. Wilson closed his eyes. Gabe swore he could see a grin on the pup's face.

He was about to close the door when a soft glow caught his attention. At first, he thought it was light coming in from the window playing tricks, but he quickly realized that the glow was coming from Magna. His eyes widened as silver threads sparked and spun, dancing across her skin. The dogs appeared to be oblivious to the swirling sparkles and faint cloud. Unsure of what in the hell was going on, he watched as it faded as quickly as it appeared.

Shaking his head, he waited several minutes to make sure she was alright before he pulled the door closed. He rested his forehead against the door. He was not imagining things. She had been glowing.

He straightened and stared at the wooden door with a sense of resolution. Magna was special. Like Kane had said, she had been through hell and back. A shiver ran through his large body. If anyone found out about her, she would be in danger here as well.

A strange, uncomfortable feeling ignited inside him. It took a few moments for him to recognize it. Fear – it was the bitter taste of fear. He'd tasted it before and didn't like it any better now than when he had served tours of duty overseas.

Drawing in a deep breath, he rolled his shoulders. They would find a way to keep her safe. Yachats was a small town. He didn't go out of his way to socialize with people here, but those who he did know were protective of the ones living here. It might be a little more difficult for

Kane. His position as one of only three doctors in the area might prove an issue.

He turned and slowly retraced his steps, crossing to the sliding doors of the living room. Opening them, he stepped outside and closed the door behind him. The wide covered deck wrapped around the house that was built into the side of the mountain.

He'd built most of it himself. The construction had been a combination of a labor of love and therapy after his return from overseas. He had added as many windows as he could throughout the house to maximize the feel of being outdoors. Whether it was sun, fog, rain, or gale force winds, he loved it all and never wanted to feel confined to a narrow, closed-in space again.

Rich natural wood and rock helped the house to blend in with the surrounding forest. Even the staircase leading down to the dock below his house was made to blend in and look as natural as possible. If there had been one thing his father had done right, it had been to buy this piece of property when he had the extra cash in his pocket.

He crossed the deck and slipped through the gate he'd installed to keep Wilson from tumbling down the stairs when he was a few weeks old. He descended the stairs with practiced ease. Once on the floating dock, he checked the dock lines to make sure they were secure before stepping onboard and checking the rest of the boat. He closed the hatches and snapped the covers around the tower.

Climbing down into the lower cabin where he had laid Magna, he made sure all the windows were closed. He was straightening the covers when something fell off the bed and hit his shoe. He looked down, noticing a thin, beaded string. Bending, he picked it up.

Holding it up, he studied the necklace. The beads were small and colorful. In the center of the row of beads lay a dark green shell pendant. The shell was about the size of a silver dollar. It filled the center of his palm when he laid it in his hand. Turning it over, he was surprised to see the interior glowed and sparkled. He stared down into the glowing colors, mesmerized. His body felt strangely light, as if he was no longer….

"What the fuc…." his voice came out strangled.

Gabe blinked, lifting a hand to rub his eyes. His hand passed through his face. He lifted his hand and stared at it in wonder. He could see through it.

Looking around him, he saw that he was no longer on his boat, but on a beach. Turning in a circle, he looked up at the stars. A frown creased his brow as he tried to identify them and came up blank.

He turned his head when he heard laughter. His hands reached out when he saw Magna running toward him. He gasped when she passed right through him. Stumbling back several steps, he barely remained standing when a man followed less than a second later.

"That was good, Magna. Coralus never even suspected what you were doing," the man laughed before he fell to the sand next to where Magna had collapsed.

A flash of jealousy hit Gabe when the man leaned over and tugged on Magna's dark hair. She giggled and lay back on the black sand crystals. Gabe couldn't help but notice how young and vibrant she looked.

She was wearing a thin, sheer green cover over a black body suit that hugged every curve. The leggings of the suit ended mid-thigh. He smiled when she dug her toes into the sand and they poked up on the other side of the hole, the rest of her feet buried.

Gabe listened in fascination to Orion's teasing and her excited response. He wished that Kane could see and hear what he was experiencing. He took a step back when she suddenly rose to her feet and swirled toward Orion with a pleading look.

Gabe made a note to watch out for Magna if she ever pouted. The look she was currently using on Orion made him think of all kinds of things he'd like to do to her. The first was put those pouty lips to use around his cock. Just the thought of that had him wishing he was there on the beach alone with Magna instead of watching a memory of her with her cousin.

Gabe's breath caught when he saw the full beauty of Magna's smile. Her dark green eyes danced with mirth and her lips made him want to taste them. Her hair danced in the wind, as if she were caught in a current. He barely heard her reply, so captivated was he by the change in her.

He turned when he saw her look up at the sky. A soft gasp escaped her, and her lips parted in awe. Gabe followed the streak of light as it flashed across the sky. In the distance, he could see the explosion of water where it landed. Sea spray rose nearly fifty feet in the air.

It suddenly dawned on him what was about to happen. This was Magna's memory of right before the alien creature took over her body. He opened his mouth to yell for her to stop. Even as he tried to follow her, he could feel the world dissolving around him. The outline of the cabin of his boat mixed with the beach and cove. He barely caught a glimpse of Magna climbing on the back of a creature that looked like a cross between a dragon and sea horse.

He swayed, and his hand shot out to steady himself. Holding very still, he fought against the disorientation. It took a minute for him to realize the sway wasn't just from him returning from wherever in the hell he had been, but also from the stormy seas. The sound of rolling thunder warned him he'd better return to the house if he didn't want to get stuck on the boat.

Turning, he grabbed the slicker that was hanging by the door. He pulled it on, pausing only long enough to safely tuck the necklace into the pocket before he stepped out and secured the hatch. Pulling the hood of the raincoat over his head, he climbed up onto the dock and headed for the stairs. Any doubt as to whether or not Magna had been telling him the truth was completely resolved in his mind. He had pulled a real-life mermaid out of the ocean and her name was Magna – the Sea Witch.

CHAPTER EIGHT

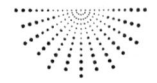

It was dark by the time Gabe heard the door to Kane's SUV slam shut outside. When Kane walked into the kitchen, he glanced around with a frown as he dropped several department store bags to the floor. Gabe returned his attention to the meal he was preparing while Kane lowered the duffle bag from his shoulder and removed his gloves and his coat.

"How is she?" Kane asked, hanging his coat on the hook by the door.

"She slept most of the day," Gabe replied.

"That's good. She was obviously exhausted, and this will give her body time to heal," Kane said with a satisfied nod.

"Yeah," Gabe murmured.

He picked up the ladle and stirred the large pot of vegetable noodle soup he'd made after coming back in from the boat earlier. He thought the soup might be better for Magna. It felt strange and rewarding at the same time to be cooking for someone else. He normally just had to worry about himself and the occasional special meal he made for the dogs. Once a week, Kane would come over and they would grill something while watching either football, basketball, or soccer.

His mind wasn't on food, but on what he'd seen and experienced today. The entire episode on the beach had shaken him. Since the weather made going out on the water impossible, cooking had been the next best thing to give him something to do with his hands.

"What's wrong?" Kane demanded.

He was quiet for a moment before he decided that perhaps showing Kane what he'd seen was better than trying to explain it. Turning away from the stove, he reached into his pocket and pulled out the necklace he'd picked up earlier. He'd wrapped it in a paper towel. He held it out to Kane with a nod.

"I found this on my boat. It obviously belongs to Magna," he quietly explained.

Kane frowned as he took the paper towel. Gabe watched as Kane carefully unwrapped the necklace. It was lying with outer side face up at the moment. Kane looked at him with a puzzled expression.

"It's beautiful," Kane observed.

Gabe ran his hand over the back of his neck before he rubbed his chin. Dropping his hand back down to his side, he nodded in agreement. He gestured with his hand.

"Let's see if the same thing happens to you that happened to me. Turn it over," he instructed.

He waited and watched. He saw Kane's eyes widen and his friend stumbled backwards a step before remaining still. What he hadn't expected was to find himself back on the beach next to Kane, as well.

"Where the hell are we?" Kane choked out, turning in a circle.

"You are locked in one of my memories," Magna replied, stepping out of the shadows until she was standing between them. "It is a loop of my last night. I captured the memory in a spell and placed it in this shell. I wanted – needed – to be able to remember who and what I was before I changed."

Gabe reached out to touch her, but his hand merely glided through her body. She turned to look at him with a sad smile before she returned her attention to the water. He heard Kane's swift hiss of breath when the memory of Magna ran down the beach and through them.

"This isn't real?" Kane asked in a hoarse voice, turning to watch the bright, laughing girl.

"It was," Magna softly replied before she walked down to the edge of the water.

"Watch and listen," Gabe cautioned.

Kane nodded, not saying anything else. The events from long ago continued to play out before his astonished eyes once again. He picked up some details he had missed before, small things. He took in the color of the water, the bright luminescence of the plants, and the sea dragons playing in the cove.

He turned his head when he heard Kane's harsh cry of warning to Magna when she ran for the water. The memory of Magna passed through the present day one. Gabe was surprised when the scene around them didn't fade, but instead became frozen. Unsure of what was going on, he walked across the sand to where Magna was standing looking out at the water. Behind him, Kane muttered a curse and followed him.

"What's happening?" Kane asked, gazing around him before stopping near where Magna stood.

Gabe shrugged. "I don't know. This didn't happen earlier," he admitted.

Magna didn't turn to look at them. "Sometimes I would stop the memory, hoping to find a way to warn myself and Orion of the dangers." She lifted a hand as if to brush away a tear. "Sometimes I just wanted to remain frozen forever at this precise moment, not moving any further ahead in time. I always loved coming here. It was a special place belonging only to Orion, Kapian, and me. We could hide from the world and all of our responsibilities, and imagine the adventures we would go on together. We were the Terrible Trio, always causing mischief and giving our parents headaches," she murmured.

"It looks and feels so real," Kane said.

"Yes... but it is all an illusion," Magna replied, her voice tired and somber.

Gabe blinked when she raised her hand, and everything faded. They were once again back in his kitchen. Kane was still standing by the door, the necklace in the palm of his hand. Magna stood near the breakfast bar that separated the kitchen from the casual dining room while he remained by the stove.

His body tensed when Magna held out her hand, palm up, and the necklace rose from Kane's upturned hand and floated through the air to land in the center of her palm. He knew he and Kane both had the same expression of awe on their faces. She closed her fingers around the necklace and lowered her hand.

"I didn't imagine it. You really can do magic," Kane said in awe.

Magna lifted her chin. "Yes. I can also breathe as I swim under the water. That is why I was called the Sea Witch," she stated, before turning her gaze to the steaming pot on the stove. "I smelled your wonderful cooking again. I'm starving."

Gabe released the breath he was holding in a strained chuckle. "One large bowl of soup coming up. I have some fresh bread and butter to go with it or would you prefer crackers?" he asked.

Magna bit her lower lip and gave him a wan smile. "Can I have both?" she asked with a hopeful expression.

Kane chuckled. "I brought you some clothes – not that I mind you running around in Gabe's shirt, we just thought you might like something else as well," he teased, bending to pick up his duffel bag and the department store bags filled with assorted clothing items. "Anything you don't like, I can return. Once you are feeling better, Gabe and I can take you to town to go shopping for more."

"Kane...," Gabe growled in warning.

Kane looked up, his eyes filled with determination. "If she is going to live here and fit in, she needs to be able to move around. I've been thinking of nothing else all day, Gabe. Trust me," Kane asserted, a thread of steel in his voice.

Gabe saw the flash of uncertainty and fear on Magna's face. He didn't want to argue in front of her. He was also mentally kicking himself in the ass for not thinking about the challenges Magna would face here. He'd been so shocked after seeing her glow and seeing her memories that his mind hadn't moved beyond that to how she was going to fit in their human world.

"I would love to see the clothing. Once I am stronger, I will be able to create my own," she confessed.

"Yes, well, that's one of the things we'll have to talk about," Kane said with a wink.

"I'll set dinner on the table," Gabe muttered.

He started to turn away, suddenly feeling like an outsider. For the first time, he wondered if the relationship that he and Kane had talked about could work. It was one thing to dream about finding a woman who would accept both of them, it was another to find and deal with one in reality.

His stomach knotted at the thought of losing Magna to his best friend. He would never let Kane know that he was dismayed by the thought. He needed to come to terms with the realization that perhaps Magna was like his first wife – horrified at the thought of being with two men at the same time.

He was so focused on his dark thoughts that he only vaguely heard Kane mention taking the items back to the bedroom and Magna's soft response. The light touch on his arm made him stiffen in surprise.

Turning his head, he found himself drowning in a pair of warm, curious green eyes. He swallowed when she slid her hand down his arm and over the hand holding the knife he had been using to slice the bread. She wove her fingers through his and gently tugged on him until he set down the knife and turned to face her.

"Thank you," she said, gazing up at him.

Gabe frowned in confusion. "What for?" he asked in a gruff voice.

Magna guided his hand down to her waist as she stepped closer. A mischievous smile, similar to the one he'd seen on her face in her memory, curved her lips. Her eyes had more of a sparkle to them as well.

"For finding my necklace," she said, sliding her right hand up his chest to his shoulder.

Gabe's eyes darkened. A hint of a smile lifted the corner of his mouth. His doubts from a few minutes earlier were beginning to evaporate in the heat that was building between them. The dark thoughts were quickly shifting to more pleasurable ones – like her on top of him and Kane leaning over her from behind.

"I'm going to kiss you," he stated in a rough voice as his arm tightened around her waist.

Magna leaned against him. "I was hoping that you would. I… enjoy the touch of your lips against mine," she confessed.

"Just wait until you feel them everywhere else," he retorted before bending and capturing her lips.

The little doubt that remained vanished when she eagerly opened for him. Her fingers threaded through the hair at his nape. The way she kneaded her fingers, lightly scraping her nails along his skin turned him on. He bent his knees slightly and slid his other hand under the thin material of the shirt she was wearing.

A muffled moan filled the air when his hand connected with soft, naked flesh. A shudder ran through him when it dawned on him that, of course, she was bare! He'd laid a shirt out, but he didn't have any under clothes for her. Hell, that would also mean that she wasn't wearing a bra.

The knowledge that the only thing separating her from his lips was the thin shirt hit him in his gut with the force of a major league slugger hitting a line drive into his stomach. His hands slid upward, taking the soft, blue material with them. She whimpered against his mouth when his left hand caressed her breast while his other hand stroked the curve of her buttock.

"Damn! You have no idea how sexy that looks," Kane exclaimed.

The sound of his friend's voice broke through the heated daze of desire. He reluctantly released Magna's lips, but kept his hand on her bare breast and buttock. His glittering eyes locked with Kane's over her head.

"You have no idea how sexy it feels," Gabe stated.

Magna tilted her head back and looked up at him with dazed eyes. "My body feels like it is on fire," she informed him. "I never knew a kiss could cause such an ache."

"You never…. Magna, if you don't mind me asking, how many lovers have you had?" Kane enquired, stepping into the kitchen.

She looked over her shoulder at Kane with a frown. "None. The creature wanted me to take Orion as my husband, but I have always thought of him as a brother," she said with a shake of her head. "I would not allow the alien to use me that way. It is why I helped Dolph when the boy approached me for assistance. The alien had me draw up a contract meant to force Orion to sacrifice himself to save his son, but I made it possible for Dolph to come to this world and find the one who could help him break the contract. Of course, I couldn't guarantee that Dolph would find a woman from this world who would match the detailed description I was forced to include in the contract," she confessed.

"Woman?" Kane asked.

"You're a virgin?" Gabe demanded at the same time.

"Yes – to both of your questions. Carly Tate and Jenny Ackerly. I told you that Carly is the one who woke Drago. Jenny is the fiery-haired woman who married Orion," she explained.

"And Mike Hallbrook?" Gabe asked, sliding his hands to her waist while at the same time pulling her shirt back down as his mind reeled at the fact that she was a virgin.

Magna tilted her head and looked up at him with a puzzled frown. "I told you, he is the one who shot me. He was with one of the witches who fought against me," she said.

Kane cleared his throat. "Why don't you go try on some of the clothes I bought you? I've laid them out across the bed. Anything you don't want, just stack it on the chair and I'll return them. I'll help Gabe get dinner on the table while you get dressed," he suggested casually.

Gabe felt Magna's reluctance when she pulled away. He bit the inside of his cheek in an effort to keep his groan from escaping. His cock was still hard as a rock. He would be lucky if he didn't end up with a set of blue balls. It didn't help when he thought of the fact that he and Kane would be Magna's first – and hopefully last – lovers.

He waited until he heard the dogs following her down the hallway before he said anything. From the painful expression that crossed Kane's face, his friend wasn't in much better shape than he was. He reached down and brushed a hand over the front of his jeans.

"A virgin," he said.

Kane grimaced. "This should change things…," he said.

"… but, it won't," Gabe finished, his hands flexing his fingers.

"You're damn right it won't," Kane chuckled. "You two looked hot. I have to tell you… that was the sexiest thing I think I've ever seen," he stated.

"Well, I'm planning on there being more. Now, help me get dinner on the table. Before anything else delays dinner, I want her healthy," Gabe replied.

"I'll check her shoulder after dinner," Kane said with a shake of his head. "I swear she makes me forget things like being a good doctor when I'm around her."

Gabe chuckled. He knew exactly what Kane was talking about. The next few weeks were going to be torture waiting for Magna to heal – yet, he wouldn't change it.

∼

Kane absently listened as Gabe worked with Wilson after they had eaten dinner and cleaned up. The pup still had a lot to learn. At eight months, the Husky's attention span was almost as long as that of a gnat – almost. He chuckled when he heard Magna giggle when Gabe told the pup to sit and the Husky fell over and showed his belly.

"I really don't remember Buck being this difficult to train," Gabe complained, glaring down at Wilson.

"If I were a changeling, I could talk to him," Magna said, resting her chin on her hand.

Kane frowned when he noticed that she appeared to be favoring her left arm and shoulder. He rose to his feet and knelt on one knee beside her.

"Is your shoulder hurting? I can give you something for the pain, if you'd like," he offered.

Magna straightened and shook her head. "It is barely throbbing," she answered with a shy smile.

Kane reached up, his fingers pausing on the buttons of the soft pastel pink, blue, and green blouse he had picked out. The colors had reminded him of Magna. The women in Yachats Mystic Boutique had been extremely helpful. In a few weeks, the three of them could go down to Portland or up to Seattle for anything else Magna might need.

"I'd like to check it," he said.

She nodded her permission. Kane expertly released the buttons. He'd only released a few of the buttons when he knew she had not tried to wear any of the bras he had purchased. That made sense considering the location of her wound and the difficulty she would have trying to put it on, but damn if it didn't throw off his concentration!

He was surprised that she had removed the bandage covering the stitches. He swallowed when he saw that not only were the stitches gone, but the only evidence of the wound was a red line. The skin was sealed.

"How is she?" Gabe asked, coming to stand next to him.

"Good," Kane replied, his fingers delicately probing the tissue around the wound. "It looks like it is almost healed."

"Healed? She had a bullet in her yesterday!" Gabe exclaimed, bending to look at her shoulder more closely.

Magna glanced down at where Kane's fingers were before she looked up at Gabe. "I would have been completely healed if I had been stronger and remained in the water," she said with a grimace.

"The area is still a little warm," Kane noticed.

Magna nodded. "I can feel the heat in my body. The metal heated the tissue as it pierced me. It is healing, but because I am still weak, it will take longer. If I could go to your ocean, the water would help," she said with a sigh of longing.

Kane looked outside. The wind was strong enough to blow the driving rain under the covered deck. He could see the shadows of the trees bending and swaying as lightning lit up the sky. The long rumble of thunder had Buck warily eyeing the doors.

"Well, swimming will have to wait for a bit," Kane chuckled.

"Kiss him, Magna."

Kane's fingers froze against Magna's skin at Gabe's rough command, his eyes locked on her face as he waited for her reaction. Magna slowly turned her head to look at him. Her green eyes turned darker. Her full lips parted.

"Kiss him, Magna, but only if you want to," Gabe repeated in a softer voice.

Kane continued to wait. The hand he had resting near her side on the couch slid closer until he was touching her thigh. The next move needed to come from her.

Her delicate fingers rose to trace his face. He couldn't resist touching the pad of her thumb with his tongue when she brushed it across his bottom lip. Her breath caught, and her eyes locked on his mouth.

His fingers curled when she leaned forward. He didn't bother to smother the slight growl of frustration when she paused a fraction of an inch from his lips. He could feel her warm breath and wanted more than anything to close the distance between them.

He didn't. This was her choice. He just wished she'd quit torturing him.

That thought flew from his mind when she tentatively touched her tongue to his bottom lip. Her tongue caressed his lip, touching, retreating, and touching again before she closed the distance. Instead of deepening the kiss, she nibbled on his lip.

"Damn, but she is driving me crazy," Gabe muttered in a hoarse voice.

Kane wanted to respond, but he was afraid to. Gabe had no idea of the meltdown that Magna was causing inside of him. He was going to have to remember this, because payback was going to be hell if he had any say in it.

His lips parted when Magna continued her exploration. Unable to keep his hands from touching her, he slid the one by her leg up under her shirt while his other hand finished unbuttoning it. His hands cupped her breasts, lifting them as his thumbs ran across the distended nipples.

She pulled back with a cry, arching toward him. Kane took advantage of her movement to bend and capture one nipple in his mouth. He pinched the other, feeling her response as she threaded her fingers through his hair and held him against her.

"Yes," she cried, her body taut.

Kane sensed Gabe moving to kneel on the couch, then Gabe combed his fingers through her thick hair, tilting her head toward him as he captured her lips in a passionate kiss. Kane continued his heated attack on her breasts, but now he added another element.

His left hand moved down to slide under the long skirt she was wearing. He paused when he reached her knee. Her legs parted, and she moved one leg enough that she could press it against him. Encouraged, he slid his hand up to her mound. He felt smooth skin instead of soft curls.

The knowledge that she was bare was too much. Things were about to quickly get out of control if they didn't stop now. Releasing her nipple, he pulled his hand out from under her skirt and straightened. Gabe felt his withdrawal and reluctantly released her lips.

"We need to give her time," Kane stated in a voice that had an edge to it.

Gabe nodded and pushed off the couch. He ran his hand through his hair, not bothering to hide the fact that he was still highly aroused. Kane could see the distress in Magna's gaze as she looked from him to Gabe and back again in confusion.

"I know, but damn. I'm hard as a rock," Gabe groaned in frustration.

"Why do I need time? I have had nothing but time. Centuries of time!" she complained, pouting at him.

With a curse, he bent and buttoned her shirt with fingers that weren't quite steady. He grimaced when Magna slapped his fingers away and waved her hand. The shirt closed and buttoned itself.

"As your doctor, I have to think of your health – both physical and mental. You've been through a traumatic event, have been basically held hostage for more than a...." His throat tightened at the thought of actually voicing the length of time.

"Centuries," she snapped.

"Centuries," he repeated with a heavy sigh. "I think Gabe and I need to be clear about the type of relationship we want with you, Magna. It is rather unorthodox."

"We both want you – as in a threesome. Me, you in the middle, and Kane. Any and every way possible, and as often as I can reload," Gabe stated in a blunt voice.

"Geez, Gabe! Can you be any more of an ass?" Kane complained.

"What? She might as well know what to expect," Gabe retorted.

"She is recovering from a horrific ordeal, has been thrown into an unfamiliar world, and doesn't even know who in the hell we are! You could try being a little more compassionate and a little less crass," Kane growled, crossing his arms and glaring at Gabe.

Gabe turned to look down at Magna with a raised eyebrow. "Are you offended?" he asked.

"No, it all sounded good to me," she replied with a grin.

Kane shook his head. "Neither of you are thinking rationally," he muttered, just as his cellphone vibrated. "Why do people decide to get hurt during the worse possible moments? I have to go back in."

"Take my truck. It's in the garage," Gabe said, pulling his keys out and tossing them to Kane.

"Thanks... and...," he started to say, stopping when he saw Gabe's wry grin.

He didn't need to say anything. Gabe knew how much this meant to him. If they were going to make the relationship work, they needed to trust each other and respect the unspoken rules – one of which was they would both be there for Magna the first time they came together.

"I might be late getting back," he warned.

"We'll be here," Gabe said.

Kane looked down at Magna. She had grown quiet. Wilson and Buck were now on each side of her on the couch. She was stroking them behind their ears. Bending down, he captured her chin in his hand and tilted her head back slightly.

"We want to take care of you, but you also need to take care of yourself. You come first – always," he murmured before brushing a kiss across her lips.

He straightened, then paused when she reached out and grabbed his hand. His throat tightened when she lifted his hand to her mouth and pressed a kiss to his palm.

"Thank you," she whispered, her eyes dark with emotion.

Kane caressed her cheek before turning and heading for the mud room door off the laundry. He pressed the garage door opener before he pulled open the door to Gabe's four-wheel drive diesel truck. He inserted the key and started the engine. For a moment, he stared blindly at the door to the house, wishing for once he'd picked a different profession. Then he shook his head and shifted the truck into reverse. Who was he kidding? If he hadn't been a doctor, he would never have met Gabe or Magna.

"Now that would have been the true tragedy," he muttered under his breath as he slowly drove down the driveway.

CHAPTER NINE

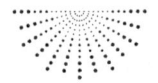

Los Angeles, California: CIA Building:

Agent Asahi Tanaka stepped into his office in the Central Intelligence Agency's Los Angeles office. He had arrived earlier than usual this morning because he had a flight out of LAX to Seattle at ten o'clock. He didn't bother with the overhead light. Instead, he turned on the small desk lamp positioned on the corner of his desk and he pressed the power button on his computer.

He walked over to the large set of windows and looked down at the street while he waited for his computer to boot up. The city never truly slept, but the early morning, and the fact that it was a weekend, meant the downtown area was relatively empty. His mind was not on the day-to-day life found in Los Angeles, though. He was thinking of a small town along the coast of Oregon.

Turning away from the view, he returned to his desk, pulled the chair out, and sat down. He quickly typed in his password. Opening the file drawer next to him, he pulled out the file titled 'Missing Persons –

Yachats, Oregon' and placed it on his desk. The contents of the file – like everything else about him – were in meticulous order.

He opened it to the first page, the transcript of his last conversation with Detective Mike Hallbrook of the Lincoln County Police Department. He carefully reread the transcript, already knowing what it said by heart.

The call from Mike had come at 4:48 on a Wednesday morning. He remembered every detail of that morning, but had documented it as well. He had been residing in the Fireside Motel in Yachats while he investigated the most recent disappearance – that of the man who had called him.

He'd seen Mike's name appear on the caller ID and known immediately he was about to get the first big break in a series of disappearances that had started nearly four decades before he'd begun working on it. He had answered the phone on the first ring.

Asahi turned the page and looked at the documents Mike had left behind. On one notepad Mike had written two words: *Ask Ruth*. Mike had retraced the words over and over until they were bold faced. Looking up, Asahi clicked on the encrypted folder on his desktop.

Inside was a video file of his interview with Ruth Hallbrook, Mike's older sister, and an audio file of the phone message Mike had left her. A smile tugged at his lips when he saw the video's placeholder showing Ruth Hallbrook's skeptical expression and determined eyes. She was going to do everything she could to find her brother, and Asahi hoped she would be successful. He directed the pointer to the audio file and clicked on it. Sitting back in his chair, he stared out of the window as he listened to the incredible story that her brother had left on her voice mail.

∽

Yachats, Oregon:

. . .

Ross Galloway stood on the dock staring moodily at the old fishing trawler that he had inherited from his dad. It had long since lost its varnished finish. Now, scars from years of use covered the tired surface. He pulled in a drag of his cigarette before exhaling the smoke into the early morning fog.

God, he hated this place. It was cold and depressing. Why anyone wanted to live along the Oregon coast where it could go from being clear and sunny in minutes to gray and damp with fog so thick you could barely see your hand in front of your face was beyond him. He would have moved away years ago if he could have afforded it. The only reason he stayed was because he was waiting for his mom to die so he could sell the house. It was the only thing worth something; the boat sure as hell wasn't.

Turning, he watched as Nathan Grumby stepped onto the dock and walked toward him. Nathan gave him a toothy grin and held up the device in his hand. Ross grunted and tossed his cigarette butt into the water.

"You're late," he said as Nathan climbed on board the trawler.

"Hey, at least I showed up! My brother was showing me some of the stuff he's found with it. It's pretty cool," Nathan replied with a shrug. "He also told me he'd kill my ass if I didn't bring this back in the same condition he loaned it to me."

Ross glanced at the expensive underwater metal detector. He gave Nathan a brief nod. Hannibal Grumby would probably do it, too. Nathan's brother was known for his hot temper. He had seen Nathan use his fists more than once down at the local tavern to beat the shit out of some overconfident preppy who thought putting on a leather jacket and riding a Harley made him a badass. Personally, Ross liked to think he was smart enough to avoid assholes like Nathan – even when he was drunk.

"Put it below, then release the ropes. I want to get the engines warmed up. We should have been out on the water a half hour ago," he stated.

Ross climbed on board the trawler, and up the short steps to the wheelhouse, then slid the door open, and walked over to the console. He turned the key to start the engines. The low rumble of the engines shook the old trawler, making every loose nut and bolt rattle. He impatiently waited for Nathan to cast off the dock lines. As soon as the boat was free, he carefully pulled away.

Nathan climbed back down from the bow of the boat and stepped into the covered bridge, rubbing his hands together to warm them before turning back to navigate out of the marina's narrow channel. Once they were clear of the 'No Wake' signs, he pressed forward on the throttle.

"So, what are you looking for that you needed Hannibal's metal detector?" Nathan asked.

Ross debated whether he should say anything, then shrugged. It wasn't like it really mattered. Whatever he found while diving would be his and only his.

"I saw something the other day and want to check it out," he said.

Nathan shook his head. "Unless you marked it, I don't see how you'll be able to find it again," he replied with a shrug. "What was it?"

"I don't know, and I did mark it," Ross retorted. "It was dark, though, so I didn't get a good look at it."

"Well, it's your boat, dude," Nathan remarked, glancing around. "Did you bring some food and something hot to drink? I didn't get a chance to grab anything and I'm freezing my ass off."

Ross jerked his head toward the cooler set to the side. "There's coffee and doughnuts in the cooler. Just save me some or you'll be swimming back," he warned.

Nathan chuckled as he turned. "I'll save you one or two," he promised.

Ross ignored his friend. Instead, he focused on the GPS position he had programmed in the other morning. Two nights ago, he had been fishing when a bright streak and loud splash had startled him. Something had fallen from the god-damn sky! Cutting his tangled net free, he'd cursed when it slipped over the side before he could grab it. The large fishing net would be a pain in the ass to replace, but it was old and had more than one hole in it. He'd hated leaving it behind, but had been afraid of losing the location of whatever in the hell it was that had fallen from the sky. He would have to come back out and see if he could locate the net when there was more light.

Following the rippling waves to the center of the area, he'd seen something interesting before he'd even focused his large spotlight down. A bright glow under the water had lit up an area half the size of a football field under his trawler before it slowly faded until only the pitch blackness of the ocean surrounded him. The spotlight hadn't helped him see more. He'd have to go down there. Afraid he would lose the location, he had programmed the spot into his GPS.

It had taken him two days to get the dive equipment he needed ready. He had to get his tanks checked and filled. They had been ready last night. While he was at the dive shop, he saw the metal detectors on display. He couldn't afford any of the nice ones, but remembered Nathan's brother had one for his work.

He had recently read an article online that mentioned a meteorite was worth its weight in gold. From the size of the splash, he hoped that it was one the size of his trawler. If it was, he would be retiring at an early age to Hawaii.

It took them nearly an hour to get to the spot where he had marked the impact. They had passed several other boats heading out, but he ignored them. He slowed, turning the boat in slow, circular patterns until he was about ten feet from the spot. Shutting off the engine, he dropped the bow anchor first. Once he knew which direction the current and the wind were blowing the boat, he nodded to Nathan to drop the stern anchor.

"Now, what?" Nathan asked, taking a sip of his coffee.

"Now I suit up," Ross said.

A shiver ran down Nathan as he looked at the chilly dark water. "Better you than me," he muttered. "I'm glad I never learned to dive."

Without replying, he pushed past Nathan and opened a storage bin to his right. Inside was his dry suit, regulator, buoyancy compensator, weight belt, and the other equipment he would need.

Forty minutes later, Ross stepped off the back of the trawler and sank down beneath the waves. He had instructed Nathan to keep an eye on the bright orange buoy he had attached to his weight belt and make sure the dive flag was raised. If he drifted too far, Nathan would pick him up. Checking his dive watch, he noted the time and direction of the boat. He pulled the pressure gauge around and glanced at it. He had a full tank of air and would need to monitor it, his depth, and his bottom time. Gripping the metal detector in one hand, he released more air in his BC and sank gracefully to the bottom.

CHAPTER TEN

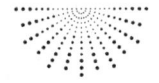

Magna woke when she heard the sound of the door closing. She lay under the thick, soft covers and stared out the large windows. It was still dark out, but she knew that it would be daylight soon.

She released a wide yawn and stretched. She hadn't slept very well for the first half of the night. Her dreams had been filled with nightmares that the alien creature still lived.

She turned her head and looked at the bedroom door when she heard the soft sound of footsteps coming down the hall. Wilson and Buck lifted their heads, wagged their tails, but didn't move. A moment later, there was a light tap on the door before it creaked open.

"Magna," Gabe's deep, rich voice called out.

The sound washed over her, filling her body with an aching need. It amazed her that just the sound of Gabe's voice could cause such an intense response inside her. She sat up, wincing when she felt her shoulder protest the movement.

Brushing her long hair back, she rubbed Buck's head when he nudged at her elbow. She grinned when Wilson jumped down off the bed and went to sit in front of the door. The pup had taken it upon himself to be her personal protector.

"You can come in. I'm awake," she responded.

Gabe pushed the door open further, glowering at Wilson when the pup refused to move. The almost hundred pounds of muscle and fur made it difficult to open the door any further. With a shake of his head, Gabe peered across at her.

"I swear I'm going to build a kennel and put his ass in it if he doesn't start behaving. Have they been bugging you?" he growled.

"No," she said, with a quick shake of her head. "They... They've been very helpful actually. I... I had trouble sleeping last night. They must have sensed it because they both came in and snuggled up next to me. I slept very well after that."

She couldn't stop her body from wiggling under the covers when Gabe's eyes swept over her tousled hair and down over her upper body. She loved the nightgown that Kane had purchased for her, but she had missed the masculine scent of Gabe that clung to the blue shirt he had given her to wear and had chosen to wear it instead.

The uncomfortable feeling inside her could also be attributed to the fact that she had been dreaming about Gabe and Kane's kisses just before she woke up. She still couldn't believe how quickly her body heated at the thought of their touch. These new reactions and feelings were overwhelming to her at times. Deep down she knew this was what Kane had been talking about and why he had stopped them from taking their passion any farther last night.

As much as she hated to admit it, she knew the decision was probably for the best for all of them. They all needed time to understand and get to know each other better. The two men had only seen small glimpses of who she really was, and she knew nothing about this new world she'd appeared in.

Except that they have accepted me without prejudice, she thought.

"I've got to take the boat out and Kane had to go into the clinic for another emergency. One of the doctors is on vacation so he has been having to work double duty. We thought it might be best if you come with me if you are feeling up to it," Gabe said in a slightly strained voice.

Her eyes widened in delight and she eagerly nodded. The thought of being out on the water filled her with a sense of excitement. These waters were new and unfamiliar to her. Her sense of curiosity kicked into high gear at the possibility of being able to explore just a little of it.

Plus, being out on the water would give her a chance to go for a swim. The water would help to heal her wound faster than anything else. She eagerly pushed the covers aside. She leaned over and brushed a quick kiss to Buck's head when he stood up on the bed next to her.

"I'd love to go," she said breathlessly, smoothing the rumpled shirt down as she stood.

"Kane said he put the rest of the clothes he bought for you in the top drawer. I'll take the dogs out. I made some breakfast for us to take with us. I'll meet you out on the deck when you're ready to go," Gabe said, motioning for the dogs to follow him.

"I will hurry," Magna promised with a small grin when both dogs looked at her before reluctantly following Gabe out of the room.

She used the bathroom and changed into the sweatpants and long-sleeved shirt that were in the top drawer. Pulling her hair to the side, she braided it before using a touch of magic at the end to bind it in place. Her shoulder was feeling much better than it had the day before but there was still a twinge. She felt sure that a quick dip in the ocean would finish the healing.

She studied her reflection in the mirror for a moment. A smile curved her lips as she lifted her hand up and ran it along her cheek. She was thinner than she liked, but she looked healthier than she had in centuries, both inside and out. The dark shadow of the creature was gone from her eyes and her skin had returned to its natural tan color instead of the sickly white pallor. Her fingers hovered over her lips as she remembered the feel of Kane and Gabe's against them. Warmth spread through her stomach along with the strange ache that had started yesterday morning. Her hand dropped back to her side and she turned away from the mirror. She didn't know what would happen next, but for the first time in centuries she was excited to find out.

"I will take care of myself... and them, definitely them," she whispered with a nod, remembering Kane's words as she exited the bedroom and headed down the hallway.

She paused as she rounded the corner to the living room. She could see Gabe through the clear glass. He was working with Wilson again, trying to convince the pup to sit down. Her heart melted when Gabe squatted down in front of the young Husky. She could see him scratching the dog as he talked. Wilson ran his tongue up Gabe's face, drawing a muffled curse from his human master before he sat down and happily thumped his tail against the decking.

Gabe stood up when the dogs turned their heads toward her. She gave Gabe an apologetic smile as she opened the door and stepped out. Both dogs immediately came to her. Reaching down, she affectionately scratched the tops of their heads between their ears.

"I didn't want to interrupt your lesson," she said.

Gabe wiped his mouth on his shirt sleeve and shrugged. "It is a continuous struggle. Wilson is learning, it will just take a lot of time and repetition. He's got a harder head than his dad," he said.

"But not his master?" she teased.

Her eyes widened when he stepped closer to her and suddenly wrapped his arm around her waist. She met the fiery desire in his gaze with a heated challenge of her own as she slid her hand up his chest.

"I wouldn't have stopped last night," he told her.

She drew in a startled breath as her body immediately heated at the memory. A rueful smile curved her lips.

"I wouldn't have either, but Kane is right. I need time to understand this world and...," her voice faded, and she turned her head to look out over the trees to the ocean.

"And...," he repeated, lifting a hand to cup her chin, forcing her to look up at him again.

She pursed her lips together. "I want you both to know who I really am. I want there to be no doubts that you are aware of who and what I was, and who I am now," she stated, refusing to cower or apologize.

Gabe's eyebrow rose at her declaration and his grin widened. "Darling, that sounds like a challenge if I ever heard one. Maybe it is us you need to know more about."

Her eyelids lowered when he brushed a hard kiss against her lips, and squeezed her butt. It felt like he'd left a burning imprint of his hand. There was no misunderstanding that he wanted her – and planned to have her.

A sigh escaped her when he stepped away and ordered the two Huskies back into the house. She followed him down the long staircase, enjoying the cool breeze and fresh scent of the ocean, though her eyes were on something a little more tantalizing – namely, the huge man in front of her and his cute ass.

∼

An hour and a half later, Gabe glanced over at Magna, worried that the bouncing of the boat might be too much for her injured arm. Satisfaction swept through him when he saw the glowing expression on her face. She was leaning against the inside of the bridge with her head stuck out of the sliding window.

She's almost as bad as the dogs, he thought in amusement. *All she needs is to have her tongue hanging out.*

A grimace pulled the smile from his face and he shifted uncomfortably when he thought about her tongue and the other things she could be doing with it. It had been too long since he'd been with a woman, he decided as his eyes ran down over Magna's profile. His body reacted as his gaze swept over the slender column of her throat and ran down over her full breasts to the curve of her ass.

A muted groan escaped him. He had always been an ass man. He loved a woman with full hips and rounded cheeks that were made for holding onto and rubbing against. Shaking his head, he pulled his dirty mind back to the present. He had to remember that she was injured and had been through a traumatic experience that would have left most people in a padded room. It wasn't as if Kane hadn't reminded him of that a million times between last night and this morning. Yet, the only thing he could think of when he was near Magna was grabbing her and bending her over! That didn't say a lot for his integrity.

"This is amazing!" Magna commented in a loud voice. "I've only been on one boat before. I usually prefer to be in the water. Raine, my sea dragon, was faster than even the fastest ship. I loved riding her through the underwater canyons."

Gabe shook his head. "When you talk about things like swimming under the water and sea dragons, I just can't wrap my head around it," he admitted. "Listen, I've got to check some sensors I set out the other day."

"What are the sensors for?" Magna asked.

"I work for the Department of Fish and Wildlife and I also do some stuff for a few universities," he explained. "Some are tracking fish migration while others are doing tests on the water; you know, temperature, currents, and pollution. Any changes to stuff like that."

Gabe saw the faintly puzzled look on her face before she turned her head and stuck it back out the window. He chuckled at the look of pure bliss on her face. Returning his attention to the water in front of him, he pulled back on the throttle when he saw a boat with the dive flag up. He turned to the port side to give it a wide berth. He didn't envy the poor sucker in the water. Even in the middle of the summer, the water wasn't much warmer than eighteen degrees Celsius on a good day.

He sped up once they were past the boat. Ten minutes later, he was slowing down again as he reached the area where he had dropped one of the sensors. It didn't take long to spot the attached bright orange float bobbing up and down on the surface. He idled up to it before cutting the engine, then grabbed the long hook attached to the wheelhouse and leaned over the side to pull it out.

"What are you going to do with it?" Magna asked, watching him with interest as he set the large tube down on the deck.

Gabe knelt down on one knee and quickly unscrewed the top. Inside was a silver box. He gently lifted it out and unhooked several long wires from it before standing back up.

"I need to download the data into the laptop," he said, turning back to the bridge. "Once I've done that, I'll reset it and drop it back overboard. I have twenty of them in all that I need to check."

"Oh," Magna replied, not sure what else to say as she really wasn't sure she understood what he was doing. Glancing back at the water, she bit her lip and sighed in uncertainty. "I want to go for a swim."

Gabe's head jerked up in surprise. For a moment, he thought he'd misunderstood her, but she was gazing at the water with such an intense look of longing he knew that he hadn't. He also knew the look on his face must have shown his displeasure because the longing was quickly replaced by disappointment.

"I... I understand if you wish for me to stay aboard your vessel," she replied in a quiet voice. "I owe you for saving my life. I will not try to leave without your permission."

"Magna," Gabe said roughly before he muttered a curse under his breath. Setting the sensor down, he walked over to where she was standing with her face turned away from him. "Honey, look at me," he softly ordered, lifting his hand to run his fingers along her jaw to her chin.

She reluctantly returned her gaze back to him.

"You owe me nothing," he said seriously. "You also owe Kane nothing.

You have the right to come and go as you please. *But...,*" he said, his voice deep and intense. "I want you to stay with us, Magna, for – a long time. There's something there, I can feel it."

"Kane—" she started to whisper, stopping when he placed his thumb along her lip.

"Wants you as badly as I do," he admitted. "You said last night that you didn't understand why you wanted to feel our hands on you. Well, I do and so does Kane. Maybe there was more to that wish you made when you cast your spell. I don't know. If you want to go for a swim, I won't stop you. You just better come back, or I swear I'll come looking for you."

A small, pleased smile curved Magna's lips at his forceful words. "I would not make myself hard to find," she teased, her eyes glowing with happiness and excitement.

"What about your shoulder?" he asked as a frown creased his brow when he glanced at the bandage sticking out from under the shirt. "Kane warned that it might look like it was healed but that he was worried that it was a little warm to his touch. I don't want him on my case for not taking care of you."

She reached up and tenderly touched his cheek, tracing her fingers down along his jaw. A shudder swept through him at the feel of her slender fingers against his skin. Turning his head, he brushed a kiss against her palm, enjoying the soft hiss of her breath when she felt him run the tip of his tongue along the center of her palm. She may be free to leave them, but he'd make damn sure she didn't want to.

"The water contains healing powers in it for my people," she whispered, slowly drawing her hand down along the skin of his neck. "I want you to kiss me again."

Gabe didn't need a second request. Hell, he didn't need the first one. He had planned to kiss her anyway. The fact that she had asked him to do so only made it sweeter.

He slid his hand around her waist, pulling her into his arms, and he bent his head, capturing her lips in a rough, passionate kiss that promised there was more to come. His left hand slid down over the curve of her ass and he squeezed it. He was rewarded with a soft moan and parted lips. Sweeping his tongue inside her mouth, he teased her until she tangled with him in an intimate dance that spoke of her own rising desire.

Gabe reluctantly pulled back, sliding his hand down between the fabric of her jogging pants and her smooth flesh. His fingers kneaded the sensitive skin and a wicked grin curved his lips at her soft, panting breaths. Brushing another kiss along her swollen lips, he slid his mouth along the curve of her jaw until his lips were just a breath away from her ear.

"Come back to us," he demanded in a deep, desire-laden voice.

"I… I will," she promised, breathless. "I want this to be real for all of us."

Gabe ran his fingers lightly across her buttocks before pressing her against him. "Oh, it's real, alright. I can't wait to show you just how real it is," he murmured. "I'll wait here for you. Go for your swim."

Gabe forced himself to pull his hand back. The moment he lost touch with her skin, he had to curl his hand into a fist so that he didn't just say 'to hell with it' and take her right then and there. There were three things stopping him from doing just that. One, her injury. He would never do anything that would hurt her or cause her pain if he could help it. At least a pain that wasn't pleasurable, he amended. Two, she deserved more than to be taken on a dirty fishing trawler. And last, Kane should be there when the time came. Right now, he was really wishing that he didn't feel that way. If Kane was late getting back to his place tonight, Gabe wasn't sure he would be able to hold off any longer, especially if Magna asked him to kiss her again.

He jerked back to the present when he felt Magna brush a kiss across his lips. "Go do what you have to do," she said with a grin as she stepped toward the side. "I will follow your boat."

"How…?" Gabe started to say before he shook his head. "How will I know you are there?"

Magna gave him a secretive smile before she sat down on the stern of the boat. "You will know," she promised before she pushed off the dive platform.

Gabe knew his mouth was hanging open, but he couldn't help it. He'd expected to hear a splash. What he had not expected was to see the water rise up and create a series of steps that slowly dissolved around her, lowering her into the frigid sea, or to see the baggy clothing she had been wearing change to a glittering green bodysuit that molded to her slender frame.

"Kane is never going to believe this," he muttered just as Magna disappeared beneath the surface.

CHAPTER ELEVEN

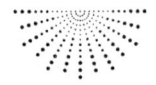

Gabe grimaced two hours later when his phone rang. The soundtrack from the movie Jaws told him that it was Kane. He chuckled when he remembered the first time Kane had heard his distinctive ringtone. The words 'You need a shrink' and 'I can prescribe medicine for that' were two phrases that came to mind.

"This is Gabe," he said after he connected the call.

"How is Magna this morning?" Kane demanded, not bothering with a welcome greeting either.

"She's fine," Gabe absently replied.

He grinned when he saw another 'sea dragon' made of water jump out in front of the trawler. Shaking his head, he couldn't stop the chuckle that escaped when the water creature did a graceful flip before dissolving. He winced when Kane snapped in his ear again.

"What the hell is so funny? Damn it! Why did Victor have to go on vacation now? What's going on?" Kane grumbled while Gabe enjoyed the show Magna had created to let him know that she was still near him.

"Calm down, man. She's fine. Hell, I'd say she is more than fine! You should see what she's doing! I'm going almost thirteen knots and she is keeping up with me as if I was dead in the water. And the things she can do with the water… Man, this is unbelievable," he said, watching as another sea dragon jumped over the bow of his boat.

"What are you talking about? Are you saying she is in the water?! I can't believe you let her go in! I said to take her with you, not let her go for a swim. Damn it, what part of 'we need to take care of her' did you not understand? She's injured, for crying out loud. What if she doesn't come back? Gabe, I trusted you to keep her safe," Kane muttered in a lower volume.

"Kane, she'll come back," he promised.

"How do you know? What if… Damn it, Gabe, what if she doesn't?" Kane replied with a loud sigh.

"Because she asked me to kiss her," Gabe bragged with a grin as he remembered Magna's body pressed up against his. "A woman doesn't kiss a man like she kissed me if she plans on leaving."

"A kiss!" Kane exclaimed in a loud voice.

Gabe grinned when he heard the muted sounds in the background. Kane must be at the local hospital. He was so glad he didn't have a regular job working around people.

"Are you in a closet? That sounded muffled," Gabe joked.

"Supply room," he said in a softer voice. "What else did you do? I knew I should have called out today. Sometimes being a doctor sucks," Kane groaned.

Gabe chuckled at the dejected sound in Kane's voice. "It was just a kiss, but it was…." He released a breath as he thought about it.

"Was what? God, Gabe, sometimes you make me want to beat the shit out of you," Kane retorted.

"Isn't that against your oath or something?" Gabe teased.

"Was what?" Kane repeated through gritted teeth.

Gabe slowed down as he neared another sensor. "Right," he replied. "The kiss was just right."

Kane's loud breath resonated in his ear. He knew that before Magna's arrival, his friend had just about given up hope of ever finding someone they could both love. It had taken a long time for Gabe to realize that they were like two halves of a whole. He was the strong, rough oaf to Kane's compassionate, fun-loving personality. The biggest thing they had in common was neither one really liked to be around other people unless they had to be. Kane had gone into the medical field out of a desire to follow in his father's footsteps. The death of both of his parents in an airplane crash had had a major impact on Kane.

His own story wasn't as nice, but he had accepted his shortcomings a long time ago. He couldn't change the past, so there was no use in dwelling on it. Instead, he moved forward and simply ignored everyone else… everyone, that is, until Kane, and now Magna. He respected and trusted Kane.

His feelings for Magna were more complicated. He hadn't fully come to terms yet with how he felt about her, but deep down, he knew that Magna was special. It was more than the fact that she was a mermaid or a witch. They were connected in a way he'd never felt with a woman before, and it both fascinated him and scared the shit out of him.

Switching the ignition to off, he grabbed the hook, only to find the sensor rising up over the side of the boat, cupped in a slender funnel of water. He reached out and grabbed it. The moment he touched it, the water swirled back around and disappeared over the side again. He quickly unscrewed the top and opened it up. Downloading the information onto the laptop, he replaced it back into the plastic marker and turned, only to stop when he saw Magna sitting on the side of the boat.

"This is the last one, isn't it?" she asked, leaning forward as she pulled her knees up so she could rest her chin on them. "I do not sense them anymore."

"Sense? You knew they were there?" Gabe asked, walking over to where she sat.

Magna straightened and scowled at him. "Of course! Anything that touches the water gives out a signal. Once I knew what they felt like, I could locate them," she explained, stopping when he ran his fingers along her arm.

"They are soft and smooth," he murmured, touching the thin scales covering her body.

"I like this form better when I swim," she replied, brushing her cheek against his hand. "Most of my people do not know magic like I do, so over the centuries, they have taken to wearing clothing made from the ocean's plants. It does not absorb water and helps protect us. I prefer creating my own."

"You're beautiful, Magna." He stroked the scales on her side, inching upward. She flushed and trembled.

"...You know," she said, "my parents are two different species – she from the land, he from the sea..." She met his gaze as she stroked his torso in return, inching downward.

He took in a breath and rumbled "They must have made it work..."

She smiled and bit her lip. "She is a witch," Magna murmured. "Of course, there was a way." Her hand slid over the front of his pants and they both surged forward to share a deep kiss that made him forget that they were on a boat off the coast. He lifted her by the waist just enough so that she could wrap her legs around him, then slid one arm under her ass while the other wrapped tightly across her back. Her own arms held him close.

He groaned when she tangled her fingers in his hair, and started to turn them when he felt Magna suddenly stiffen in his arms. Pulling back, he looked down into her distressed face, and carefully lowered her back to the deck.

"Did I hurt you?" he demanded, cautiously touching her shoulder.

"No, don't you feel it?" she asked, turning to look out at the ocean.

Gabe frowned and shook his head. "No. What do you feel?" he asked, coming to stand behind her.

"It is calling for help," she whispered. "I have to go."

Gabe's hands tightened on Magna's hips when she tried to take a step toward the side of the boat. His eyes scanned the horizon. He didn't see anything, but he had no doubt that she could sense more than he could. Her body was taut with tension and her skin rippled with color.

"Be careful," he finally said, releasing her and stepping back. "I'll follow you."

He watched as Magna climbed up onto the side of the boat and gracefully dove into the water. Grabbing the sensor, he tossed it overboard again before hurrying to the bridge. Starting the engine, he pressed the throttle forward and made a wide turn back the way they had come. Even with the engines at the max, he could see that Magna was outdistancing him as the jumping sea dragons grew smaller and smaller in the distance.

A hoarse curse escaped him when they disappeared altogether from his sight. He pulled the throttle back until the boat slowed enough that he could scan the rippling waves. Running his hands through his hair, he stared ahead of him. Except for the one dive boat they had passed earlier, he saw nothing out of the ordinary.

"Kane is going to kill me," he muttered, pushing the throttle forward again.

∽

Magna slowed until she hung in the ebb and flow of the current just below the surface of the water. She felt it again. It wasn't far away now. She twisted and kicked out, pulling on the current in the water to propel herself forward. The water shifted around her, pushing her forward at a greater speed than she would have normally been able to swim. It was a trick that Orion had taught her when they were younger. She had just added a touch of her own magic.

She twisted to a stop, startled when a creature suddenly rose up in front of her. Cursing herself for being foolish and inattentive, she barely avoided hitting it. It was solid black except for the thin shield of clear glass covering its dark eyes. Strange hoses protruded from each side of the shield covering its face and a series of tiny bubbles escaped from one corner of its mouth. Magna stared back at it in fascination for a moment before she heard the distressed cry again. Turning, she swam away toward it.

Her heart thundered several minutes later when she finally found the source of the distress cries. She studied the massive creatures surrounding it. They reminded her a little of the huge mammals that lived in the oceans of her world, only they were a smaller version. There were ten of them nearby, though there were only three that held her attention. Two of the large creatures were holding up a smaller one. The small one had a net tangled around its fins, back, and tail. The female and her calf were the ones making the distress calls while the others hovered nearby for support.

"It is alright," Magna said soothingly as she swam closer. "I will help free your little one."

Magna slowly circled the three creatures. They were a mixture of dark gray on top and light gray, almost white along their stomachs. Frowning, she saw that the net was beginning to cut into the tail section of the infant and without the support of the other two, it would be unable to stay afloat. She tried tugging on the thick cord to loosen it, but it was too tight. She needed something sharp to cut the thick, rope-like material. She cursed herself that she had been using all of her restored energy to play with Gabe. She was stronger, and manipulating water didn't drain her as much as actually using her magic, but it still used the precious energy she had regained.

She turned in the water, her arms floating outward, and closed her eyes. Her fingers spread wide, searching for the familiar signature of

Gabe's boat. A sigh of relief filled her when she felt the familiar vibration in the water. He wasn't far.

With a wave of her hand, she propelled a large funnel of water toward the boat. Relief flooded her when the vibrations increased – he had seen her signal. She stretched her hands out in front of her and surfaced so that he could see her. Treading water, her gaze locked with his as he drew closer and shifted the boat into neutral. She swam over to him.

"I need a knife to cut the netting," she said, glancing up at him when he leaned over the side of the boat. "The infant is trapped in it. We will need to remove the net so that it does not happen to another creature."

"Here," Gabe said, pulling the long knife he carried when out on the boat from the sheath at his waist and unfolding it so that it was open. "Damn careless fisherman. I should be able to tell whose it is, if it still has the ID tag on it. They are supposed to notify the Fish and Wildlife if they lose a net."

"It shouldn't take long," Magna replied, wrapping her fingers around the handle.

Gabe nodded, but held onto the knife for a fraction of a second longer. "Just be careful," he said in a quiet voice. "That water is pretty damn cold, but I'll come in there after you."

Magna chuckled and rose up in on a surge of water to press a quick kiss to his lips. Her eyes twinkled with mischief as she let a trickle of the cold water run down the back of his shirt. His softly muttered curse against her lips drew a giggle from her before she sank back down.

"I find it very refreshing," she teased, before turning to disappear beneath the waves.

"I just bet you do," Gabe said softly as he watched her swim just below the surface to where the pod of whales hovered protectively around the younger one.

CHAPTER TWELVE

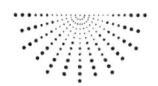

Ross threw his mask and fins up to Nathan before he clumsily climbed up the ladder attached to the side of the boat. The moment he was on the deck, he turned and scanned the area around him. He undid the clasps on his buoyancy compensator, better known as a BC, when he felt Nathan lift the tank behind him.

"You weren't down very long this last time," Nathan said in surprise. "Did you find what you were looking for?"

Ross cast an impatient look at Nathan as he shrugged out of the vest. Ripping the hood of his dry suit off, he tossed it onto the pile of other equipment he had handed to Nathan. Refusing to answer, he climbed along the side of the trawler and up to the bow. Standing on the higher platform allowed him to see further.

"Where are the binoculars?" Ross called out over his shoulder.

Nathan disappeared into the bridge before reappearing with a battered black case in his hands. He climbed up and handed the case to Ross before standing beside him in confused silence. Ross yanked the binoculars out of the case and raised them to his eyes.

He saw the familiar shape of Gabe Lightcloud's boat as he turned in a circle with the binoculars, and was on his second full turn when he caught the spray of a group of whales near Gabe. He muttered a curse under his breath when he realized that they were too far away for him to see what was happening.

Lowering the binoculars, he stood still for a moment before making up his mind. He looked grimly at Nathan, who was staring out at the water trying to figure out what was going on. He grabbed the case that had fallen to the deck and began climbing back down to the lower level.

"Secure the gear," Ross ordered, unzipping the dry suit and stepping out of it.

"Where are we going? You never did say if you found what you were looking for," Nathan complained. "Hannibal said I could only use the metal detector for one day. He's got a job up in Poulsbo so he needs it for tomorrow."

Ross threw another impatient look at Nathan. "I won't need it anymore," he replied in a curt tone. "Now pack up the gear. I don't want it rolling all over the place."

"It's a good thing you're paying me," Nathan grumbled under his breath. "I should have asked for more money, though, if you're going to be bossing me around so much. 'Nathan, do this. Nathan, do that.' Man, didn't your mother ever teach you to ask or say please?"

Ross ignored Nathan's grumbling and started the engines. He pushed down on the throttle as he made a wide turn. He needed to get closer. Something told him that whatever in the hell he'd seen down there had something to do with Lightcloud. He could feel it in his bones.

The image of the tantalizing female flashed through his memory. There was no doubt in his mind that she wasn't human. She had appeared out of nowhere. He couldn't wait to check the underwater camera that had been mounted to the side of his mask. He hoped that it had still been working. Whoever, or whatever, that girl had been, she was real and the key to him getting out of Yachats.

"Get the camera off my mask," Ross yelled over the sound of the engine.

Nathan sighed and turned back to the locker where he had just stored everything. "You told me to put everything away," he snapped.

Ross threw Nathan a heated look, then returned his attention to the boat ahead of him. He pulled back on the throttle as they drew closer. He nodded to Nathan when he held out the tiny camera sealed in the clear plastic case. Opening the outer casing, Ross plucked the camera out of it and slid it into his pocket.

This was one thing he didn't want anyone else to know about, especially Nathan. He knew Nathan would tell his older brother if he even had an inkling of what might be on the camera, and not just his brother. Nathan was one of the town's loudmouths, especially after a few beers.

"Grab the dock line and put out a couple of bumpers," Ross ordered. Then as he turned away, he grabbed Nathan's arm. "Don't say a word about what I was doing. Now, keep your mouth shut and let me do the talking."

"Sure, Ross," Nathan mumbled. "I don't like Gabe that much. He's the only guy I know that's meaner than Hannibal."

Ross nodded. "Good," he said before turning his attention to where Gabe Lightcloud stood near the stern of his boat scowling at them. "Hey, Gabe. Everything okay?"

∽

Gabe watched as Ross Galloway idled toward him. His gaze flickered to the pod of whales before returning to the boat. A wave of impatience, irritation, and fear washed through him. He hoped that Magna realized that they had company and was smart enough to remain hidden from view.

"Ross, what's up?" Gabe responded, catching the line that Nathan threw at him. "I'm working."

"Are you counting whales now, Gabe?" Nathan joked before clamping his lips together when Ross cast him a nasty warning look.

"What were you diving for?" Gabe asked, ignoring Nathan.

Ross shrugged and leaned against the side of the boat. "I thought something had caught in the prop," he replied before looking beyond Gabe to where the whales were hovering. "Unusual for them to just hang out like this," he observed. "Are they sick?"

Gabe glanced over his shoulder. His mouth tightened at the searching look in Ross's eyes. The man had a reputation for being hard. He really couldn't blame him, though. Ross's father hadn't been much better than his own. The only thing Ross had in his favor was that his mom had stuck around, something that Gabe's hadn't bothered to do.

"I'm waiting for some help," Gabe lied. "Some asswipe cut his net and left it. The calf is tangled in it."

Ross's lips tightened, and he looked away. Gabe narrowed his eyes, and casually turned his head to look at Ross's empty net.

"Looks like you're missing one," Gabe commented as he met Ross's gaze.

Ross looked back at the winch and shrugged. "It's at the house. I tore it and needed to repair it before I used it again. I thought I'd check out some new areas while the weather was good," he said. "So, who's coming to help you?"

"Ross could do it," Nathan suddenly said. "He's got the equipment."

"No!" Ross and Gabe both said at the same time.

Nathan blanched and shoved his hands in the front pockets of his jeans. "I was just suggesting, is all," he complained, looking away from the two men glaring at him.

"I have it under control," Gabe reassured Nathan before turning in irritation when his cell phone rang. "Listen, why don't you guys take off? Too many boats around might spook the pod. I've got help… coming," he added as he threw the dock line back to Nathan and turned away to grab his phone off the shelf near the ladder leading up to the roof of the bridge. "Speak."

～

Ross nodded to Nathan, but didn't move away as the other man pulled the bumpers back into the boat. Instead, he focused on listening to Gabe's conversation for as long as he could. A tight smile curved his lips when he heard him mention Kane's name and the softly hissed words 'she's in the water'. He had heard the rumors that the two men liked to share a woman. He wondered if the good doctor and Gabe had found something a little more interesting to share between themselves.

He lifted his hand and waved to Gabe when the other man turned and glared at him. Turning, he walked back to the bridge and started the engine again. His hand moved briefly to the front pocket of his jeans. The reassuring feel of the camera told him that he would soon know if he had been seeing things or not.

～

Magna gingerly sawed through the heavy line, freeing the calf one slice at a time. She worked on his entangled tail first, knowing that he would need it to help keep himself afloat and afraid of the damage it was already doing. She paused and focused a wave of healing energy into one particularly deep cut. It felt good to be helping other creatures instead of killing or enslaving them. She worked her way from tail to nose, paying close attention around his fins and mouth. She trailed her hand along its side, whispering to it as she worked. The two adults that had remained close watched her with attentive, curious expressions. A soft giggle escaped her when the calf tossed its head, shaking free of the netting that covered part of its mouth.

Swimming downward, Magna maneuvered the rest of the netting away as the calf jerked and pushed down with its tail. She knew the adults were interested in her, but they were also eager to move away from the danger. She held on to one end of the net with her left hand as she turned to watch the three whales join their pod. Soon, she could sense them moving farther out to sea.

Releasing a sigh, she tightened her grip on the net and checked to make sure that the other boat that had come up a short while ago was far enough away that they wouldn't be able to see her if she surfaced. Satisfied that it was, she kicked her feet and rose upward. She watched as Gabe talked into the strange device that he had pressed against his ear. A smile lit her face when he froze the moment he saw her and quickly pocketed the device.

Several minutes later, he had pulled the boat close to her and was retrieving the discarded net with the winch. Magna waited until it was completely out of the water before calling a surge to lift her to the side of boat. Stepping onto the side, she gasped when she felt Gabe's hands wrap around her waist and lower her to the deck.

"Thank you," Gabe whispered as he pulled her closer.

Magna frowned as she stared up at him. "For what?" she asked, puzzled.

"For coming back to us," he said before capturing her lips in a kiss that heated her blood.

CHAPTER THIRTEEN

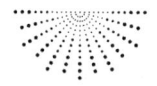

Kane stood at the end of the dock waiting for them, an apprehensive scowl on his normally cheerful face. They had barely bumped against the wooden structure before he was climbing over the side. Magna giggled when he wrapped his arms around her and buried his face against her neck.

"It's not funny," he muttered, pressing a hot kiss to her neck.

"What is wrong?" she asked, pulling back far enough to gaze up at him.

Kane shot a heated look at Gabe. "I was afraid you wouldn't come back," he reluctantly admitted. "When Gabe said you had gone for a swim… I just… You have me twisted in a knot."

Hell, he could hardly think straight. He knew he probably sounded like a pouty little boy, but he didn't care. His arms tightened around her before he pulled back to look at her in concern.

"Your shoulder …," he started to say.

Magna smiled up at him with glowing eyes. "It is completely healed," she said.

Kane's gaze softened, and he brushed a strand of her hair back from her face. His finger ran down her cheek to her neck, pausing on the thin line he felt there, the doctor in him curious about the physical differences between her and a human.

"Touch me," she whispered, seeming to understand his curiosity. "You will not hurt me."

Kane glanced at where Gabe had stopped to watch them. He could see in his friend's face that Gabe understood he needed this time with Magna. Returning his gaze to Magna's neck, he deftly followed along the long thin line. The 'scales' were really just a slightly different texture of skin in a mixture of blues. From a distance, it looked like a delicate tattoo.

"How do you breathe underwater and above ground?" he asked.

Magna opened her mouth to respond, then closed it and frowned at something behind him. Turning, he watched as Ross Galloway stepped off the path and onto the dock. He instinctively pulled Magna closer to his body at the same time as Gabe hissed a warning.

The three of them watched as Ross walked closer. The hair on the back of Kane's neck stood up when Ross's eyes locked on Magna. He swallowed down the desire to push her behind himself. Instead, Kane turned to face the other man as he came to a stop next to the boat.

"Ross," Kane said, tipping his head in greeting.

Ross returned his nod before his eyes swept over the back of the boat, pausing on the tattered remains of the net before sliding away. He returned his attention back to Magna before Gabe moved to block his view.

"What do you want?" Gabe asked bluntly.

Ross chuckled and nodded his head to the net. "I came to see if you were able to free the calf that was caught," he said with a shrug.

"Since when have you ever given a damn about the environment?" Gabe demanded, folding his arms across his chest.

"Since I found my net missing," Ross replied with an easy grin. "I thought it was still in the shed. It looks like someone borrowed it. I was hoping you had been able to retrieve the one wrapped around the calf. I'd like to take a look at it and see if it is mine."

Kane watched the suspicious look cross Gabe's face, but there wasn't a lot his friend could say. His arm curled around Magna's waist and he decided that it was a good time to excuse the two of them. Gabe could handle Ross on his own.

"If you'll excuse us, I know Magna is probably starving," Kane said, standing to one side as Ross climbed over the side.

"Magna? An unusual name for an unusual woman," Ross observed, stopping in front of her. "The whales were pretty cool. Did you get to see the calf?"

Magna gave Ross a tight smile and nodded. "Yes. The calf was afraid, but his mother was there to calm him. He learned a valuable lesson and has promised to use care in the future."

"*He* promised?" Ross repeated with a raised eyebrow.

Kane's arm tightened, and he pulled Magna around Ross. He climbed up on one of the lockers and stepped up onto the dock before reaching down to offer Magna his hand. He almost came unglued when Ross wrapped his hand around Magna's upper arm as she stepped up onto the locker.

"Nice tattoos. I don't think I've ever seen any like them before," Ross commented, staring at Magna's neck.

"I'm sure you haven't," she said, pulling her arm free and reaching for Kane's hand.

Kane glanced at Gabe over Magna's head as he helped her up onto the dock. He saw the fury in Gabe's eyes, but he also saw the unease. Something wasn't right.

"I'll meet you up at the house," Kane told Gabe. "Have a good evening, Ross."

Ross didn't turn back around to Gabe until Kane and Magna walked down the dock and left his sight as they climbed the stairs leading up to the house, but when he did, the fury and suspicion in Gabe's eyes were hard to miss.

"Nice looking woman," he commented casually. "I don't think I've ever seen her around here before."

Gabe's jaw tightened. "That's because she's not from this area," he retorted, before jerking his head toward the net. "Is it your net or not? The tag that's supposed to be on it is gone."

Ross walked over and touched the net with the toe of his boot. He could see some of the old patches he had done on it. It was the one he had cut loose the other morning. His mind wasn't on the net, though, it was on the woman. She was definitely the one he had seen underwater.

"Whoever stole it likely wouldn't have kept the tag on it," he replied with a wry grin. "It's hard to tell, but it looks like it is mine. I was going to file a police report, but figured it wouldn't do any good, then I thought I'd better check with you first."

"I'll have to report it," Gabe said, folding his arms across his chest again. "You might want to go ahead and file that report, otherwise you'll be looking at a hefty fine."

Ross shook his head. "I don't think it is necessary to report it. No harm done, after all," he said, locking eyes with Gabe in a silent battle of wills.

"It's my job," Gabe stated.

Ross scowled. The last thing he wanted was the hassle of paperwork. A slow smile curved his lips as it occurred to him that Gabe would want it even less.

"Strange that neither Nathan nor I saw Magna on your boat when we pulled up," he commented, looking back at Gabe.

"She was there," Gabe stated in a cool voice.

"Not a lot of places to hide and your bridge is pretty open," Ross observed with a shrug.

"She wasn't hiding and she was there," Gabe repeated, not budging.

Ross rubbed his jaw and nodded. "If you say so," he said, turning to climb back off the boat. He paused after he was safely on the dock and glanced back at Gabe. "It's strange, I thought I saw something when I was diving. I guess I'll have to put that in the report if you insist on filing one."

The shuttered look in Gabe's eyes told him that he had hit a sensitive nerve. Triumph filled him when Gabe glanced down at the net. Ross waited, knowing that the other man was wondering how much he knew, or thought he knew.

"I guess no harm was done," Gabe finally said with a shrug. "Just don't let it happen again."

"I won't," Ross promised. "Perhaps I'll see Magna around town. I hope you have a good evening."

Ross turned away and walked down the dock when Gabe didn't reply. Earlier, he had debated if he should come and confront Gabe or not. Now, he was glad he had. He had looked at the video on the camera. There had been something there, but it had been fuzzy, just a blur and a faint outline before the damn battery had died. This visit had given him concrete proof that he had seen a woman, Magna, and that she wasn't your typical female – a fact that Gabe and Kane were trying to hide.

Shoving his hands in his pockets, he climbed along the uneven path that cut through the trees up to the road. It was a bit more difficult hike than using the stairs, but for once he enjoyed the exercise.

He returned to his truck and climbed in. The house was barely visible through the trees on the side of the mountain. Pulling out a cigarette, he placed it between his lips and lit it with the lighter from the console next to him. Drawing in a deep breath, he slowly released a series of smoke rings. Now, he just needed to figure out a way to profit from his knowledge.

CHAPTER FOURTEEN

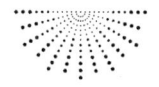

"I've seen that man before," Magna murmured as she and Kane climbed the steps.

"You... Where?" Kane demanded, grabbing her upper arm when he suddenly turned in front of her.

"He came up out of the depths as I was swimming," she reluctantly admitted, biting her lip and looking back down toward the dock. "It took a moment for me to understand why I recognized him. He was wearing some funny clothing and a mask over his face, but I recognized his eyes."

"Damn it," Kane cursed, running his left hand through his hair. "We've got to warn Gabe. This could mean trouble."

Magna took a deep breath and closed her eyes. "If it will cause you and Gabe trouble," she said quietly. "I can leave. I won't let you two be harmed because of me. Never again will I be responsible for harm to another."

Kane slid his hand down her arm and pulled her close. The feel of his warm body against hers sent a shaft of longing through her. After centuries of horrible loneliness, she didn't know if she was strong enough to return to the darkness and solitude. She would rather die than have to live like that again.

"No," he whispered against her temple. "We'll figure something out."

Magna felt tears burn the back of her eyes. Burying her face against his chest, she breathed in the soothing scent of his skin. Fear battled with the knowledge that perhaps this was fate's way of punishing her for all her previous misdeeds. What better way than for her to fall in love with Kane and Gabe, only to have them ripped away from her as she had done to so many others back in her world?

She lifted her head when she heard footsteps coming up the stairs. Glancing over her shoulder, her gaze locked on Gabe's grim face. The feeling of dread built inside her until certain knowledge pierced her like the metal from Mike Hallbrook's weapon, ripping through her with a pain that threatened to overwhelm her.

"He knows," she whispered, staring down at Gabe.

"Yes," Gabe replied in a quiet voice. "He knows."

∼

They returned to the house, each lost in their own thoughts. Magna called to Buck and Wilson when they entered, and the two Huskies raced toward her. Kane and Gabe disappeared into the kitchen. She could hear them preparing a meal and quietly talking.

She laughed when Wilson ran to his basket of toys and started pulling them out one at a time and bringing them to her. Every time she would try to pick one up, he would grab the toy and hold it in his mouth until she sat still.

"He's a clown. A total disgrace to Huskies around the world," Gabe said, shaking his head when he peered over the bar to see what she was laughing about.

"I think he is adorable," she responded.

That earned a lick up her cheek. A giggle escaped her when Buck started to join in. Soon, the two dogs were competing to see who could pile the most toys on her.

"I told you they didn't need any more toys," Kane dryly replied.

"I'd rather buy them another toy than have them eating my furniture," Gabe retorted.

Magna knew that they were all avoiding talking about what had happened earlier. She wasn't sure why the man knowing of her existence would cause so much worry – unless he also knew what she had done.

Was there a way for a man of this world to know that she was the dreaded Sea Witch? If there was, would the people of this world attack Gabe and Kane because they had helped her? She buried her face against Buck's soft fur as a wave of pain struck her.

Drawing in a deep breath, she pulled back and looked into Buck's sweet eyes. She would wait and grow stronger. If danger appeared, she would escape to the ocean and watch them from a distance like her father had watched her mother.

"Dinner!" Kane called out.

Magna laughed when both dogs took off for the kitchen, almost knocking her onto her back. She rose off the floor and followed them. A grin lit her face when she saw Wilson dancing around Gabe as he tried to put the food on the table.

"Down, you damn dog. No, this is not for you. Damn it, Kane. I told you to say supper! You have to say supper. Wilson thinks dinner is for him," he growled.

"Well, why didn't you train him with supper instead? Who calls out supper? Everyone I know says dinner," Kane argued.

"I didn't think about it, okay?" Gabe retorted.

Magna bit her lip as she sat down at the table. She whispered a simple spell and snapped her fingers. Two dog bones suddenly appeared under the table, and she picked up the fork next to her plate. She sighed when she saw her hand tremble.

"How did your day go?" she asked.

Kane shrugged. "Not bad. No heart attacks, a few stitches, a minor car accident, and some fevers and ear infections," he said, sliding several large broiled shrimp, fresh vegetables, rice, and warm rolls onto her plate.

She grinned up at him with an appreciative smile. He winked at her before he stepped back around the table and sat down across from her. Her stomach growled as she drew in a deep breath of the delicious aromas from the food. She decided food tasted so much better when she didn't have to hunt it and eat it raw.

"How do you treat those who come to you?" she asked, curious.

She listened, fascinated. The world Kane was describing was so different from any of the kingdoms she had visited. Even on her mother's isle, those who were ill visited a local healer for healing stones, spells, or potions. Those who were very ill might need the touch of a gifted healer, one who could connect with the patient.

"So, Gabe said you rescued a whale calf today?" Kane asked.

"Yes. His mother was very upset. She had even warned him to stay away from the net," she said with a wave of her fork. "He really shouldn't have snuck away from her."

"It was Ross's net. He said it was stolen," Gabe said, his lips twisting in disbelief.

"So, the whales told you that the calf snuck away from his mother?" Kane asked, enjoying watching her eat as much as he was listening to her.

She nodded, her mouth full and her plate almost empty. With a sigh, she picked up a piece of shrimp. She was hungrier than she'd realized.

"Yes," she mumbled around the food in her mouth. "The leader of the pod was concerned the others might get tangled. He isn't very happy with you humans."

"I'm sure he isn't," Kane chuckled ruefully, glancing at where Gabe was quietly sitting.

"He also said his species was thinking about banding together to do something about you land creatures' habit of making the water a mess," she replied casually with a twinkle in her eyes.

Kane leaned forward. "He really said that?" he asked with an incredulous stare.

Magna burst out, laughing. "No, not really! I could see evidence of your pollution in my swim. You should see your face!" she said with a giggle.

"I'll show you my face," Kane growled as he pushed back his chair.

Her squeal of delight rang through the room as Kane came around the table and she dropped her fork and slid out of her chair. Racing to escape, she made it as far as the living room before he scooped her up in his arms.

"You looked so funny," Magna laughed, feeling light-hearted and young again.

"Yeah, well, take this," Kane teased, tickling her sides.

"Oh! No fair," she gasped.

"How about this?" Kane asked, his voice deepening.

She opened for him the moment his lips touched hers. The combination of everything that had happened melted into this one moment. She wanted him. She wanted Gabe. She wanted something that she could hold onto and never let go.

Wrapping her arms around Kane's neck, she threaded her fingers through his hair. She kissed him as if there were no tomorrows. When he reluctantly pulled back, she continued to press desperate kisses along his jaw.

"Love me, Kane. Please. I want you and Gabe," she murmured, running her tongue across the tip of his ear. "I have been alone for so long. I don't want to be alone any longer."

"Kane," Gabe's voice behind them sounded taut with need.

Magna partially turned in Kane's arms. Her eyes were luminous with desire. She wouldn't take no for an answer. She was stronger, healthier now. Her body had healed, and her mind was in a better place than it had been in centuries.

"Love me, Gabe," she requested, not looking away from him.

"Bedroom, now," Gabe ordered, his fingers moving to his shirt.

"Gabe," Kane said hesitantly.

Gabe shook his head. "I don't need to be told how to make love to a woman, Kane. You should know that by now," he said, his shirt already hanging open.

Kane took a deep breath. "Remember she is a virgin," he reminded Gabe in a quiet voice.

"I'll remember," Gabe said.

Magna gasped when Gabe suddenly pulled her out of Kane's arms and into his. He bent and scooped her up. "Coming?" Gabe asked Kane, grinning mischievously. Magna looked over Gabe's shoulder excitedly as he walked toward the bedroom.

"I'd really like for you both to be there," she called.

"Well, shit," Kane muttered as he reached down and pulled his sweater and the thin, black shirt under it over his head.

Magna's eyes widened in appreciation at the display of Kane's hard muscles and flat stomach. He might be leaner than Gabe and not have the same amount of hair on his chest that Gabe did, but he made her mouth water. She swore she had found the perfect combination between the two men.

Her appreciation grew as Kane continued to shed his clothing as he followed them down the hall. By the time they reached Gabe's bedroom, Kane was nude. He walked over and jerked the covers back down to the end of the bed.

Magna held onto Gabe's strong shoulders as he placed her feet on the floor. Her toes curled into the thick rug next to his bed while he shrugged out of his shirt and tossed it to the side. Within less than a minute, he, too, was standing proudly naked before her.

"There's only one person with too many clothes on," Kane commented to Gabe. "Do you want to remove them, or do you want me to?" he asked.

"I'll take the top, you take the bottom," Gabe countered.

Magna's heart raced as Kane stepped behind her, unsure of exactly how they were going to do this. He gripped her sweatpants and pulled them and her panties down at the same time. Her breath hiccupped when he followed the movement with his lips. The feel of his lips moving over her bare buttocks made her body heat up. Moisture pooled between her legs.

It didn't help that Gabe reached down and pulled her long sweater off over her head. He tossed the top aside and reached for her breasts, lifting them up. His hot mouth closed over her right nipple at the same time as Kane slid his hand between her legs.

She felt his fingers pressing through the soft folds protecting her channel. Her hips jerked when she felt a slight sting as he bit her left buttock. The hot moisture increased until she swore he had ignited a fire in her belly. The ache between her legs grew, as did the throbbing of her nipples. She didn't realize that they could be both super sensitive and painful at that the same time.

"I want to lick her," Kane groaned, pressing his finger deeper.

"Kane," Magna panted, her arms tightening around Gabe's head so he couldn't pull away from her breasts. "Harder, Gabe."

She cried out when Gabe nipped her distended nipple, making it throb even more before he transferred his attention to her left nipple. While Gabe was driving her crazy by making her breasts ache for more, Kane was making her weak in the knees.

"Get her on the bed," Kane ordered.

Magna gasped, her body stretching upward when she felt Kane stand behind her. She could feel his cock throbbing against her buttocks. Her body instinctively melted against his, seeking relief from the empty feeling he had left when he had removed his fingers.

Gabe released her nipple and straightened. He climbed on the bed, drawing her with him. She followed, crawling on her hands and knees when he sat with his back against the headboard and his legs spread. Her eyes were glued to the thatch of dark curls and his long, thick shaft. His penis pulsed with his desire. His cock was long, thick, and the bulbous head had a light film of moisture beading on the tip.

Magna wasn't even aware that she was bending down until her mouth wrapped around the end of Gabe's cock. It was as if some primitive instinct was guiding her. Pleasure poured through her when she not only heard Gabe's reaction, but felt his response.

Her own breath caught when she felt Kane's fingers again. This time, he was rubbing the small nub that had grown to the size of a pebble. His touch was both excruciating and exquisite. A shudder ran through her and she opened for him, spreading her legs even more.

Gabe tangled his left hand in her hair while his right hand played with her breasts which were gently swaying in time with the movement of her mouth. He leaned his head back against the headboard and watched her slowly slide her mouth up and down his cock.

A whimper escaped her when Gabe began guiding her head up and down faster while at the same time Kane stretched her with his fingers. It was as if the two of them were working in unison to make her body ignite into flames. She could feel the moisture of her desire begin to run down the inside of her thigh. Kane growled in satisfaction and tweaked her swollen nub with his finger, drawing a prolonged cry from her.

Magna was locked in a world of pleasure when Kane rose up behind her and aligned his cock with her feminine channel. He leaned forward enough to wrap his arm around her and once again torment her nub as he pushed into her.

Unwilling to break the connection she had with Gabe, she moaned around his cock as Kane's long, smooth shaft stroked the lining of her channel. She felt the slight hesitation when he came to the barrier marking her maidenhood.

Another whimper slipped out when he started to pull back, as if to withdraw from her. The feel of Gabe's hand releasing her hair and reaching down so he could pinch both of her nipples had her bending forward to suck him all the way down. At the same time, Kane surged forward and through the barrier, claiming her with a loud groan as he sank his cock as far as it would go inside her. He continued to play with her clit until she was bucking, trying to throw him off as her orgasm built.

In a double assault on her body, Gabe rocked his hips while playing with her throbbing nipples. Kane, sensing she was close to having her first orgasm, grasped her hips, his shaft moving in and out of her with increasing speed now that her body had adjusted to him.

Kane drove deeper and deeper into her which caused Gabe's cock to slide farther down her throat, and Magna was overcome. Her mouth and body tightened around both men, pulling long moans of pleasure and a flood of seed from them as they all came.

"Yes!" Kane groaned, his head falling back as he emptied himself into her.

"Beautiful," Gabe uttered in a hoarse voice, watching as Magna swallowed his cock, his hands still holding her breasts firmly in his hands. "Aw, baby, yes!"

A shudder went through her. Her body trembled when she felt Kane slowly pull his cock out of her. Her lips tightened, trying to hold onto Gabe when Kane reached down and wrapped his arms around her waist.

"What are you doing?" she whimpered, reaching for Gabe.

"Shower time, baby, then Kane and I will trade places," Gabe chuckled.

"Yeah, we are not letting you off this easy, sweetheart," Kane added, sliding off the bed and reaching for her.

Magna looked back at both of the men and grinned. "Thank the Goddess for that!" she giggled as they pulled her to her feet.

∼

Later that night, Gabe pulled free of them, and said he needed to check on the dogs. Twenty minutes later, Magna was sleeping contentedly in Kane's arms, but Gabe still hadn't returned.

Kane slipped from the bed, threw on his jeans and a shirt, and walked into the kitchen. Grabbing a beer out of the refrigerator, he opened the back door and stepped out onto the deck where Gabe was standing, looking out at the ocean over the treetops. He walked over and leaned against the railing.

"She asleep?" Gabe asked.

"Yeah, finally," Kane replied. "You should have stayed with us."

Kane watched as Gabe lifted the beer bottle to his lips, taking a long swig before he lowered it. He knew his friend well enough to know that Gabe needed time to accept what was happening. Things were moving fast, even for them. This wasn't like any of their other relationships; this one was serious.

Gabe finally looked down at his hands and spoke. "I needed to think," he finally admitted. "That isn't easy to do with her lying between us."

"So, what are we going to do?" Kane asked, turning around so he was facing the house.

"We aren't letting her go," Gabe retorted in a harsh voice.

Kane glanced at him before turning his attention back to the darkened living area. He could see the hallway leading to the back part of the house. It had been hard for him to leave Magna, but he knew that he and Gabe needed to talk. Magna's safety and all of their futures were at stake.

His gut tightened when he realized what Gabe was alluding to.

"Ross could be trouble," Kane said moodily.

Gabe shrugged. "He has no proof of anything. If nothing else happens, he won't have any fuel to start something," he muttered. "Without fuel, a fire can't burn."

"What if he doesn't let it go?" Kane insisted. "She's been through enough."

∽

Gabe looked down at his hands before he straightened and turned to stare into the house he had built with Kane's help. The house and the boat had always been his pride and joy. He loved living along the coast and being out on the water.

He had been twelve the first time he'd seen the view from the side of the mountain. He'd been out late, as usual. His old man hadn't cared what he did as long as he didn't get into any trouble with the law. He had sat in almost this exact spot and made a vow that one day he would build a home here so he could stare out at the water.

He had worked and saved every dime he made from that summer on. When his dad became sick and couldn't fish anymore, he had taken over running the boat. His gaze moved to his rough hands. When he was eighteen, the economy tanked, and his dad had sold the boat. He got his high school equivalency and enlisted in the military.

He had also married. That had been the biggest mistake of his life. Louisa was a small-town girl looking for a ticket to the easy life. He had been young, horny, and she'd said the right things, at the right time.

Less than a year later, he was divorced and being shipped off to another base while his ex-wife took the last dime they had in their checking account. Life was a bitch, but he'd found out a week after the divorce that if you sold the puppies, it wasn't so bad.

The month after the divorce was finalized, he received two letters in the mail. The first certified letter was from an attorney for his dad who had died a week after the divorce was final. It turned out that his dad had known about his obsession with the property and purchased the land with the money from the sale of the boat.

The second certified letter stated the mother he'd never known had died soon after his dad and had left him a modest inheritance from her life insurance policy. Free of Louisa, he'd been able to focus on the money he would need to build the house of his dreams and replace the boat he had sold.

During his tour of duty, he had discovered a love for learning. At first, he had just been content to read anything he could get his hands on, but soon he had wanted to know more. He fulfilled that hunger by enrolling in online classes.

Meanwhile, he had taken any assignment that offered a bonus. On his second of four tours, a fire fight had left him with two bullet wounds, which had brought him to the base where Kane was stationed.

Their friendship grew enough over the course of their deployment that Kane was drawn to Lincoln County when he got out. Gabe had returned two years later with enough money to buy the materials to build his house and buy the boat he now had. Together, they had outfitted the boat, then built the house. He had stayed with Kane at his place on the outskirts of town while his house was under construction. He had moved in after they finished it a little over a year ago.

Kane divided his time between both places. When his friend was on call or had to work, he stayed at his own place. Otherwise, Kane usually hung out at his, since they were usually working together on a project or out on the boat anyway.

Gabe sighed and answered Kane's question.

"If he doesn't let it go, we disappear with her," he said.

CHAPTER FIFTEEN

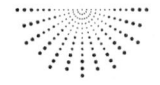

"So, how long did you say you were going to be staying?" Patty asked, rocking on her heels and looking pointedly at where Asahi was sitting at Mike's old desk.

"I didn't," Asahi stated.

He ignored Patty's glare. She had been doing that a lot since he arrived late this afternoon. The one thing he couldn't ignore was her tapping the pencil against the notebook in her hand. It might have been a nervous gesture, except for the glare she was presently shooting at him, which almost certainly made it an intentionally irritating gesture.

"He's coming back," Patty stated.

Asahi looked up and replied, "No… He is not."

Patty's eyes widened and filled with tears. "You can't know that for certain," she insisted.

"I do not require any more assistance at this time, Miss…," Asahi said, resting his forearms on the desk.

A flash of rebellion flickered across Patty's face. "You're the CIA, you figure it out," she snapped, turning on her heel. "I'm late to pick up my son. Don't forget to lock the front door when you leave."

Asahi waited until the bell over the front door of the police station jingled and the door slammed before he sat back in the chair. Patricia 'Patty' LaBelle had not been pleased to see him when he walked into the police station an hour ago. The receptionist had been like a chihuahua nipping at his heels. He pursed his lips when a slight shudder ran through him at the visual.

He looked down with distaste at the tattered state of the file he had requested from Patty. Coffee stains, a few oil marks, and what looked like crusted frosting covered the exterior of the folder. His memory flashed to the empty donut bag in the trashcan next to Patty's desk and he wondered if she had purposely coated the file before bringing it back to him.

Perhaps he shouldn't have been quite so blunt when he ordered Patty to provide him with the files he needed and leave him alone… and he probably shouldn't have turned into Mike Hallbrook's office instead of the empty storage room she'd tried to direct him to. Oh well. He was here now… with this disgusting folder.

Carefully gripping the folder by the corner, he opened it. Inside, he discovered the papers were in pristine condition and chronological order. He turned the pages, pausing when he saw the photograph of a local fisherman. Lifting it up, he recognized the name. Ross Galloway had been a suspect in each of the previous disappearances. He scanned the information, noting that Ross liked to visit The Underground Pub.

Asahi looked up at the clock on the wall. His eyebrow rose at the message written across the black background of the clock in iridescent white letters: *The White Pearl*. Below that was the owner's name – Pearl St. Claire – and the address. Shaking his head, he decided that the entire office had been decorated with local thrift shop blue light specials.

Another glance at the clock told him that if he left now, he would have time for a quick visit to Mike Hallbrook's former home before stopping at the Underground Pub for dinner. He removed the stack of papers from the ruined folder. Testing the file drawer on each side of the desk, he was surprised when they both opened. Inside one was a green tennis ball, dog bowl, and leash. In the other drawer were empty folders and an assortment of forms. He pulled out one of the new folders and inserted the stack of papers before closing both drawers and tossing the soiled folder into the trashcan.

Asahi rose out of the chair and exited the office. There was something special about Yachats. This was not the first time an unexplained phenomenon had occurred in the area. There had to be a connection. He was determined to discover what it was and solve a cold case that had lingered unexplained and unresolved for more than forty years.

Locking the front door, he pocketed the keys Patty had reluctantly handed him. He crossed the sidewalk, unlocking the white SUV rental car with the touch of a button as he went, then opened the door, and slid in. Pressing the start button, he shifted and slowly reversed out of the parking space. Ruth Hallbrook had given him permission to search the house with the understanding that nothing was to be disturbed or destroyed in the process. She planned on being here in a couple of weeks and would be staying in the house.

Asahi honestly didn't expect to discover any new information from the house. He had already been there once before. No, his best opportunity would come from talking to Ross Galloway. He hoped the man was in the mood to share what he knew.

∼

Ross applied the brakes and used his turn signal before turning into the narrow driveway of his mother's house. It was a small, wooden structure painted in a dark sea blue with white shutters. The house wasn't much, but it was in good shape for its age.

He shifted the truck into park and turned off the ignition. Sitting in the dark, he lit up another cigarette. His mom hated that he smoked so much, and out of respect for her, he never did so in front of her. He inhaled a deep breath, letting the addictive nicotine fill his lungs, and looked at the house with a critical eye.

The right shutter was drooping again. He needed to replace the hinge and make sure the wood wasn't rotting. He'd just finished painting the damn place three months ago. There was always something that needed to be repaired. Between the boat and this house, it was a never-ending job.

He knew he was procrastinating. As much as he cared about his mom, he hated going in the house. It brought back too many bad memories, even after all these years. Dropping the remains of his cigarette into the can he used as an ashtray, he released a tired sigh. Tonight would be a short visit. He'd see what new project his mom wanted done, then make an excuse to leave early, and head down to the Underground for a bite to eat and a beer or two before he headed back to his own place.

He had a lot on his mind. Without any conclusive video of the strange woman he'd seen today, he would have to find another way to cash in on what he knew – without getting killed. Hell, with the disappearances of Carly Tate, Jenny Ackerly, and now Mike Hallbrook, everyone was walking around looking over their shoulders.

Pushing the door to his truck open, he slid out and shut it behind him. A frown creased his brow when the front porch light didn't come on. Usually his mom turned the light on the moment the lights from his truck flashed in the living room window.

He walked around the front of the truck and up the short walkway. Taking the steps two at a time, he paused and rapped on the front door twice. Concern tugged at him when there was no answer.

Gripping the doorknob, he pushed open the door. The house was dark. His hand slid down to the knife at his waist. He pulled it free. There was no way his mom would have left the front door unlocked if she had gone anywhere.

"Mom," Ross called out, his eyes moving over the immaculate living room.

His hand tightened on the handle of the knife when there was no answer. At the end of the hall, he could see the soft glow of a light. He silently walked down the hallway, his footsteps muted by the worn rug.

A smothered curse escaped him when he looked in the room and saw his mother lying on the floor. Sheathing his knife, he rushed forward and knelt beside her. His fingers trembled as he gently rolled her over onto her back and felt for a pulse. He released a sigh of relief when she moaned softly.

"Hang on. I'll call for help," he softly ordered, pulling his cellphone out of his back pocket and dialing emergency services. "Yes, this is Ross Galloway. I'm at Margaret Galloway's house on Main Street. I need an ambulance."

"Ross," Margaret murmured, her voice thin and barely audible.

Ross gripped his mother's hand when she moved it. "Yes, I'll stay on the line," he said to the emergency responder. "I'm here. What happened?"

Margaret Galloway's eyelashes slowly lifted to reveal tired eyes filled with pain. Ross could feel the weakness in her grip. She tried to smile, but instead moaned.

"Fell. I… love… you, Ross. I always have," she murmured before closing her eyes.

Ross released her hand when he heard the siren. Rising to his feet, he hurried back down the hall and opened the front door. The next twenty minutes were a blur as he answered questions as the paramedics attended his mom.

Standing to the side, he watched as they wheeled her out to the ambulance. He automatically locked the door as he followed them. A numbness started to fill him as he slid into his truck.

His mind wandered as he followed the ambulance, falling farther behind when he had to pause at the red light. He watched it disappear around the corner and wondered when life had become so complicated. Unexpected sorrow hit him when he realized that he could lose the one thing in the world that actually mattered to him – the only person who gave a damn about him.

∽

Asahi nodded and thanked the nurse. When he'd gone to the Underground Pub, and Ross had not shown up, he had been disappointed. It wasn't until he had been about to leave that he had heard Dorothy, the waitress, ask a man who entered where Ross was. The man had said he'd seen an ambulance leaving Margaret Galloway's house with Ross following behind it.

After careful consideration, he'd decided that while it might be insensitive to still attempt to talk to Ross, people tended to be more forthcoming with information when they were in stressful situations.

Though he and Ross had never met, Asahi recognized him from the photo in the office file. Ross was farther down the hall, sitting in one of the hard chairs outside one of the doors. Tired, troubled eyes looked up at him when he drew closer. Asahi motioned to the seat next to Ross. The other man shrugged in response.

"Are you a doctor?" Ross asked, sitting forward and resting his elbows on his knees.

"No, CIA," Asahi responded.

Ross's head jerked up and for a moment his expression was devoid of everything but surprise. Then a sardonic smile curved Ross's lips for a brief second.

"Are you here for me or for my mom?" he asked with a neutral expression and a slightly sarcastic tone.

"Would your mother know anything about the disappearances?" Asahi asked.

Ross stared at him for a moment as if he had lost his mind, then he suddenly rose. Asahi's gaze followed the other man as he turned in a circle, releasing a string of colorful expletives. Ross finally came to a stop, faced Asahi, and crossed his arms.

"What do you want to know?" With visible effort, Ross managed to keep himself from yelling in the small hallway connecting rooms of sick people, but his resentment was obvious. "I told Mike Hallbrook," he continued without waiting for a response, his fingers twitching with agitation, "that I had nothing to do with Carly Tate or Jenny Ackerly's disappearances, then he up and disappears, too. I'll tell you the same thing I told the FBI when they came, I didn't have anything to do with any of their disappearances!"

"I know," Asahi calmly replied.

That clearly threw Ross for a loop. The man opened his mouth, then closed it, a frown darkening his expression. Asahi rose from his seat as Ross finally responded.

"You know? How do you know?" Ross demanded, dropping his arms to his sides.

Asahi glanced down the hall where several nurses were standing, then politely motioned to the chair next to him.

He wasn't sure if Ross would sit at first. After several seconds of silence, Ross released another curse and walked over to sit down. Asahi sat down set to him.

"Mike Hallbrook called me several weeks after he disappeared," Asahi began.

Ross looked at him with a hint of suspicion. "Then why are you here and why was I being grilled by the FBI about his disappearance?" he demanded in exasperation. He ran his fingers through his short hair. "Hell, everyone in town thinks I'm either a serial killer or a bad luck magnet. Well, they already thought the last, but I'm not a murderer."

Asahi's lips twitched at the incredulous expression on Ross's face. "Mr.

Galloway, have you ever noticed anything out of the ordinary, possibly extraterrestrial, in the area?" he asked.

The sudden flare of unease was noticeable in Ross's face before the man turned his eyes away. Asahi's gaze narrowed on Ross's clenched hands.

"I don't know what you are talking about," Ross lied, then rose from his seat again and stepped away, looking up and down the hallway before his gaze turned to the closed door next to them. His mouth was tight.

Asahi rose from his seat. "I think you do. What have you seen and where?" he pressed.

"Listen..., I'm not sure...." He stopped when the door opened.

"Ross, you can go in now," the doctor said, his gaze sweeping from Ross to Asahi and back to Ross.

There was a look that passed between the doctor and Ross, and as the doctor stepped out of the room, the brief glance he sent Asahi was brimming with suspicion.

"Thanks, Kane," Ross mumbled, nodding to both of them before he disappeared through the door.

Asahi glanced at the name tag on the doctor's white coat – Dr. Field. He made a mental note to do some research on the man. His thoughtful gaze moved from the doctor to the closed door and back again.

"Can I help you?" Kane asked, his jaw tight with tension.

"No, thank you. I believe I have everything I need for the moment," Asahi quietly stated with a bow of his head.

He turned and retraced his steps down the corridor to the exit. A tingling between his shoulder blades told him that Dr. Field was watching him. He would have to reread the reports. There was more going on here than Mike Hallbrook had discovered. He was sure he had found another piece to add to the puzzle, and as his grandfather had once told him, each piece to a puzzle helped clarify the overall picture once you knew where it connected. The key was to be patient and diligent.

CHAPTER SIXTEEN

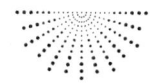

Over the course of the next two and a half weeks, life began settling down into a pattern. Magna helped Gabe out on the boat during the day, and the nights were spent in his and Kane's arms. She was grateful that there had been no sign of Ross yet.

She hummed under her breath. The daily swims, good food, and incredible nights were having a positive effect on her both mentally and physically. Mentally, she felt stronger, healthier, and happier than she had since the night the alien creature took over her body.

She would be the first to admit a large part of her healing had come from Gabe and Kane. Their tender caresses, teasing, and acceptance was helping calm the nightmares she still had. Though at first, she had been afraid to share the horrors of the things she had been forced to do, worried that it would turn the men against her, that fear had died when Kane had shared some of the things he and Gabe had gone through overseas. She had become ever more certain that they truly cared and wanted to help her, and she had hesitantly shared some of her memories with them. When it became too difficult to speak, she had shown them through a memory spell.

After each event, they had held her. Sometimes they would talk about it, sometimes they would merely hold her while she cried. Other times, they would sit on the deck and stare at the ocean in silence or go for long walks with the dogs until she was ready to store the memory away.

The good food, exercise, and loving had also physically benefited her. She was no longer frail and skeletal. Laughter, something she had missed, came more easily each day. It was hard not to laugh between the antics of the dogs – especially Wilson – and the two men. She was gaining weight, the dark circles and gaunt look had disappeared, and she could use her magic again without feeling exhausted. For the first time in centuries, she was happy.

A startled laugh escaped her when Kane wrapped an arm around her waist, and pressed a heated kiss to her neck. It was Saturday morning and he was off for the weekend. Thankfully, the doctor who had been on vacation had returned yesterday, so he would have more time to spend with them.

He had been asleep when she had quietly crawled out of bed. Poor Gabe had been woken up an hour earlier by the two dogs, and whispered to her to go back to sleep while he took the dogs for a run. She tilted her head and pressed a kiss to Kane's cheek when he peered over her shoulder.

"What are you doing?" Kane asked.

"I am trying to understand the directions in this book," she said with a sigh. "I used a spell to translate it so I could read it, but it still doesn't make much sense."

She made a face at him when he chuckled. The food she was making looked nothing like the picture above the recipe. She was trying to make pancakes from scratch. There was flour, sugar and eggs all over the counter from where the mixer had flung the ingredients in the large bowl she had found in one of the cabinets. So, now she knew that you should not raise the tool when the blades were still moving.

"Let me help you," he murmured, brushing his lips along her shoulder where the oversized t-shirt had slipped down. "Can you turn it back to English?"

With a frustrated sigh, she waved her hand over the page. The words shimmered and floated off the page before settling back down into a pattern and sequence that he recognized. He read the instructions, and saw that she had placed all the ingredients into the large bowl like she was supposed to. It looked like it was the mixer that was causing her problem.

"Here, let me show you how to use this," he offered in a quiet voice, motioning for her to pick up the handheld mixer. His hand enveloped hers, and he covered her thumb. Together they pushed the button until it moved to the first line. "Start like this, moving it in a slow circle."

Warmth spread through her as he gently moved her hand with his. He slid his other hand around her waist, pulling her close, and she shivered with need. She liked cooking like this. A satisfied smile curved her lips when the mixture in the bowl turned into the creamy liquid shown in the pictures. When all of the ingredients were mixed, he slid the button down until the mixing tool turned off.

"And that, my beautiful mermaid, is how you use a mixer," Kane said in a husky voice.

"If you keep showing her how to use my kitchen appliances like that, she'll be laid out on the table with us eating her up," Gabe said dryly from the door.

"Or I could be eating both of you," she said before her eyes widened in amusement. "What happened to you?"

She fought the urge to laugh. Gabe stood on the thick mat in front of the door leading outside. A small, but growing, pool of water dripped from his body. It took a moment for her to realize that there was a light rain coming down outside. A giggle escaped her when both dogs suddenly shook, sending a shower of wet droplets all around them and pulling an irritated curse from Gabe.

"Wilson decided he would take the scenic route this morning," Gabe muttered with a crooked smile. "I need a shower."

Her lips twitched at the blatant invitation in his eyes. Shaking her head, she held up the spoon and grinned. It was hard to resist him when he looked at her like that, but she knew what would happen if she ended up in the shower, and it wouldn't be breakfast.

"I'm cooking," she stated proudly. "A thing called pancakes. They sounded very interesting."

Gabe's lips drooped and he gave her a pouty look. She had fallen for it once already. Remembering what had happened when she did caused a heated blush to rise up her neck.

"Kane can cook them," Gabe said with a twinkle in his eyes at her red cheeks.

"No…," Magna started to say when she felt a little push from Kane.

"Go on," Kane said with a grin. "I've got this. You need a shower, too. You're covered in flour and egg yolk."

Magna swallowed at the predatory look that came into Gabe's eyes.

"Gabe," she whispered in anticipation.

Something told her she was about to be well and truly loved, again. Her cheeks weren't the only thing that started to warm up when he took a step closer to her.

"You're all mine this time, Magna," he said with exaggerated wickedness. He glanced at where Kane was rolling his eyes. "Don't be in a hurry to cook them. This might take a while."

Kane raised an eyebrow and returned Gabe's look. "If you take too long, I might just join you."

"Doesn't taking the dogs for another run sound like more fun?" Gabe teased, grabbing Magna's hand.

She barely had time to glance over her shoulder at Kane, worried he would be upset. Instead, he winked at her with a genuine smile and turned away, murmuring just loud enough for them to hear that 'unlike some people', he knew better than to go running in the rain.

Gabe scoffed and called back, "Just give us a head start!"

Magna giggled as Gabe pulled her along behind him down the hall to his bedroom. Her heart raced when he firmly closed the door.

"I don't mind if Kane comes in, but those damn dogs are going to have to wait to get any attention from you this morning," he growled, pulling her around and pressing her up against the door.

The sound of clothing being torn pulled a startled squeak out of her. He kissed her until she was breathless while he pulled the remains of the old t-shirt away from her body. Her hands ran up his chest to the back of his head as his lips moved to her jaw and he cupped her breasts.

She half-closed her eyes. *This is way better than trying to cook*, she thought with a sigh.

∼

Gabe knew he should probably go easy on her, but he wanted her so damn bad. He and Kane had talked about the need to go slow, to give her time, but all of their best-laid plans disappeared out of his mind the second he put his hands on Magna. Hell, if he had his way, they might never get out of the bedroom.

His hands moved over her body with precision, removing their clothing until there were no barriers between them. Pulling her into the bathroom, he turned on the large shower. Once again, he was thankful he had taken the extra step to install a hot-water-on-demand system in the house. It heated quickly and stayed hot indefinitely. No worries of being in the middle of making love, only to get a cold shower!

He guided her in, gritting his teeth when her hands wrapped around his cock and stroked him. He looked down, enjoying watching her touch him. A light hiss filled the shower when her finger ran over the tip before skimming around the head of his cock.

He reached down and gripped her wrists when she moved to cup his balls. If he didn't stop her now, he would be coming like a schoolboy watching his first adult movie.

"My turn," he stated.

"Why is it always your or Kane's turn first?" she complained with a delightful pout.

Gabe leaned down and pressed a hard kiss to her lips. "Your pleasure will always come before ours," he swore.

"Always?" she asked, her eyes shimmering with emotion.

"Always," he promised. "Now, turn around and grip the bar."

She looked at him with a confused expression for a second before she turned. Gabe knew if he didn't have her look away, his efforts to hold on long enough for Kane to join them would be doomed. Alone time with Magna was wonderful, but this relationship was about the three of them. Gabe was wishing now that he hadn't teased Kane so much. What if he really did take his damn time with those pancakes?

Picking up the bar of soap, he lathered his hands and began a full out assault on her body, determined to bring her to a peak over and over. His hands ran over her shoulders and down her arms before retracing their path and moving to her breasts. Only when she was panting and rubbing her ass against his crotch did he move further down. He paid close attention to her smooth womanhood. He had guessed that after all she had been through, grooming wouldn't have been a top priority, so the hairless state had to be natural, but he had asked her a while ago, and she'd told him that the women of the sea people did not have hair between their legs.

Her hips rocked with his hand movements and soft moans escaped her as she bent her head forward. His hands slid to the rounded cheeks of her gorgeous ass. He reverently ran his fingers along the valley between her cheeks. Curious about how she'd respond, he guided her to bend over more.

"Put your hands on the bench," he requested.

Magna released the bar and placed her hands on the bench. The move opened her up to him. Soaping his hands again, he ran them over her buttocks, kneading them. A smile of pleasure crossed his face when her hips lifted. She was a natural.

His fingers moved deeper until he rubbed against her tight rosette. A shudder ran through her, but she didn't resist. His cock throbbed. He wanted to take her ass while Kane buried his cock in her pussy. Where the hell was he?

"Take her."

Oh thank god, Gabe thought as his head jerked up and he noticed Kane standing outside the shower door, staring hungrily at Magna. He could see from Kane's damp hair that he had taken a shower in the other bathroom.

Then he hesitated. "She isn't ready," he replied in a tight voice.

"What am I not ready for?" Magna groaned, rubbing against his hand.

"Both of us," Gabe replied.

"Yes, I am," she groaned, tilting her head back.

"She *is* ready. Look at her, Gabe. She wants you," Kane said.

Gabe looked down. Magna was rubbing her ass against his hand. The vision of them taking her at the same time burned inside of him. A shudder ran down his long frame.

He bent and wrapped his arm around her waist. "Go with Kane. I'll be there in a moment," he said, pressing a kiss to her shoulder.

"Not long," Magna insisted, looking at him over her shoulder.

"Not long," Gabe promised.

A satisfied smile curved Kane's lips. He opened the door to the shower and helped Magna out. Wrapping a towel around her, he led her into the bedroom. He knew that Kane would get Magna ready for the two of them, and Gabe would be able to hear everything that was going on in the other room. He quickly washed and rinsed, his body thrumming with desire.

Turning off the shower, he pulled the towel off the rack and dried his body, then opened a drawer, and pulled out the lube and a condom. He cursed when he saw his fingers tremble.

Walking into the bedroom, he paused halfway to the bed, watching as Magna slowly impaled herself on Kane's cock. Kane's hand rose and he played with her breasts, bringing her to a peak and holding her there.

"Lean forward, baby. Kiss me," Kane encouraged, motioning for Gabe to climb on behind her. "Kiss me while Gabe gets you ready."

"Yes," Magna murmured.

Gabe tore the condom package open with his teeth and removed it from the envelope. Fitting it over his cock, he drew in a deep breath. He was so excited; his cock was extremely sensitive and his balls were beginning to hurt from the tension. Flipping the top of the lubricant, he squeezed a little onto the palm of his hand before coating the condom. He climbed on the bed and positioned himself behind Magna. He caressed her ass. Once again, he felt her rock back against him.

"You are about to feel fuller than you've ever felt before, sweetheart," he warned, his hand sliding down between her buttocks.

"Gabe," Magna panted, her head turning so she could look at him over her shoulder.

"Focus on Kane, honey. Relax, enjoy, and focus on him," Gabe gritted out as he aligned his cock behind her.

He slowly rocked his hips, letting her adjust, listening to her quiet pants before he felt her body open and accept him. The feeling of fullness sent a ricocheting wave of pleasure through him. He could feel every movement when Kane began to rock his hips. Gripping Magna, he controlled the rhythm, moving in opposition to Kane until they were in sync. Magna's cries grew louder and more wild the deeper and faster they went until she stiffened.

"Damn, Gabe," Kane groaned, his body stiffening as he thrust upward. "Oh, Magna. Oh, baby."

Sweat broke out on Gabe's forehead while he waited for Kane's orgasm to finish. Magna's body was still locked between them. He could feel her pulsing around Kane. With a loud groan, Kane pulled free.

Gabe leaned forward, his fingers biting into Magna's hips as he rocked faster and faster. Her loud pants turned to begging as her body reached the precipice again. Her saw her fingers dig into Kane's shoulders and felt her tightening around his cock as she came. The tight squeeze was his undoing and he emptied the tension of his aching balls in a continuous pulsing wave that drained him.

It took him several minutes to gather enough strength to pull out of her and slide off the bed. Magna had collapsed on Kane who was holding her tightly against his body. Gabe gazed down at her peaceful face for a moment before he turned to the bathroom.

"I'll clean up and get a washcloth and towel to clean her," he said.

"Gabe," Kane softly called after him.

He looked over his shoulder, pausing in the doorway to the bathroom. "Yeah?" he said.

"I love her. I'm never letting her go," Kane informed him.

"I love her, too, man. She's ours," he replied before he disappeared into the bathroom once more.

∼

The sound of the rain hitting the roof of his truck made Ross glad he had canceled taking his boat out today. He sighed as he stared out of the windshield of his truck. The rain had picked up over the last hour. The dreary weather matched his mood. There didn't appear to be any chance of him getting close to the woman. Hell, she seldom left the house. The only time she did was to go out on the boat with Gabe.

He unconsciously patted his front pocket, looking for his cigarettes before he sighed as he remembered he had tossed them out. The last couple of weeks had been brutal, but they had also made him realize that he was still human, no matter how hard his dad had tried to beat that out of him when he was younger. He'd had a lot to think about in that time, and even more to do. His thoughts turned to his mom and he released a sigh of regret.

While they had never been close when he was growing up, he realized their distant relationship had been because of her fear of his dad, rather than a dislike of having him as her son. He realized now that she had tried to protect him the only way she knew how, by letting him run free and keeping him away from the house as much as possible.

Once again, he wished he hadn't promised his mom that he would quit smoking. He might be a lot of things, but there was one thing he had sworn he would never do; he would never break a promise he had given. A man was only as good as his word. If he didn't give it, that was one thing, but if he did… if he did, he needed to live up to it, no matter how difficult or painful the promise was.

Leaning back, he closed his eyes. He had only made two other promises in his life. The first had come the day his dad had died and his mother was crying. He had been twelve years old when he laid his hand on her shoulder at the cemetery and promised her that he would take care of her.

That was the day he had started to grow into a man who would never have to live in the shadows of fear and brutality again. He had worked down at the docks and anywhere else he could for the next two years. At fourteen, he started taking his dad's old fishing trawler out at night.

He had kept his promise to her until two weeks ago. For years he had stopped by her house three times a week – two days a week for dinner and one day to do any work she needed done. Now, there was nothing left but empty memories and guilt that he hadn't seen how sick she was sooner.

He swallowed as he remembered Kane and one of the new doctors in town coming out of her room after quietly talking to her. He had been waiting in the corridor outside her hospital room. Rising, both men had nodded to him in greeting, but he could see the resignation in their eyes.

Walking into her room, he had been shaken by how fragile she looked against the pristine white sheets. She hadn't cried, just nodded to him to come sit by her. She had looked tired, and her eyes had silently searched his face.

Sitting down in the hard chair that he'd pulled up next to the bed, he had held her hand, something he hadn't done since he was a child. It still tore him up when he remembered the sadness and pain in her eyes.

"I'm dying," she had whispered.

"How… How long?" he had asked, thinking in the back of his mind that it wasn't right for a thirty-year-old man to want to cry. "How do you know? Surely…."

His mom had shaken her head and leaned back against the bright white pillow. "I found out six months ago when I went to Portland," she said tiredly, closing her eyes. "I haven't been feeling too good for a while. The cancer had already spread."

"There are other hospitals," he started to argue before pressing his lips tightly together when she opened her eyes and stared at him in resignation.

"Maybe if they had caught it in time," she whispered. "It is all over my body, Ross. They wanted to do things that would give me a couple of extra months, but I wanted quality, not quantity. I'm in a good place. You've made sure of that. You've worked so hard for so many years. I don't… We've never had much, but I've put money back for years and kept up on a life insurance policy. I wanted you to have something, just in case. I want you to know I love you, son. I always have. You were the one thing in my life that I did right. I don't ever want you to think otherwise. I'm proud of you, Ross. I always have been. You've grown into a good man, despite…."

Ross opened his eyes, remembering how her voice had faded. He had to give his mom credit. In all her life, she never spoke bad about anyone, especially his father.

He stared blindly out of the window. It still shook him that after all these years of thinking he had been taking care of her, she had secretly been looking after him. His fists clenched and he looked down at them, trying to lock the grief back in the closet he had pushed it into.

She had slipped into a coma that night and died three days later. He had sat by her side, talking to her. For the first time in his life, he shared his dreams, talked about his fears, and hoped that she could hear him. The funeral had been yesterday afternoon. Only a handful of people had come out in the rain to say goodbye, but he hadn't cared. He had been there and he had kept his promise. Now, there was nothing tying him to the small town. Nothing but an unusual woman who he just wanted to know whether she was real or not before he left.

Picking up the card the funeral home had created, he looked down at the picture of his mom when she was young. The second promise he had made had been to himself. He had sworn that he would never hurt a woman the way his dad had hurt his mom. Deep down, he knew that Magna didn't want to be found. He had seen the fear in her eyes when he had grabbed her arm. It had been more than being exposed as some strange creature. There had been a deep sadness in her eyes that he had recognized in his mother's eyes.

Drawing in a deep breath, he pocketed the obituary and leaned forward to start his truck. There were some things in life better left unknown, he reluctantly decided. Perhaps, she was one of them.

Putting the truck into drive, he slowly pulled out from where he'd been parked along the edge of the road down the hill from Gabe Lightcloud's house. A new sense of peace, one he had never felt before swept through him. He would put his affairs in order and start looking for a new place to live. He had always fancied living on an island somewhere in the world.

Somewhere warm, he decided as he drove away.

He drove by a dark sedan, unaware that he had been the focus of a quiet surveillance. The woman behind the wheel watched him drive by before her gaze turned to the house on the side of the mountain. A frown darkened her brow and she pulled up her phone to access the address. Several minutes later, she had accessed the database at work. Gabe Lightcloud, former Army Ranger, decorated war hero, worked for the government at the United States Fish and Wildlife Department. No arrests. Yet, he was definitely someone of interest, she thought as she watched the white SUV that had been following Ross Galloway for the past couple of weeks. What did the CIA want with Ross? Missing persons within the United States were usually handled by the FBI. Nothing that she had researched had shown Ross to be an international threat – hell, the guy had never been out of the country before.

She watched as another SUV came down the road and turned up the drive. She recognized it as another vehicle of interest to the CIA agent, because it belonged to Dr. Kane Field.

Tonya Maitland reached into the passenger seat next to her and pulled up the report she had on Asahi Tanaka. It felt strange for her to be following one of the government's agents. Granted, it was her job as an investigative reporter. In her mind, they all worked for the same cause – to keep the people safe.

"What is the connection? Mike Hallbrook said Ross Galloway wasn't behind the disappearances, yet, he has the attention of the CIA. Not only that, we now have a decorated military hero and a local doctor with military experience involved. Curious, very, very curious," Tonya murmured, starting her car and doing a U-turn.

She paused at the bottom of the hill. Tanaka was turning left, which meant he was returning to the motel. Deciding that she had a better chance of learning something from Ross, she turned right and headed toward town. Glancing at the clock on the dash, she decided it was about time to offer him a cold beer.

CHAPTER SEVENTEEN

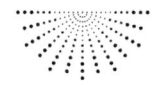

The rains from last night had cleared and the sun was shining. Magna grinned as she walked beside the two men along the brightly colored shops lining the street. Kane had talked Gabe into taking a day off so they could go shopping together. She knew her excitement was as much about seeing her new world as it was about buying anything. This was her first trip out among the residents.

Gabe had not been happy when Kane decided that she needed more clothes. He had argued that he was perfectly happy with her not wearing any at all. Kane had not been impressed with Gabe's reasoning. Gabe on the other hand said that if she insisted on wearing any clothes, his shirts worked just fine. At that point, Kane had dragged Gabe into the kitchen.

"I want to take her places," Kane argued. "She can't do that wearing your shirts."

"What kind of places do you want to take her to? She goes out on the boat," Gabe retorted.

The sound of Kane gritting his teeth had Magna wincing. He only did that when he was really upset. Standing in the passage between the kitchen and dining room, she had bit her lip to keep from pleading with Gabe.

"She deserves more," she heard Kane finally respond in a quiet voice. "I want to take her to dinner, to the movies, and show her some of our world. She deserves that, Gabe. She was held a prisoner long enough. I don't want her to ever feel like that with us."

Gabe's face had tightened into a stiff mask before he released a long breath and his shoulders slumped in resignation. She knew he was afraid for her, and that knowledge warmed her heart.

"You're right," he muttered, running his hand over the back of his neck. "It's just…." his voice faded when he saw her watching him.

"It's just what?" she asked, gazing back at him.

His face softened. "What if someone realizes that you aren't human?" Gabe muttered.

She smiled, knowing that wouldn't be an issue now that she was strong again. Walking over to him, she wound her arms around his waist and laid her head on his chest. He immediately wrapped his arms around her, tightly holding her against his broad frame. A moment later, she felt Kane's warm body pressed up behind her, sandwiching her between them. She released a contented sigh. This is what it felt like to be loved. Tilting her head back, she looked up at him with a serious expression.

"I can use a glamour spell," she assured him. "No one will be able to tell I'm not human, I promise. I have also been watching your magic box so I know how people speak in your world, not that I am likely to talk to anyone. Your world and mine are really not all that different," she added with an excited expression.

A half hour later, they had departed. She had barely been able to contain her fascination with Gabe's truck and how it worked. Then, there were the roads and the houses and the lights and the…. Well, the list had gone on and on, drawing laughter from the two men as they competed to answer her questions as fast as she asked them.

Gabe had pulled up in front of a long row of storefronts. People milled about, enjoying the beautiful weather. She glanced up at the sky, shielding her eyes. Above them, seagulls swooped down, hoping to find a tidbit of food that someone had dropped.

"Here, try these," Gabe said.

He was holding out a pair of the dark eye shields similar to what he and Kane were wearing over their eyes. She giggled when Kane suddenly placed a bright yellow hat on her head. The combination of the eye covering and the hat made it easier to see everything.

"Thank you," she laughed, tugging down the hat on her head to make sure it didn't blow off.

"Where to next?" Gabe asked, his tone a little more relaxed than it had been when they first arrived.

She knew why. So far, the spell she had cast had worked beautifully. They were on their third shop and not one person had given her more than a dozen looks – all because of who she was with, not because of who she was. The girl at the last boutique had been very vocal about that!

It was a good thing that Magna had sworn she'd never use her magic for harm again, or the girl would have ended up with a very large pimple on her nose, though if she had touched Gabe's arm or tried to hand Kane the little piece of paper one more time, then all bets would have been off. The thought that she could be jealous and petty amused her because she had never thought of herself as being either before.

She grinned at all the bags both men had in their hands. She had an assortment of new outfits, including lingerie.

She sighed. Everything would have been perfect if she didn't have the darkness of all the things she had done in her previous life hanging over her head. If only she could know being here had reversed her spells, then everything would be perfect.

"What's the matter?" Gabe asked, immediately sensing the change in her mood.

Magna shook her head. There was nothing he or Kane could do to help her. It was something she would either have to come to terms with or find a way to resolve. She leaned against Kane when he wrapped his arm around her waist.

"I know what she needs," Kane said with a crooked grin. "Food! I'm starving."

Her face lit up. "Food does sound wonderful," she admitted, glancing at some of the buildings that overlooked the water. "Can we sit outside? Perhaps near the water?" she asked with a hopeful look.

"I know just the place," Kane said, turning to hand the packages to Gabe. "Why don't you take these back to the truck while Magna and I get a table down at Luna's. Afterwards, we can grab an ice cream."

"Okay," Gabe grumbled, trying to hold onto the slippery bags. "I want a beer."

Kane chuckled. "I think we both deserve one after all this marathon shopping," he said with a twinkle in his eyes as he pulled her down the sidewalk.

She looked over her shoulder, watching Gabe walk away. She immediately missed his comforting presence. With a loud sigh, she turned and followed Kane. They walked up the hill to a set of colorful buildings. She watched as the cars passed by them, wondering where everyone was going. This world was different from her own in so many ways. The isles where everyone lived were small enough to make it across on foot in just a few days. They did not have the massive metal machines, but used a simpler rail system that connected each town, both above and below the water on the Isle of the Serpent. Once they reached their destination, most residents used push carts or their sea dragons to carry the larger items.

She tilted her face again. It truly was a beautiful day. There was a light breeze coming in off the water that kept the temperature just right. She didn't understand why the people here did not just walk to their destinations. It hadn't taken long for them to reach the nondescript building and the walking felt good after being cooped up inside.

"It doesn't look like much, but they have good food," Kane promised with a reassuring smile as they walked through the doorway into the dim interior. He turned when a waitress came up to them. "We'd like to sit outside, please."

"Sure," the young hostess replied with a bright smile. "Follow me. It's such a beautiful day, I don't blame you."

They followed her as she weaved around the tables set up inside and out onto a large, covered deck situated outside.

"Your waitress will be with you in just a moment," the young girl said.

"Thank you," Kane replied, sliding into a corner spot.

A moment later, another girl came out, placed the menus on the table, and gave them a brief review of the specials for the day. Magna wanted to roll her eyes when the young waitress kept smiling at Kane and didn't even bother to acknowledge that she was sitting there.

"Two lagers on tap and a water with lemon. We are waiting for one more," Kane said.

"I'll bring them right out," the girl replied with another bright smile before turning away.

Magna shook her head and peered over her sunglasses at Kane. "I should have put a glamour spell on you and Gabe, too. Do the women of your world all act like this around men or only you and him?" she inquired with a raised eyebrow.

Kane chuckled. "They are jealous."

She gave him a skeptical look, and he smiled. "Trust me, you have nothing to worry about," he promised. "I need to go to the restroom. Gabe should be here any minute."

She smiled sardonically. "I can take care of myself for a short time," she teased with a dismissive wave of her hand. "I will wait for Gabe and our drinks."

She tilted her head when he leaned over and brushed a kiss across her lips.

"I'll be right back," he promised.

He made it almost halfway to the door before he worriedly glanced over his shoulder. She shook her head in amusement. She had been waiting to see how long it would take for him to glance back. He had made it almost three seconds longer than the last time.

Both men had been very protective of her all day. She had told them no one would be able to tell she was different. She had perfected that art during the years she had been under the control of the alien creature.

She pursed her lips together when a wave of depression hit her despite the beauty of the day. A part of her knew the guilt she was feeling came from having her strength back. As strange as it sounded, knowing that she was powerful enough to undo some of the damage she had committed was causing an internal conflict that she wasn't sure how to resolve. If she could just return to her world long enough to see if her spells had reversed, she knew it would help.

She was so lost in her thoughts that she didn't realize that someone else had approached the table. She blinked at the shadow blocking the sun. The smile on her lips wavered before fading. Instead, of Gabe or the waitress, another familiar face stood next to the table. It was the man from the water.

"Hello," Ross said, stuffing his hands into the front pockets of his jeans.

She pushed back against the choking fear. Her gaze moved over his face, trying to gauge what he wanted. He looked tired and there was a faint air of uncertainty about him.

"Hello," she finally said.

A Few Minutes Ago:

Ross looked up and froze. Kane and Magna were walking through the restaurant. He couldn't believe it. He was sitting at a table in the back corner where it was darker, so they didn't see him when they walked by.

He had finished signing the papers down at the realtor's office thirty minutes before and had stopped in to grab a bite to eat before he went down to the docks. His gaze followed them as they went outside. A few minutes later, Kane came back in and headed to the restroom.

Realizing this might be his only chance to get an answer to his question, he slid out of his seat and made his way outside to where the woman was sitting by herself. Swallowing, he stared at her. She looked different – healthier and happier than he remembered. His mind went blank when she looked up at him and he saw the fear. For a moment, it reminded him of the look in his mom's eyes when his dad had come home drunk. Pushing the memory away, he finally spoke.

"Hello," he greeted in an uneasy voice.

He watched as she raised a nervous hand to tuck a loose strand of hair behind her ear. His eyes moved over her face down to her neck. The markings he had seen before were gone, and he could have sworn she'd had thin scars along each side of her throat as well.

"Hello," she responded quietly, a slight tremor in her voice.

He glanced back at the doors before refocusing his gaze on her face. "Listen, I don't want to frighten you. I know I came off too strong. It's just… things are different now. I don't really care who you are or why you are here. I just need to know if what I saw was real. I want to know… just for my own peace of mind. I won't tell anyone else," he said in a hesitant voice. She bit her lip and continued to stare up at him in silence.

The silence extended another few seconds before she drew in a breath. "Yes," she whispered.

He took a deep breath. "Where are you from? How?" Ross muttered, raising a hand to rub over the back of his neck.

Her eyes softened as she continued to watch him. He knew he looked tired and rough. He hadn't had a decent night's sleep in over two weeks.

"The world I come from… It is different from yours in many ways. It is very beautiful, but I am happier here," she finally said, looking down at the shell lying on the table. Picking it up, she nibbled on her lip again as she studied it.

"Why did you leave?" Ross asked. "I mean, this isn't a bad place to come to, but why would you leave a world that you obviously loved?"

She looked up at him and a sad smile twisted her lips. "Some things are best left unknown," she responded quietly, gripping the shell in her hand before holding it out to him.

He reached out and took the shell from her, turning it over and over in his hand. He'd seen this same type of shell before. He didn't know what it was called, but it was common in the area.

"What's this?" he asked, looking back at her face with a puzzled expression.

"A gift," she murmured before her head turned and she looked back toward the door. "Gabe and Kane are coming."

He grimaced and slid the shell into his pocket. He knew with the two men there, he wouldn't learn anything else. Hell, if Gabe discovered he knew anything, he might be wearing concrete-filled boots and feeding the fish before he had a chance to ask another question. Deciding it was better to retreat, he gave her one of his famous crooked smiles before nodding his head in farewell.

"Thank you for telling me. I… I wish you happiness, mermaid," he said.

"As do I you, Ross. Good luck on your journey," Magna replied in a soft voice tinged with an emotion he didn't understand.

Ross paused as he started to turn, a frown creasing his brow, before he nodded again and walked away. He slipped out the back exit along the docks. For the first time in two weeks, he felt lighter.

A smile curved his lips as he fingered the shell in his pocket. A quick glance up at the sky showed clear skies. He had planned on talking to one of the guys down at the docks who was interested in buying his boat, but instead, he decided he would take it out one last time.

Today is a beautiful day to be out on the water, he thought, feeling good.

∼

Magna watched as Ross walked away. A sense of remorse swept through her. Perhaps there was a darkness inside her that wasn't part of the alien creature. She glanced down at the small pile of shells that decorated the center of the table. Picking up another one, she stared at it. She had cast a spell on the one she had given to Ross. The next time he picked it up, he would think of her, and when he did… she shook her head.

She pushed down on the guilt threatening to choke her and gazed out over the water. This human would be another dark mark against her soul that she would have to live with until she could find a way to make it right.

She looked up when she heard familiar laughter, and she forced a smile to her lips when she saw them threading their way through the tables toward her. Behind them, the waitress followed with their drinks and a tray of food.

"Food's on; I ordered inside. I hope you don't mind," Kane said with a grin as he slid into the seat next to her while Gabe sat in the one on the other side of her.

"I thought I saw Ross," Gabe murmured, glancing at her in concern while the waitress placed their drinks on the table.

She reluctantly nodded. "He came to say hello," she admitted, picking up her glass of ice water and taking a sip.

She could feel both men stiffen at her softly spoken words. They both remained quiet until the waitress had finished serving their food. She knew the moment the woman was gone, they would demand to know what Ross had wanted. She wouldn't lie to them. She owed them more than that.

"What did he want?" Gabe hissed under his breath, his eyes flashing with fury.

Her gaze softened. "You don't need to worry. He just wanted to know... He just wanted to know if what he saw was real," she clarified.

Kane leaned closer to her and picked up her left hand, holding it in his. "What did you tell him?" he asked in a quiet voice.

Magna turned her head and stared into his eyes with a sad smile. "I told him 'yes', that I was not from this world," she murmured.

Gabe's breath exploded past his lips in a long hiss. "That's it, we've got to go," he growled, starting to stand. "We can grab the dogs and be on the road in less than an hour."

Magna reached out, gripped his forearm and furiously shook her head. "No," she said, begging him to understand what she was about to tell him. "I... I took care of it. He won't be a threat to us."

"Magna, what did you do?" Kane asked in a quiet voice, sending a warning glance at Gabe, who was slowly sitting back down. "How do you know he won't be a threat?"

Magna bit her bottom lip as tears filled her eyes. "I put a spell on the shell I gave him. The next time he thinks of me, he'll be whisked away," she admitted in a soft voice.

"Whisked? The only way you'll be safe is if you send him to another world!" Gabe muttered, running his hand down over his face.

Magna nodded. "Exactly," she responded, her voice filled with regret.

"Magna," Kane said, reaching out and turning her chin so that she had to look at him. "Where are you sending him?"

"To my world," she answered in a voice that was barely audible.

Gabe's soft chuckle startled her and she pulled free of Kane's grasp to stare at him in shock. The sound grew until both men were laughing. She scowled, unsure of what they found so funny.

"This is not funny!" she snapped, clenching her fists. "Did neither of you understand what I just said? What I have done?"

Gabe picked up his beer and took a deep gulp of it before he set it back down on the table and grinned at her. "Yeah, we heard you. It was a hell of a lot better than our plan." he said, grinning at Kane.

"And what plan was that?" Magna demanded, folding her arms and glaring back and forth between the two men sitting on either side of her.

"Take your pick," Kane said, picking up a chip off his plate and waving it. "It was either kill Ross, grow a set of fins, or live on a deserted island somewhere. I'd much rather Ross have to deal with it. Besides, he won't go unless he thinks of you, right?"

"Yes," Magna said in confusion.

"Then, it is up to him whether he stays or goes," Kane said with a nonchalant shrug, popping another chip into his mouth.

"Well, you've also got to remember that he's been saying for years that he wanted to get the hell out of this area. I'd say he is about to get his wish," Gabe added with a raised eyebrow.

Magna's eyes widened and a slow smile grew on her face. "He did?" she asked with a hopeful expression. "Then I was not bad to give him the spell?"

Kane leaned over and brushed a kiss along her cheek. "No, I'd say you've given him a gift he'll never regret," he informed her, glancing over her shoulder at Gabe and winking.

"Definitely," Gabe said around a mouthful of food.

Magna picked up her sandwich and looked at it, suddenly hungry again. Maybe she was looking at this wrong. If Ross wanted to leave, but had been unable to do so, then her granting him his wish was a good thing, she reasoned.

"So, we are going for ice cream after this?" she asked before taking a bite of her sandwich.

CHAPTER EIGHTEEN

Tonya frowned, watching the woman and the two men. She impatiently fingered the glass of unsweetened ice tea the waitress had refilled, and ground her teeth in frustration.

Her attempts to make contact with Ross Galloway had been futile. It was like he had become a hermit since his mother passed away two weeks ago. Tonya had gone to all of his old haunts, and the only thing she had learned was that he needed better friends to hang out with. Nathan Grumby and his brother, Hannibal, made her want to take a shower with bleach.

The only thing she had discovered from them, beside the fact that she never wanted to have to be near either one of them again, especially Hannibal, was that Ross Galloway hated to fish and liked to fuck. The conversation had quickly gone downhill at that point, and Nathan had eventually taken the hint, but Hannibal had needed a ball-busting to get the message.

It didn't help that Asahi had also disappeared on her. His rental car records showed that he had returned the car at the Seattle airport. He didn't strike her as the kind of guy who would give up so easily.

That had left her following Ross, and now she was torn. Watching Ross from across the room, she had seen his immediate reaction when Dr. Field and a woman walked into the restaurant. Knowing what she did about the good doctor, Tonya had dismissed Ross's sudden interest in the man. It had to be the woman.

Her theory had proven to be correct. The moment Dr. Field had gone to the bathroom, Ross had been out of his seat and heading for the woman. Now, it could have been because she was beautiful, but there was something off. She knew what a guy interested in a pretty face looked like and that wasn't the expression on Ross's face. No, he was so intensely determined, it was like he *needed* to talk to her, and he clearly didn't want Dr. Field or the other man to know he was there.

Her first thought was the woman might have been a jilted lover. The flash of fear on the woman's face and her defensive posture could have been due to a relationship gone bad. Tonya had read that Ross's father had been an abusive bastard. A lot of times the apple didn't fall far from the tree, but as far as she knew, it didn't match Ross's M.O.

Galloway could have been stalking the woman. It would explain why he had been sitting outside Lightcloud's house. She huffed in aggravation. At the rate she was going, she would end up with more questions than answers.

Her frustration grew when she saw the woman talking to Ross, and it was clear that Ross was earnest and apologetic and… well, he was more than nervous… he was afraid, she decided. His mannerisms, posture, and expression held an edge of real fear. It could have been because of the two men that she'd come here with, but the way he watched her every move gave Tonya the feeling that it was the woman who made him apprehensive.

Her eyes narrowed when the woman picked up one of the shells on the table and handed it to Ross. Tonya would have loved to have ripped the sunglasses off the woman's face. She really wanted to see her eyes. Eyes told a lot about a person.

"Do you need anything else?" the waitress asked Tonya, distracting her for a moment.

"No, just the bill," Tonya replied in a curt tone.

The waitress gave her a leery look and nodded. "I'll be right back," the young girl said.

Returning her gaze to the woman, she grimaced when she saw Ross disappearing out the back entrance, and wavered between following him or waiting. Deciding she could catch up with Ross, she focused on the couple. It was obvious that the three of them were intimate. The constant touches of both men, the smiles the woman was giving them, and the answering looks in the men's eyes all spoke of an intimate relationship.

Tonya shook her head. More power to the woman if she could handle two men. Personally, Tonya wasn't sure one was worth it. Most of the men in her experience were shallow, immature, and demanding. Adopting a dog would be easier and more rewarding. Adopting a cat was perfect; they only asked for minimal attention and came potty-trained by nature.

She breathed a sigh of relief when the woman rose. The larger of the two men started to rise as well, and the woman scowled down at him and pointed her finger. A smile tugged at Tonya's lips when the man grumbled but sat down.

If the woman could handle a fierce ex-Army Ranger with a look and a point of her finger – not to mention two men at the same time – Tonya was going to rule out Ross and physical abuse. She rose to her feet when the woman passed by her.

Following her to the Ladies' room, she turned to the sink as the woman entered one of the stalls. She studied herself in the mirror. Running her fingers through her shoulder-length, dark brown hair, she pulled out the lip balm from the front pocket of her jeans and applied a thin layer to her lips.

She was just replacing the tube of lip balm when the toilet flushed and the door to the stall opened behind her. Her gaze ran over the woman's face. She had removed her sunglasses and Tonya caught a glimpse of the woman's unusual dark green eyes. Moving to the side so she could get to the sink, Tonya gave the woman a friendly smile.

"Beautiful day out. I'm so excited that it has finally stopped raining," Tonya commented.

The woman returned her smile with a cautious one. "Yes, it is very beautiful," she replied.

"I'm not from around here. Do you have any suggestions about what I might find interesting?" Tonya asked, turning to look at the woman. "Oh, sorry, I'm Tonya, by the way," she added.

The woman shook her head apologetically. "My name is Magna. I'm afraid I don't know much. I've only been here a few weeks."

"Oh, where are you from? I'm from New York," Tonya shared.

A warning bell went off inside Tonya as she finally put her finger on what it was about Magna that had felt off from the moment she had come out of the stall. It was like Tonya was seeing her, but she wasn't really seeing her – which made absolutely no sense. Sometimes her instincts were helpful, and sometimes, they really weren't, but Tonya *was* interested to see a look of confusion cross Magna's face. "Is New York far from here?" she asked with a hesitant smile.

"You don't know where New York is?" she asked in disbelief. Magna was clearly foreign, but what were the odds that she wouldn't have a vague idea of the location of a place so famous?

Magna's smile wavered, and her eyes became wary. Tonya felt like kicking her own ass. She could almost see Magna withdrawing from her.

"I have to return to my companions," she said, slowly stepping toward the door.

"I didn't catch where you are from," Tonya said, reaching out to stop Magna from leaving.

Magna paused and frowned. She shook her head and looked at the bathroom door.

"My home is far away from this world. I hope you have a wonderful day," Magna said, pulling open the door.

Tonya absently nodded. Out of the corner of her eye, she could see Magna's reflection in the mirror hanging on the wall above the sink. A line of dark blue tattoos lining Magna's throat caught her attention, but when Tonya turned her head and looked at the woman as the door closed, she didn't see them.

A shiver of unease ran through Tonya. Rubbing her hands along the sides of her jeans, Tonya bit her lip as she remembered something. She pulled her cellphone out of her pocket and leaned against the wall. Doing a Google search to confirm, she paled and shook her head in disbelief. She lifted her hand and rubbed her suddenly aching brow with her fingers.

"CIA handles fucking space aliens?" she whispered, wondering how on earth she could have forgotten that little tidbit of information.

She straightened when the door opened again and two giggling teenage girls stepped inside. Grabbing the door, she exited behind them. Weaving her way through the tables, she paused at the entrance to the patio. The table where the three had been sitting was empty.

"Damn," she muttered, realizing she had a lot more homework to do before she called it a night.

~

Magna laid out on the lounge on the deck and laughed as Wilson retrieved the toy she had thrown, brought it close enough to be just out of her reach, and lay down, happily gnawing on the toy. She was exhausted from their day and glad to be home where she could remove her shoes and return to wearing one of Gabe's shirts. A smile curved her lips as she remembered Kane's reaction when she emerged from the bedroom.

She moved her arms over her head and stretched. Her body was still tingling from what had happened next. A soft moan slipped out when the soft material of the shirt rubbed against her sensitive nipples.

Closing her eyes, she captured the memory and held it close. Maybe someday she would collect a hundred shells – no a thousand – and inside each one she would store a memory of the men so she could relive the feeling of their hands and mouths on her again and again. She wanted to hold them close to her heart, so they could replace the nightmares. She drew in a deep, contented breath as she remembered Kane's words when she'd stepped into the kitchen wearing nothing but Gabe's shirt.

"Do you have any idea how much I want to rip that shirt off of you?" Kane had groaned, his gaze running down her body and causing a swift wave of fire to ignite inside her.

Gabe had chuckled, his eyes alight with mischief. "Too late, I already did that," he replied.

She'd shaken her head in mock irritation. "Neither you nor I will have any more clothing if you two rip all his shirts," she stated, placing her hands on her hips.

Kane had looked at Gabe with a raised eyebrow. Gabe grinned and shrugged.

"I can go topless," he volunteered.

"Oh, you two are impossible. Is sex with me the only thing you two think about?" she'd demanded with a toss of her head.

"Yes!" both men answered at the same time.

"Then, what are you waiting for?" she'd asked with a suggestive smile. "An invitation?"

She probably shouldn't have turned her back to them and lifted up the shirt to reveal she wasn't wearing anything under it. She'd barely made it into the dining room before they had her bent over one of the thick padded chairs. Her lips curved as she relived what had happened next, and her fingers moved down between her legs.

∼

Shortly before dinner:

"Did I mention that I love the way you two think?" she moaned, watching as Gabe removed his shirt.

"Did I mention I'm calling your ass?" Gabe responded, tossing his shirt to the side and reaching for the button on his jeans.

"I want her mouth," Kane muttered, unzipping his pants.

"I always wanted to try it on the dining room table," Gabe said in a thick voice.

Kane released a strained chuckle. "I'm just glad you didn't choose a cheap one," he replied, moving around to the front of the chair.

Magna's lips parted on a gasp when she felt Gabe's strong fingers reach around and grip the front of the shirt she was wearing. Buttons went flying, revealing her unbound breasts. She cried out when Kane pinched her nipples at the same time Gabe slid his fingers inside her vagina.

"Hot damn, but she is ready for me," he groaned, pulling his fingers out and aligning his cock with her moist and ready channel.

"Slide your mouth around me, Magna. I want to watch Gabe take you from behind while you are eating me," Kane ordered.

∼

Magna groaned and her body arched at the memory. A soft sigh escaped her and her eyelids fluttered open. Her face flushed when she realized that Gabe and Kane were standing on each side of the lounge, their eyes glued to her hands.

"I was thinking about earlier," she admitted, giving them both a weak smile.

"Why didn't you tell us?" Kane demanded, his throat moving up and down when she pulled her hand away from her clit.

Her cheeks flushed a rosy red when Gabe released a soft growl as she closed her legs. Sitting up, she pulled her shirt down over her hips, and gripped his hands when he held them out. She gasped when he pulled her into his arms.

"I didn't want to interrupt what you were watching," she confessed.

"Yeah, well, next time, interrupt us. I'd much rather watch you come than see some sweaty guys kick around a ball," Gabe informed her.

She laughed, wrapping her arms around his neck. "Well then, I'll have to make sure I come in next time and see if you are interested in watching me instead," she teased, playing with the hair at his nape.

"I think it is time to do a little watching," Kane said with a grin.

"I think we are into some major Overtime," Gabe retorted.

"Overtime? What is overtime?" Magna asked.

She wasn't sure she wanted to know after the two men looked at each other and grinned. Two hours later, she couldn't even think anymore. She had been so thoroughly loved that she didn't even notice falling asleep.

CHAPTER NINETEEN

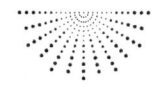

Several days later, Gabe stood at the counter of the local hardware store. He needed a few items for the house and his boat.

Gabe listened half-heartedly to the gossip Fred Albert was sharing. Fred had owned Fred's Hardware, Marine, and the Five and Dime for the last twenty-five years. His wife Mildred had once told Gabe that when Fred died, she was going to have him stuffed and put in the window. Personally, Gabe wasn't sure the woman had been joking.

"I heard the Coast Guard found Ross's boat today anchored offshore," Fred said as he rang up the items. "They think he must have gotten tangled up in one of his nets and fallen overboard."

"Why do they think that?" Gabe asked, glancing at the front of the store where Magna was looking at some garden statues.

The man shrugged as he bagged the items he had just rung up. "One of the nets was missing," he said. "Shame. Ross's mom died just a few weeks or so ago and he had her place up for sale. I heard he was going to sell everything and move to Hawaii."

"Yeah, a shame," Gabe nodded distractedly.

"I need to get the other bolts you ordered," Fred added. "They're in the back."

"No problem, I'm in no hurry," Gabe commented, glancing over his shoulder when the door opened and a woman in her mid-thirties came in. "I forgot I needed some rope for a bow line as well. Mine is getting a little frayed."

∽

Magna glanced up when the door opened. She had been admiring a small statue of a mermaid that would look cute on the back deck when a woman carrying a bundle of papers came in. The woman took down a picture in the front window and replaced it with another one. Curious, Magna walked over to see the picture on the front of the papers.

A soft gasp escaped her when she recognized the intense eyes of the male who had shot her. The woman, hearing her swift intake of breath, turned to look at her. Magna stumbled backwards when the woman took several steps closer.

"Do you know him?" the woman demanded. "Do you know where he is? Have you seen him?"

Magna forced her eyes away from the paper in the woman's hand and up to her face. The woman's dark blue eyes refused to allow her to look away. Unable to stop the automatic response, she nodded.

"Where? Where did you see him?" the woman pleaded. "When? Please. I need to find him. He is the only family I have left. Please."

Magna searched for Gabe's huge form. The desperation in the woman's eyes was too much for her to ignore. That same look haunted her dreams at night. Eyes of the men, women, and children she had turned to stone. The eyes of a parent pleading for their child. Her mother and father's eyes as she turned them to stone.

Licking her lips, she nodded toward the door. The woman sucked in a breath and nodded in reply, then hurried to the door and opened it. Magna followed her out, making sure the door closed behind them.

She looked up and down the sidewalk to make sure that they were alone. Still afraid, she walked a short distance away until she reached a narrow alley between the buildings, far enough away from the door to the store that they would not be disturbed.

"Who is he to you?" she asked the woman.

The woman gripped the papers tightly against her chest. "Mike is my baby brother," the woman replied in an earnest voice. "We... He's all I've got. If you know anything, I would appreciate your help."

Magna could see the grief in the other woman's eyes. "What is your name?" she quietly asked.

"Ruth Hallbrook," Ruth immediately replied. Magna watched Ruth turn over one of the papers and look at the picture of her brother. "No one knows what happened to him. He left me a message, but it didn't make any sense. He said he had met someone and that I would probably never see him again. That isn't like Mike. We promised each other after our folks died.... I can't... I can't think of him being lost or gone forever. I need to bring him home."

"What if he doesn't want to come home?" Magna asked in a quiet voice.

Ruth drew in a deep breath, staring at Magna. "Why wouldn't he...? You know where he is, don't you?" she asked harshly, her eyes widening in disbelief and anger.

Magna lowered her gaze. "Yes," she responded, looking up when Gabe came out of the hardware store. She could see the slightly wild expression in his eyes. The emotion was almost identical to the look in Ruth Hallbrook's eyes. "Gabe."

His head immediately turned toward where she and Ruth were standing, and as he walked over to the alley, he looked into her troubled eyes before his gaze moved to the papers in Ruth's hand. She grimaced when he released a muttered curse before he nodded in understanding.

"How about we get a cup of coffee?" he finally said with a sigh.

Ruth looked back and forth between them before she nodded. "Where?" she asked, lifting her chin in determination.

"My place," he replied in frustration. "You can follow us. Kane should be home by the time we get there."

"How do I know…?" Ruth started to say, her eyes narrowing with suspicion.

Magna turned and touched Ruth's arm. She gave her a reassuring smile. Helping Ruth would also help herself. Releasing as many demons as she had would take time, but deep down she hoped that someday she could set them all free.

"It will be alright," Magna promised. "I… owe your brother a great debt."

She could feel Ruth's skeptical eyes on her and Gabe before she gave them both a brief, sharp nod. They walked toward Gabe's truck. Ruth had parked next to them.

Magna climbed in the truck when Gabe opened the door for her. She watched him hurry around to the driver's side. He opened the door and climbed in, then stashed the shopping bags behind their seats.

"I hope you know what you are doing," he said, inserting the key and turning the ignition.

Magna looked at him with a haunted expression. "How did you feel when you thought I was gone?" she countered, waiting for him to answer. She continued when he didn't say anything. "Mike Hallbrook is the only family she has left."

Gabe looked at her, then at the car waiting for them to pull out. He reached over and squeezed her hands. She smiled when he shook his head in resignation.

"It terrified the hell out of me," he admitted, shifting the truck into reverse and pulling out of the parking space.

"Exactly," she replied, clasping her hands in her lap.

She drew in a deep breath as he drove through town. She stared out of the window, checking the mirror for the dark blue sedan that was following them. This was another wrong that she could right. Each one helped her feel a small measure of redemption.

"How much are you going to tell her?" he finally asked as he turned onto the road leading to his house.

"Everything. She deserves to know the truth," she said quietly.

Gabe reached over and grasped her hand again. "Then what?" he muttered.

"Then... I will give her a shell," Magna whispered.

∽

Ruth Hallbrook bit her lip as she followed the truck in front of her. She couldn't decide if she was crazy or suicidal. Still, if there was the remotest chance of finding her brother, she'd take the risk. Glancing down, she fumbled for the card the FBI Agent had given her this morning.

She would have thought between the FBI and the CIA, someone would have found Mike by now! The state police sure weren't going to. They said that since Mike had called and left her a message saying he had voluntarily left, there was nothing they could do. She had told them exactly what they could do. Of course, she'd come close to going to jail for that little conversation.

Pressing the dial button on her phone, she tapped out the number while trying to keep her eyes on the road. Hell, if something happened to her, well, she wanted at least one person to give a damn! She lifted the phone to her ear when it began to ring.

"Maitland."

"Hello, Agent Maitland, this is Ruth Hallbrook," Ruth said, turning on the turn signal. She glanced both ways before turning left. "You said I should call you if I found out anything else about my brother, Mike Hallbrook."

"Yes, thank you for calling. Can you tell me what you've discovered?" Tonya asked.

"I'm not exactly sure yet. I was hanging up new reward posters down at the hardware store and I met a woman there who said she knew him and where he is. I'm on my way to her house to talk with her," Ruth said.

"Ms. Hallbrook, I don't think that is a good idea. Can you tell me the name of the woman and where she—?" Tonya was saying as Ruth accelerated up the winding road.

"Hello? Agent Maitland? Hell…o? Can you hear me?" Ruth asked. She glanced at her phone. No Service. "Damn it! You'd think by now the phone company would be able to have cell reception in even the most remote places. I knew I should have switched services when it was time to renew."

She had two choices: keep following the only lead she had to finding her brother, or tuck tail and run. Since she didn't even know the meaning of the latter, she tossed her cellphone onto the seat next to her. She could always call when she got back to Mike's house – if she made it back there.

She began to feel a little better about her decision by the time she pulled up outside the house. There was another SUV parked out front and a man in a jacket standing outside of it, waiting for the couple. Ruth raised her eyebrows when the man walked over to the passenger side of the truck, helped the woman out of it, and placed a passionate kiss on her lips. She could have sworn the woman was with the man named Gabe.

She swallowed as she slowed to a stop and turned off the ignition. The woman was surrounded by both men now and they each looked like they were very possessive of her.

To each their own, Ruth thought with a soft whistle.

Personally, she had bombed at handling one man, and her ex-husband had been the epitome of a wuss! Pushing open the driver's door, she cursed when she realized that she had forgotten to unbuckle her seatbelt. Clicking the release, she slid out and stood up just as the man named Gabe walked over. For a moment, she wondered if she had made a mistake. There was definitely something intimidating about him. Both of the men, actually.

"I'll tell you this now, I won't let you hurt Magna," he warned in a soft voice. "She has been through hell and back."

Ruth blinked in surprise. This was not at all what she had been expecting. Raising an eyebrow, she looked back at him with a steady gaze.

"All I want to do is find my brother. If she helps me do that, I'll have my lips superglued before I hurt her," Ruth swore.

Gabe released an unexpected chuckle. "That damn stuff works really well," he warned, surprising her again.

She nodded and smiled in return, relaxing a little at his teasing. "I'd much rather use glue than get stitches any day," she remarked.

"Oh God! You mean there are two of you in the world?" the other man groaned with a shake of his head.

Ruth looked at Gabe with a raised eyebrow. If she wasn't careful, her face was gonna get stuck this way, but what the hell, the surprises kept on coming.

"He's a doctor," Gabe mumbled.

"That figures," Ruth chuckled.

"Please come in," Magna said, turning and heading inside. "Oh, I have to warn you that we have two—"

"Damn it, Wilson! Will you get out of the way? Buck, you'd better not be learning any bad habits," Gabe warned.

"Ah, the sweet sound of pet ownership. I gave Mike a golden retriever for his birthday several months ago," Ruth commented with a knowing grin before her smile faded.

"Wilson is still young," Magna laughed.

"My name is Kane Field. Would you care for something to drink, Miss…? "

"Ruth Hallbrook."

He smiled. "We have coffee, tea, juice, and beer."

"Coffee would be great," Ruth replied, stepping into the kitchen. "You have a beautiful home."

"Thank you," Magna said, smiling giddily because it really was home – the three of them had a home together. "Please, come into the living room. I love being able to see the ocean from it," Magna encouraged.

Ruth took off her coat and handed it to Gabe when he held his hand out. She followed Magna into the other room. The entire house screamed peace and unity.

Gabe followed them in and started the gas fireplace. Ruth stood by large glass doors and looked out over the treetops to the ocean. She turned when Kane returned with a tray, a pot of coffee, and small dishes that she suspected contained cream and sugar. In addition to the coffee, there was a large glass of water.

She watched Kane set the tray down, wondering what she would learn here today. Gabe immediately picked up the glass of water and handed it to Magna. She walked over to the chair across from the couch and sat down as Kane poured her a cup of coffee.

"Cream and sugar?" he asked.

Ruth released a pretend shudder. "Black, please. I hate ruining a perfectly good cup of coffee by putting anything in it," she joked, taking the cup from him.

Amusement danced in her eyes when Kane sat down on one side of Magna while Gabe sat on the other. Both men had an air of being on edge while Magna appeared calm and relaxed. Ruth drank several sips of her coffee before she looked at Magna.

"Where is my brother?" she asked.

Magna returned her steady gaze with one of her own. "He is in my world," she replied.

"Your…. Where is that?" Ruth asked, leaning forward and placing her cup on the tray before she sat back.

"Perhaps I should start at the beginning," Magna said, opening her hand and holding out a necklace with a beautiful green shell in the center of her palm. "Take the necklace and turn it over. I will be there with you."

"You'll be where with me?" Ruth asked, leaning forward and taking the necklace.

She turned the shell over, admiring it. Her eyes widened when she saw the glowing center. Looking up to ask Magna about it, her voice froze on a soft croak. The living room was gone.

Looking down, she saw that her booted feet were in sand. She turned in a slow circle, trying to understand what in the hell had happened and where in the hell she was. Her eyes scanned the area. Thick palms, along with other glowing plants she had never seen before, created a thick forest on one side of her. To her right, the beach wound down along a rocky coast. To her left, tall cliffs rose out of the ocean. In front of her, the lone figure of a woman stood by the water, staring out at it.

Unsure of what to do, she walked across the sand to the edge of the water, and stood slightly behind Magna. Neither one of them spoke. Ruth's gaze was on the creatures playing in the cove.

"That is my cousin, Orion, with the sea dragons," Magna said, turning to look at her. "My name is Magna. I am the Sea Witch. My mother is from the Isle of Magic, one of seven kingdoms in the realm of the Seven Kingdoms. My father is from the Isle of the Sea Serpent. He is what you would call a merman. My home was both above and below the water."

"We... Are you saying we aren't on Earth anymore?" Ruth asked in a hesitant voice.

Magna lifted her hand and waved it through the air. "Our bodies are still in the living room of Gabe's house, but our minds are in one of my memories of the Isle of the Sea Serpent. I stored this memory before my body was inhabited by an alien creature that threatened to destroy my world," she explained.

Orion and the sea dragons suddenly faded away, and Ruth turned when she heard the sound of laughter. She watched a much younger version of Magna running down the beach toward them. Orion followed, laughing and teasing her.

Ruth turned when she saw a flash of light streak across the sky. Her eyes widened when it hit the water with a tremendous splash. Turning her gaze back to Magna, she saw the sadness in the other woman's eyes.

"A creature was within that meteor. It took over my body, most of my mind, and my magic. It forced me to do horrible things to my people." The anguish vibrating Magna's voice was starkly moving. "I fought him as best I could, but I knew I would need help if I were to destroy him," Magna murmured, staring at the frozen scene before them.

"What did you do?" Ruth asked.

Magna lifted a hand to her cheek. Ruth blinked when the hand passed through her face. Magna didn't appear to realize it. She continued with her story.

"I was finally able to create a spell to destroy it, but in order for it to work, I needed a weapon not of our world that could weaken me. I tried for over a century to end my life, but each time, the creature prevented it. He had learned from my memories how to defend himself against all the weapons of our world," she said in a weary voice.

"That is why you needed Mike," Ruth deduced.

Magna nodded. "I was growing too weak to bind the creature to me for much longer. He was hungry for power and would have moved to a different host, perhaps one more powerful than I. Over time, I set in motion a series of events. I needed Drago, the Dragon King, to wake. Only his fire, fueled by the heat of vengeance and grief, could burn through the tentacles of the alien. I also needed the power of my cousin's trident to create an electrical field that would stop the alien from communicating with the nightmarish creatures it had created. And finally, ... I needed the weapon your brother carried, the one that fired the metal ball, to strike me so that the alien would think I was dying," she said, reaching up to touch her left shoulder.

Ruth blinked in surprise. "Are you telling me that my brother shot you?" she asked incredulously.

Magna nodded. "Yes. It was the only way. The creature would have forced me to kill King Oray. With Drago and Orion attacking it in the throne room, and the other rulers and their armies attacking it from the outside, the alien no longer saw me as the most serious threat. I told your brother to save King Oray and escape with the others while I released a spell strong enough to destroy the evil creature. Anyone remaining in the room would have been killed," she said.

"But... if the others escaped and you didn't, wouldn't you have been killed along with the creature?" Ruth asked in confusion, looking out at the huge splash.

"I was supposed to die.... I wanted to die. My death...." Magna stopped and shook her head before she lifted her hand and waved it. "Instead, I woke here," she softly replied.

Ruth gasped when she saw the living room of Gabe's house reappear around them. She blinked several times and gripped the arms of the chair. She looked at where Magna leaned against Kane.

"But, what about my brother? I know he came back. He left me a partial message. The damn voicemail cut off too soon," Ruth said.

Magna lifted her head. "He is in my world. He was with a young witch from the Isle of Magic. She had a family. I suspect he returned to the Seven Kingdoms because she could not come here," she murmured.

Ruth was silent as she absorbed everything she had just learned. Rising to her feet, she stepped back over to the doors. It was another beautiful day. Drawing in a deep breath, she finally turned and looked at Magna with a fierce expression.

"How do I get to this 'Seven Kingdoms' place?" Ruth asked.

Magna looked back at her. She rose to her feet and stepped around the coffee table. Ruth swallowed when Magna stopped in front of her and looked into her eyes with a serious expression.

"Open your hand," Magna requested.

Ruth held out her hand and opened it. Magna waved her hand over Ruth's palm, and a red shell the size of a large coin, appeared in the middle of it.

"When you are ready to leave, go to the beach where your brother disappeared and make a wish. The shell will guide you. Keep the shell close to you. If you ever wish to return here, you will need it," Magna warned.

Ruth nodded. "I... I can't tell you how strange this all sounds, but if it means finding my brother...." She shook her head and looked down at the red shell in her hand. "Thank you," she murmured, her fingers closing around the shell.

"I hope you find what you are looking for," Magna said.

Ruth could feel the smile growing on her face. She laughed. Looking at Magna, then at the two men who were now standing and silently watching the exchange, she couldn't help but be thankful that she hadn't given up.

"Thank you so much," she repeated, knowing that she would find her brother and kick his ass for not taking her with him.

CHAPTER TWENTY

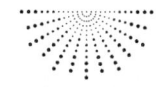

Several weeks later, Kane stepped down onto the dock as Gabe's trawler rounded the bend. Shoving his hands in his pockets, he waited until the boat idled up to the dock. Magna threw the dock line at him, and he caught it automatically. A smile curved his lips. She was becoming a pro at being a deckhand.

"What's wrong?" Gabe demanded, stepping out of the wheelhouse.

Kane could feel Gabe's sharp gaze on his face. He must be losing his touch at keeping his thoughts hidden, he thought. Of course, the fact that he was home early could have also been a clue.

"The whole town is crawling with police and the media," he responded, bending and tying off the lines.

"Why?" Magna worriedly asked, pushing a swathe of long hair back from her face.

"It seems there have been two more disappearances to add to the growing list," Kane replied.

Magna grimaced. "This was not what I expected to happen when I opened the first portal," she said with a sigh.

"Don't worry about it. They'll leave when the next big story breaks. We just have to trust that Ruth didn't tell anyone anything," Gabe reassured her, wrapping his arm around her waist.

"She promised that she wouldn't. I believe her," Magna said, looking up at him.

Kane reached up and touched her cheek. She turned her head, and he brushed a kiss across her lips.

"We'll keep a low profile for a little while. I hear a lot of what is going on around town. The nurses and patients are loving the excitement. So are the merchants. Fred down at the hardware store is getting his fifteen minutes of fame and his wife is happy because business is booming," he said.

Magna's lips drooped. "Does this mean we will not be able to go out tonight?" she asked.

"Yes," Gabe stated.

"No," Kane replied at the same time. "We need to keep a low profile, not a non-existent one. The locals know we go to the pub every Friday night. If we don't show up, they'll think we've disappeared as well."

"Then, you go. Magna and I can stay here. I'm sure we can find something to do," Gabe retorted with a grin.

"Like hell," Kane grumbled. "You get to be with her all day. You can go to the pub and I'll stay here and keep Magna entertained."

Magna shot him and Gabe an exasperated look. "Is sex the only thing you two ever think about?" she growled.

Kane laughed. "The answer to that question is still yes – Yes, we only think of sex when we are around you," Kane replied with a wry grin.

He released a soft groan and he knew he and Gabe were doomed when she lowered her head and her bottom lip stuck out a tiny bit. What was bad about the pouty, disappointed expression was that he knew Magna was completely unaware of it and the effect her disappointment was having on both of them. Friday nights had become their unofficial date nights. She loved it when they took her out to wine and dine her.

"As long as she uses the glamour spell, no one will know," Gabe reluctantly conceded, pressing a kiss to her hair.

Kane nodded. "People would wonder. Someone from the media is bound to be there and Dorothy might mention that we were missing. That would cause more suspicion than us showing up," he added.

Magna's head lifted and she looked at them with a growing expression of hope. The glimmer of excitement made Kane want to bury his hands in her hair along with his body.

"Does this mean we are going on our date?" she asked.

Gabe chuckled and playfully smacked her on the rear. "Yes. I need to secure the boat. Why don't you and Kane go up to the house and get cleaned up? It won't take me long," he suggested.

Magna bit her lip and tilted her head. Kane loved the way her eyes darkened. He could feel his body tighten as she ran her eyes over his face and down his body. A pleased growl swept through his mind when her eyes lingered on the front of his pants. She had to know exactly what she was doing to him.

"I need to get cleaned up. Didn't you say something about missing me?" she asked cheekily, confirming his suspicion when she reached out and ran her hand along the front of his dress slacks.

His eyes narrowed at her invitation. "Gabe, take your time," he retorted, grabbing her hand.

Gabe chuckled and nodded. "I need to get cleaned up, too. If you are still in the shower by the time I get back up there, it won't be my fault that you'll have company. Can't let you have all the fun," he said, turning and stepping back onto the boat.

"Like you haven't already had some fun today," Magna retorted.

"Might I remind you about earlier this afternoon on the bunk below deck?"

"Damn, top, bottom, or behind?" Kane asked.

"None of your damn business," Gabe growled over his shoulder.

"All three," Magna replied with a grin.

Kane groaned, his mind exploding with ideas. He wondered how Magna would feel about taking their love-making up a notch. They had been holding back – a little – until she was stronger and they felt all three of them were completely comfortable with their relationship.

He'd be the first to admit he still had twinges of jealousy when he was working and Gabe had Magna all to himself. Fortunately, Gabe appeared to realize that and often gave him time alone with Magna. His and Gabe's biggest challenge had been making sure that they gave Magna her own alone time.

He had mentioned it to Gabe and they had both agreed several weeks ago that they needed to do two things: give her space and take her out. One of those things had worked better than the other.

The first time they had left her alone, Gabe had worked on some furniture he was building in his workshop while Kane had retreated to the study to read. Keeping their hands and minds occupied was the only way they could keep them both off of her.

Of course, neither activities worked. Gabe had come inside a million times for one reason or another, while Kane couldn't help but notice every sound Magna made. When the house had grown quiet, Kane had risen again to find her sitting on the lounge on the deck with the two dogs and was the first to see the hurt in her eyes.

Their conversation was still fresh in his mind as he grabbed her hand and walked with her up the steps to the house. He listened as she shared her day on the water, but his mind remembered the conversation that had given him insight into the nightmares she tried to conceal from them.

. . .

Two weeks before:

Kane stood by the glass door, torn between sticking to his and Gabe's decision to give Magna space and his desire to make sure she was alright. The latter finally won out when he saw her draw her knees up, wrap her arms around her legs, and bow her head. Buck was the first to whine and lay his head on the chair next to her.

Opening the door, he stepped out. The soft sound of a sob tore a hole through his heart. Silently walking over to the lounge, he sat down on the edge and stroked her back. She slowly lifted her head and wiped at the tears coursing down her cheeks.

"What's wrong?" he murmured, wiping his thumb across her damp skin.

Her bottom lip trembled. "What have I done?" she choked out in a confused voice. "All morning, you and Gabe have avoided me."

He groaned and waved his hand for her to put her legs down so he could hold her. Drawing her into his arms, he rocked her as she buried her face against his shoulder. A wave of regret shot through him. They should have handled this better, or at the very least explained the motives behind their behavior instead of just putting them into action. It had never occurred to him that she might think they were mad at her.

"You've done everything right. Gabe and I are the idiots here. We decided we were being too demanding and that you needed some space. I don't know if you are aware of this, but whenever we are close to you, it is a bit difficult for us to keep our hands and mouths off of you," he teased, stroking her back.

She raised her head and studied his face, then she gently punched him on the shoulder.

"And you both thought I had a problem with that? Do you have any idea how long I have been alone? Centuries! I do not need, nor do I want, any alone time for the foreseeable future. When I am alone...." She paused and drew in a shaky breath, her eyes growing distraught before she continued. "When I am alone, the darkness begins to swallow me. I see and hear the voices of those who I have hurt. Only when I am with Gabe and you can I feel the warmth and hope that one day, I can do something to make things right again. Not knowing..." her voice faded and she shook her head in regret. "I need you both to help me keep the ghosts away."

Her barely audible words were like a knife, slicing through his gut. He and Gabe had clearly not truly understood the depth of the pain Magna had been hiding.

"Then you'll never be alone again," he swore.

At that moment, a realization came to him. There was a reason why he and Gabe had connected like brothers, even with their different backgrounds. They had been destined to find the one woman who needed both of them.

Their relationship ensured that one or both of them would always be there for Magna. She would never be left alone to face the ghosts of her past. The epiphany answered a question that had been nagging at him for years and gave him a sense of contentment.

"I'm sorry, Magna," Gabe's deep voice said from the shadows of the deck. Kane watched as Gabe stepped forward and motioned for Buck to move so he could sit down on the lounge next to Magna. "We should have explained."

She turned her head and gave him a watery smile. "I understand now. Thank you. You both think of my comfort and wellbeing. I'm still learning how to accept that," she admitted.

"Well, we aren't doing a very damn good job of it," Gabe growled, raising an eyebrow at Kane.

"We'll do better. Did we mention we are going to start doing a date night?" Kane commented with a grin.

Magna frowned. "What is date night?" she had asked.

"What are you smiling about?" Magna asked, bringing him back to the present as they reached the top deck.

Kane chuckled. "I was thinking of your response when we told you what date night was all about," he admitted with a grin.

"Oh," Magna replied, blushing.

"I see you remember as well," he replied.

Her eyes lit up with amusement. "How could I forget? You tasted so good," she retorted with a toss of her head.

A smothered oath escaped him and he turned, pressing her back against the glass doors. He captured her lips in a passionate kiss. His hands wrapped around her wrists and he lifted her arms up above her head. The movement forced her breasts up. Pressing his hips against her, he made sure she had no doubt in her mind about the effect she had on him.

Pulling back, he trailed his lips along her jaw to her neck. He pressed small, heated kisses along the smooth scales. She moaned and arched against him, rubbing her hips in a rocking motion.

"How would you feel if Gabe and I showed you a few other ways to have fun in the bedroom?" he murmured near her ear.

She moaned when he ran his tongue along her neck. The slight taste of salt told him she had been swimming. Even the thought of how beautiful she was underwater turned him on.

"Does it have to be done in the bedroom?" she breathed.

"What?" he asked, pulling back to look down at her. He had been lost in the thought of her hair flowing around her and the tight, green body suit she wore when she swam. "Does what have to be done only in the bedroom?"

She smiled innocently up at him. "The other fun ways?" she inquired.

His mind went blank for a brief moment before a rush of erotic thoughts flooded his brain. A soft chuckle escaped him as he thought of how to answer her. He finally decided showing her would be more fun.

"No, the other fun can happen anywhere," he promised, and lowered his head again.

∽

Magna clapped her hands as another local resident stepped away from the microphone. She ignored Kane and Gabe's pain-filled expressions. Granted, the woman hadn't been as talented as the man who'd performed before her, but at least she had tried.

"I don't know why they can't move Karaoke night to another night," Gabe said, lifting his beer bottle to his lips.

"I told you that we should have gone back to the truck for the earplugs," Kane muttered.

"You are both being very mean. The woman's singing was not that bad," Magna chided, draining the last of the water in her glass before she rose to her feet in determination.

Both men rose at the same time. They had been particularly protective tonight. Kane had been right about the explosion of people in the area. The Underground Pub was packed tonight with people from all over the country. Main Street was lined with news vehicles.

"Where are you going?" Gabe growled.

"I want to sing," Magna stated.

"What?!" Both men practically shouted at the same time.

She wasn't the only one who turned to look at them. A group of people at the table next to them turned to see what was going on. The four men looked her over with appreciative glances.

"Go ahead, let her sing," one of the men encouraged.

"Magna," Gabe started to say, before two other men from another table cheered her on to perform.

"Let her sing, Gabe. I'm sure Magna can belt one out better than Betty Lou did. We all need to have our ears sanitized after that," their waitress, Dorothy, stated as she placed two more beers and a glass of water on the table before retrieving their empty bottles and glasses. "You show them how it's done, Magna."

Magna grinned at the encouragement. She carefully weaved her way to the small stage that had been erected in the corner. Walt sat next to the controls. He smiled at her when she stepped onto the stage.

"Pick a song and press the green button. All you have to do is follow the words on the screen," he instructed, leaning back against the wall.

Magna nodded. She already knew which song she wanted to sing. This one was one from her world. With a wave of her hand, she added it to the list. Pressing the selection, her finger hovered over the green button. It had been centuries since she had sung. She and her mother used to sing together all the time.

Tears burned her eyes. Perhaps this had been a mistake. The memory of her mother and father's faces as they hardened to stone sent a shaft of pain through her. Looking up, she searched the crowd for Gabe and Kane.

"Go on, darling. Sing," someone yelled.

Her eyes locked on the faces of the two men who accepted her for being her and had become everything to her. Love swelled inside her. Her finger pressed the green button on the screen and the familiar music of a love song from her world filled the inside of the dimly lit pub. Everyone and everything around her disappeared except the two men she loved as she began to sing in the words of her people.

Ashure, King of the Pirates, had once teased her that she had the voice of a siren. After the alien had taken over her body, he had looked at her mournfully and told her she had the soul of one.

'Careful, Magna,' he'd warned softly, *'or one day you might find out what happens to those who lose a soul like that.'*

She sang from her heart and soul, and her voice wove a spell around her audience, profoundly impacting them. Her voice quavered with emotion while pulling the listeners in until they could feel her longing, her hope, and the love she felt to the marrow of their bones.

She was unaware that one of the people who had encouraged her to sing was a reporter who was now filming her. She wasn't aware that Dorothy was standing frozen next to the table, her hands laden with fresh drinks forgotten by the customers waiting for them. Neither was she aware that the owner and chief cook of the pub, along with those working in the kitchen had come out. All she knew was that she needed to convey her love to the two men in the simple but beautiful song her mother had sung to her father for as long as she could remember.

Her voice faded away as the music ended. The room was silent until she stepped down off the stage, then the people stood and began clapping. They parted as she passed to where Gabe and Kane had started forward to meet her halfway.

"Magna," Gabe said, his voice thick with emotion.

"Can we please leave?" she whispered, gazing up at him with eyes shimmering with grief and tears.

"This way," Kane murmured, his arm protectively wrapping around her.

Magna was grateful for the fact that both men shielded her as they exited the pub. A shudder ran through her when she heard a shout from the reporter who had encouraged her to sing. She shook her head, a sense of panic beginning to sweep through her as another wave of grief hit her.

"I shouldn't have sung that song," she said, drawing in a deep breath of fresh, salty air as they emerged from the pub.

"Why?" Kane asked, his arm tightening around her when she turned toward the dock instead of the where they had parked his SUV.

She shook her head, needing time to get her emotions under control. Pulling away, she walked to the end of the dock and stood looking out over the water. She could feel it calling to her.

"What happened?" Gabe quietly asked, stopping behind her.

She gripped the railing and stared down at the water. Tonight had shown her once again that as hard as she tried to forget or accept the things she had done; the darkness would always haunt her. The memory of her mother's eyes as Magna turned to strike her dead surfaced in her mind.

"My mother used to sing that song to my father. It is a love song. I wanted to sing the song to both of you. I wanted you to feel my love for you both," she explained.

"We felt it. The song…. Hell, Magna, you had me feeling unglued. All I wanted to do was to wrap my arms around you, hold you, and never let you go," Gabe said.

"I second that," Kane added before he turned her to face them. "Something happened. I could actually feel your grief."

The tears she was trying to hold back overflowed. "I can't do this. I thought I could, but I can't. I see their eyes and hear their cries. It reminds me of the monster I was," she sobbed, wrapping her arms around her waist. "I have to… I have to go back. I have to try to undo some of the evil I did, even if it means…."

"Even if it means what?" Gabe demanded.

She looked up at them, her heart in her eyes. "Even if it means my death," she murmured.

"No!"

She winced when they both hissed at her. "I need time to think," she said, shaking her head. "I will come back to the house later."

"Magna," Gabe growled in warning, his voice growing deep and rough.

"I need to think," she repeated. She waved her hands and the jeans and black sweater changed to a black body suit.

"No!" Gabe hissed, his hand shooting out to stop her from disappearing through the opening where an emergency ladder hung.

"Let her go, Gabe," Kane ordered. His voice softened, his eyes glittering with emotion when he said, "Come back to us, Magna."

She nodded, unable to say any more. She dove off the side of the dock into the dark waters, thankful that the dock had been deserted. The soothing water swept around her and she called to the current to propel her out of the cove. Once she cleared the mouth of the narrow inlet, she swam several miles out before descending into a dark abyss similar to her lair in the world she had left behind.

∼

Los Angeles, California:

Asahi looked up from the papers inside the file he had received from Mike Hallbrook after The Phone Call, as he'd started to think of it – that unforgettable call when Mike Hallbrook had told him there really were monsters out there.

He pressed his fingers to the bridge of his nose and pinched it, trying to relieve some of the tension headache. He knew it was from staring at the same documents for hours, but that wasn't going to stop him from staring longer.

Refocusing his attention on the report in front of him, his mind wandered to his last conversation with Mike.

"Are they real?" he remembered asking.

Mike Hallbrook's one word answer had sent a piercing shockwave through the agent.

"*Yes.*"

Asahi looked up at the television when a familiar name on it caught his attention. He lowered the file to his lap and reached for the remote. Turning up the volume and instinctively hitting the record button, he listened to the reporter.

"Despite the unusual disappearances in Yachats, Oregon, and the possible threat of a serial killer, residents refuse to be intimidated." Behind him a woman was singing at the microphone and her song could be heard in the background of the reporter's broadcast.

Asahi ignored the rest of the man's commentary as an intense wave of eerie familiarity struck him in the gut. He reached up and paused the broadcast, thankful for the technology that made that possible.

Frowning, he looked down at the file he held. Thumbing through the pages, he pulled out an enlarged photograph of Carly Tate and Jenny Ackerly standing together with several small children, obviously their own. The original had been left by Mike to prove both women were alive, happy, and healthy, but Asahi had scanned, enlarged, and printed the new version to get a better look at the tapestry behind them, hoping it might give him a clue as to the women's location.

He leaned forward, opened the small drawer in the end table, and pulled out a magnifying glass. He glanced up at the image on the paused television before returning his gaze to the tapestry behind the two women.

Moving the magnifying glass over the photograph, he narrowed in on the background above the two women. In the tapestry, there was a woven figure of a woman standing next to a throne. On one side of the tapestry was an image of a massive black dragon. On the other side was the picture of a merman holding a blazing trident. He couldn't see the two figures below due to the women and children standing in front of them, but he could sure as hell recognize the depiction of a gun being fired.

His eyes moved back to the figure of the woman standing on the platform next to an empty chair. She had dark hair that flowed around her shoulders and vivid green eyes. Blood stained her left shoulder as she raised her arms toward the swirling black mass floating above her. She looked like a villain from a fairy tale.

The more he carefully studied the image, the more he could feel the connection between the woman in the tapestry and the woman on the stage. He pressed play. Her song was haunting, but it was the words that she sang that truly captured his attention. She was singing the chorus in a language he'd never heard from anyone, save one. Someone who had disappeared over forty years ago before suddenly reappearing again. Someone who had spoken of another world with fantastic creatures and a beautiful woman who he had believed to be a sorceress. The man who had raised him – his grandfather.

Saving the recording, he picked up his cellphone on the table next to him and pressed the number he had programmed into his Favorites.

"May I help you?" a voice asked on the other end.

"Yes, I'd like to make reservations to Portland. I will need a rental car and lodging as well," Asahi quietly stated, staring at the photograph in his hand.

EPILOGUE

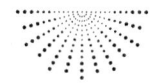

Magna lowered her hands to her side. The water danced around her for a moment, as if trying to tease a smile from her tired lips. She gave in, running her fingers through it as it retreated over the side of the dock.

She felt better, more in control, than she had felt last night. As the light of the sun had broken over the coast, she had watched it with a sense of resolve. She could no longer hide from who she had been. If she was to have a new life and future, she needed to come to terms with her past.

She was not a martyr, but neither was she a coward. One thing she was, though, was the Sea Witch. Over the centuries she had learned a lot about the other kingdoms and the people who lived there.

"It's about time," Gabe said in a blunt voice.

A rueful smile curved her lips. She had known the two men would be waiting for her. That was the kind of men they were and she loved them for it.

"I love you, Gabe," she said. Her eyes scanned Kane's tired face. "Thank you for everything, Kane. I love you so much."

"You better not be here to say goodbye. Tell us that you're staying," Gabe demanded.

"Give her a chance," Kane snapped, stepping forward. "Come upstairs. We'll make some breakfast for you and we can talk there."

She nodded. Each man took up a position beside her. A small smile curved her tired lips when they both captured her hand and held on as if they were afraid she would disappear.

Twenty minutes later, they were sitting at the dining table. Wilson and Buck were lying on each side of her chair. They had taken up the position that Kane and Gabe had reluctantly relinquished so they could prepare breakfast.

"What are you going to do?" Kane finally asked when they finished eating.

She laid her fork down on her empty plate and gazed across at both men. Her expression was serene now that she knew what she had to do. Lifting her chin, she cupped her hands together to keep them from trembling.

"I'm going back," she said with a determined look. She raised her hand when Gabe opened his mouth. "I have to if I… if we are ever to be happy and if I am to find anything in myself worth redeeming. I have to know if my parents were freed from the spell I cast. They aren't the only ones, but it is their eyes – my mother's eyes – that I see every time I look in the mirror."

Gabe leaned forward, his forearms on the table and his hands flat on the surface. She looked into his intense, dark brown eyes. She could see the confusion, denial, and fear in them.

"Will you be in danger?" Gabe demanded.

Her gaze softened. She would not lie to him or Kane. They had already done so much for her.

"Yes. If I am seen, I will be hunted. If I'm captured, I will more than likely be sentenced to death," she honestly replied.

"Damn it," Gabe muttered, thrusting his chair back and rising out of his chair. She watched as he took several steps toward the kitchen before he turned and ran both of his hands through his hair. "You can't go. We'll find another way. You could send me... or Kane. One of us could go and find out if the spells you cast were broken."

Magna shook her head. "You would know nothing of the kingdoms. You couldn't travel between them. If the spells weren't broken.... No, Gabe. I must be the one to return," she quietly insisted.

"Kane..., will you try to talk some sense into her, please?" Gabe demanded.

She swallowed. She had expected Gabe's resistance to her going. All night, she had thought of each argument he could make and how to handle them. Her gaze moved to Kane. She hadn't been sure how he would handle her decision. Her eyes pleaded with him to understand.

"Nothing we say will change your mind, will it?" Kane quietly asked her.

She shook her head. "I can't, Kane. It is slowly killing me, the not knowing," she replied.

Her heart broke when she saw the pain in his eyes before he lowered his head. His fingers curled into fists until his knuckles shone white. A shudder ran through his lean frame before he pushed his chair back and rose.

She stared at his face. His mouth was compressed into a straight line. She saw him look at Gabe.

"You'd better come back to us," Kane ordered in a guttural tone. "You'd better fucking come back to us, Magna."

Her bottom lip trembled and she turned her gaze to Gabe. He released a loud curse before he gave a brief, sharp nod. Rising out of her seat, she walked around the table and stopped in front of him.

"I will come back. I love you both too much not to. I want the life you have shown me. I will… come… back," she promised in a slow, deliberate tone.

"You'd better, or I swear I'll find a way to come to your world and get you," he swore.

"That goes for me too," Kane added in a somber voice. "What do you need us to do?"

"I want to leave tomorrow. There is a rock formation off the coast. I will guide you to it. There is a link between our worlds there that I can use," she explained.

"How long will you be gone?" Gabe asked.

"I have calculated it will take me a month to do everything I need to do," she quietly answered.

"A month!" Kane exclaimed, paling.

She nodded. "I… have a lot of things to correct," she said.

"One month, Magna. Not one day more. We will be in the same spot waiting for you," Gabe stated.

Magna could sense the cost of this concession. She wrapped her arms around both of them. They folded around her, each absorbing what little comfort she could give to them and them to her. She had to believe everything would be alright. The Goddess could not give her this taste of happiness after so much heartache only to rip it away.

Please, she begged, closing her eyes when she felt Kane's lips press against her neck and Gabe's against her forehead. *Please help me do what I must and then return.*

∽

"One month," Gabe said in a tight voice as she stepped up to the edge of his trawler and sat down.

"I will be back. If I return sooner, I will come to the dock," she said.

"Whatever you do, be safe," Kane added, bending and brushing a kiss to her lips.

She blinked, trying not to cry. "I will be back. I will be safe. I'm going before I start crying again," she snapped.

"Wait!" Gabe said.

Magna turned an exasperated look to him. "What now?" she demanded.

Her heart melted when he gave her a crooked smile before he bent and kissed her. "I love you, my beautiful Sea Witch," he said before he straightened and stood back.

Magna nodded and turned. With a wave of her hand, a staircase of water rose up. She kept her back to the two men, afraid she would lose her courage. Unable to stop herself, she glanced over her shoulder a second before she disappeared under the waves.

Beckoning the current to help her, she shot forward. Soon, she had entered a small opening in the rock offshore and was traveling through a kaleidoscope of turbulent water. Within minutes, she was in a beautiful cavern that glowed.

She swam over to the beach with pink sand and rose out of the water. Dozens of juvenile sea dragons squeaked, their eyes wide, their little bodies shuffling with excitement. Her head turned and she lifted a finger to her lips. They dove from their perch on the rocks walls into the pool of water. Turning back around, she waved her hand, and changed her appearance.

No one looked twice when one of the royal guards exited the protected entrance of the pool. The guard continued up the path to the tunnel that led out to the sea. All around him, visitors from other kingdoms milled around. He could see the smiling faces and hear the joy in their voices. The guard paused and looked up at the crystal dome that covered the underwater kingdom of the Sea King. All the damage had been repaired.

"Orion!" the breathless voice of a woman called out.

The guard turned and watched as Orion strolled with two young boys. The fiery-haired woman was carrying a small child in her arms. For a moment, the guard stood watching the family walk by him.

Stepping into the shadows, the guard turned and waved his hand over himself. Now, an old woman stood in the alcove along the outer wall of the palace. She turned and made her way to the departure tubes.

"Pardon me, you dropped this," a familiar voice said.

The old woman turned. Her eyes widened in disbelief when Kapian, the Captain of the Guard, held out a pink scarf. He frowned as he stared down at her.

"Thank you," the old woman replied in a soft voice.

His fingers paused and he studied her face. "Do I know you?" he asked.

The old woman gave him a sad smile. "Perhaps once upon a time," she responded, taking the scarf from him.

She stepped into the departure tubes before he could respond. Her hand rose and she splayed it on the glass as she returned his look. A small, crooked smile curved her lips when the tube filled with water and she felt her body rising.

Tearing her gaze away, she shot upwards toward the surface, her body twisting and shimmering as it changed back to her normal appearance. She didn't see Kapian's eyes widen or the way he stepped forward to watch her as she disappeared into the ocean above, and she was unaware that she looked nothing like the Sea Witch any longer. She looked very much like the young, beautiful woman she had been destined to grow up into.

∼

She was determined to restore the dragons first. The most difficult part would be traversing the Isle of the Dragon without Drago knowing she was there.

She recruited the help of several sea mammals to help her transport the stone statues from under the sea closer to the isle's shore. Her hope was to bring them into the shallows, then change them where she knew the dragons could survive.

The first stone figures she found were Drago's parents. Her heart hurt when she saw their frozen features.

As she brought them near the isle, shock coursed through her when she saw dragons flying overhead. The only thing that saved her from being seen was the fact that she was swimming under the mammals who were helping her. Unable to believe what she was seeing from under the water, she took a chance and surfaced.

Her eyes widened when she saw the cliffs lined with dragons of all ages, shapes, and sizes. Excitement built inside her. Her spells had been broken – but her safeguards had kept those in danger still frozen. Drago's parents had fallen into the deepest part of the ocean. They would never have survived long enough to swim to the surface if the spell she had cast on them had been undone while they were still there.

The realization that most of those she had harmed – including her parents – had already been released from her spells filled her with joy. She ducked under the surface when a powerful black dragon, followed by his guard, flew over her. They were heading back to the tall cliffs.

Turning toward the two majestic dragons still frozen, Magna sank down below them. With a whisper, she unwove the spell binding them. The male dragon stretched, the outer crust of the stone cracking and falling away. Drago's father turned, his large wings pushing at the water and his tail snapping back and forth.

Magna watched as the male dragon saw his mate. His front claws grasped her as she began to wake. From far below them, she watched as they broke the surface of the water, each clinging to the other as their wings lifted them higher. Only when she was certain that they were safe did she return to the surface.

In the distance, she heard the loud cry rise up as the dragons along the cliff recognized the older King and his Queen. Her eyes moved to where Drago had shifted and stood on the cliff, a small child in his arms while Carly Tate stood next to him with two small boys. They all turned in unison at the cry.

Moments later, she watched as Drago stepped forward and embraced his mother before he did the same to his father. A smile of satisfaction curved her lips when the Queen embraced Carly before bending to the two boys.

Her smile wavered when Drago suddenly turned and looked out at the ocean. His eyes scanned the waters. Sinking down, she disappeared back into the depths.

Day by day she searched for more wrongs to right, and safely unweave the spells, one by one. Now, her journey and her mission were coming to an end. Her heart was in her throat as she returned to the Isle of Magic and the quaint cove where her parents lived. She had come here last, knowing it would be the most difficult part of her journey.

A soft cry escaped her when she saw the elderly sea dragon swimming among a group of young. The sea dragon turned toward her as the young scattered. For a moment, the glazed eyes didn't appear to recognize her. When they did, the sea dragon surged forward.

"Oh, Raine, I have missed you so much," Magna whispered, stroking the beautiful head.

"Magna?"

Magna's head turned when she heard the hesitant voice of her father. The tears she had been holding back overflowed, mixing with the seawater. Unable to help herself, she swam forward.

"Father," she cried.

Pain filled her when his hands shot out and he held her away from him. She knew her eyes pleaded with him to forgive her. Her body trembled as she waited to see what he would do.

"Magna," he whispered, uncertainty and emotion making his voice waver.

"I love you," she choked. "I'm so sorry. I didn't... the creature... it made me...."

"The creature?" her father asked, searching her eyes.

Magna's eyes softened. "Gone. Dead," she replied.

"Are you sure?" Kell asked. He wanted so badly to believe her.

Magna nodded. "Yes. It no longer dwells inside me," she promised.

"Where have you been? Why have you returned? If you are seen...." Kell's voice faded.

Magna's eyes softened. "I had to undo what I could. Where is mother?" she asked.

Kell hesitated. Magna smiled ruefully, her heart in her eyes. She couldn't blame him for his mistrust. Slowly reaching out, she gave him a hug.

"You once told me that as long as I remembered who I was and I believed, I could do anything. I did that, Papa," she murmured. "I remembered."

Kell trembled before his arms swept tightly around her. He held her close, reminding Magna of all the times he'd done this when she was little. She finally pulled away and gave him a trembling smile.

"Come, your mother is in the garden," he said, grasping her hand.

They swam to shore, slowly emerging from the water. Kell scanned the area. They lived in an isolated spot, but occasionally someone from the village would come by to visit. Nodding to Magna, they crossed the beach and walked along the wide path to the small cottage that she remembered visiting when she was a child.

"We live here full-time now. We had no use for the larger home and prefer the simpler life," her father told her.

Pain flashed through Magna. "It is because of me," she murmured.

Kell turned and looked at her with a frown. "We make our own choices, Magna. This cottage is near the water and allows your mother to have her garden. I can raise the sea dragons as well," he reassured her.

Magna nodded. Her gaze swept over the beautiful flowers growing all around the cottage. Her mother had always loved to grow things. Stepping around the side of the house, she heard her mother's soft voice as she hummed.

"Momma," Magna softly called.

Seline straightened from her examination of a plant when she heard her name. Her eyes widened and her basket tumbled from her hands to the ground. Her eyes darted from Magna's damp face to her husband's and back again. Seline took a step forward, her hand lifting.

"Magna?" she asked, her voice thick with emotion.

Magna nodded. "I'm me."

"Oh, Magna," Seline cried, rushing forward.

Magna met her mother halfway. They wrapped their arms around each other and held each other close. Both were sobbing. Seline finally leaned back and cupped her face, searching it as if trying to memorize every new detail.

"You did it. You found a way," her mother said.

"Yes. I… I've met two men. They are from another world, a world where I don't have to be afraid," she told her mother, finally knowing that everything would be alright.

∽

Exactly one month after Magna left Earth:

. . .

Gabe leaned over the side, searching the waters. It was a beautiful day. He and Kane had made the trip as the sun was rising over the coast to the spot where they had last seen Magna.

He swore the last month had been the longest of his life. Hell, even Wilson and Buck had moped around the house. He and Kane had tried to act like life was normal, but the emptiness had been eating away at them all. Neither one of them had slept a wink last night, impatient for the hours to slowly crawl by.

"Do you see her?" Kane asked, pulling Gabe back to the present as he scanned the rolling waves from the stern of the trawler.

"Not yet," Gabe replied, standing on the back of his boat staring out at the waves. "She'll come back. She promised."

"I know. I just wish she would hurry," Kane muttered as he ran his hand down over his face.

"She'll come back," Gabe repeated in a firm voice. "I told her I'd come after her ass if she didn't."

Kane gave a gruff laugh and leaned against the rigging. "Fat chance of that," he retorted before he released a breath of relief when he saw a water spout suddenly dance on the surface. "There she is!"

"I told you she'd be back," Gabe muttered, leaning against the side.

Both men watched Magna as she waved to them before disappearing under the surface of the water. Kane laughed as she emerged next to the boat seconds later, and he reached out as the water rose to lift her to their level. He didn't care if he got soaked with the icy liquid as long as he had Magna back in his arms.

"Did it work?" he asked in a rough voice as he wrapped his arms around her and held her against his chest.

"Yes," she breathed, leaning back enough to give him and Gabe a brilliant smile.

"You were gone longer than you said," Gabe muttered as he grabbed her other hand and pulled her out of Kane's arms and into his. "We expected you back hours ago."

Kane groaned when Magna chuckled at the slight pout on Gabe's lips, then reached up and brushed her lips across Gabe's bottom lip. The protest on his own lips faded when she turned and pressed her mouth against his as well. He immediately wrapped his arms around her waist and pulled her close. It was only when Gabe grunted that he reluctantly pulled back.

"There was something else I needed to do before I came back," she paused to draw in a deep breath. "I went to see my parents."

Gabe's hands stilled on her hips. "How did it go?" he asked in a cautious tone.

"It went well. They believed me and understand what happened was not really me," she replied in a soft voice.

"Will they want you to return? I mean, of course they will, but do they understand that it isn't safe for you to go back?" Kane asked in a strained voice. "I'll be honest, the last month has been total hell without you. I... We can't lose you, Magna. We love you."

She pressed her warm palm against his skin and he leaned his cheek into her hand. "You won't lose me. I love you both and won't ever leave you," she promised before she turned her gaze out to the water. "Yes, they understand it would not be safe for me to go back. I hope you and Gabe...." her voice faded when she heard Gabe's swiftly inhaled breath.

"Kane," Gabe muttered, following Magna's gaze.

"They are only here to visit," Magna softly said. "They wanted to meet both of you."

A few yards from the boat, two figures gazed back at them. Her father's vivid green eyes were inscrutable, but through the clear bubble surrounding her mother, Gabe could see that she was clearly curious and worried. The woman had the same glossy black hair that Magna did, and the man's short white hair was bright in the sunlight.

"Mother, Father, it is safe," Magna called to the couple in the water.

Kane swallowed as the couple disappeared beneath the waves before reappearing next to the boat a few seconds later. He pulled Magna to him and Gabe stepped back to give them room. The clear bubble rose on a wave of water. The moment Magna's mother was over the boat, the wave retreated and the bubble dissolved. Gabe reached out and steadied the older woman before stepping back when the burly man cleared the boat's side and stood next to her, wrapping his arm around her.

"This is my father, Kell, and my mother, Seline," Magna introduced as she wrapped her arm around Gabe's waist to pull him closer to her.

Gabe cleared his throat. "Hi," he muttered, staring back at the tall man.

The man bowed his head in greeting. "Thank you for helping our daughter," the man said.

Gabe relaxed and nodded. "No problem," he said with a crooked grin. "She's not going back."

"Gabe," Kane growled under his breath.

Magna giggled and blushed. "Gabe speaks his mind," she explained with a happy grin.

Seline chuckled, her eyes twinkling with amusement. "Magna said the same thing," she said.

Kell nodded. "It would not be safe for Magna to return," he agreed. "Even if she were to petition for forgiveness from Orion, many would rather see her dead, regardless of the truth."

Gabe's face darkened into a fierce scowl. "Not happening," he retorted in a steely voice. "She's ours."

Kane studied Magna's parents. They both just nodded in agreement. He drew in a breath of relief. He felt much better now.

"How were you able to travel back here and how long do you plan to visit?" Kane asked in a hesitant voice. "So far, we've been able to keep Magna's identity quiet."

"There is a passage between our worlds," Seline admitted. "It is not well known and it is guarded. Magna shared an invisibility spell that she learned while on the Isle of Magic. We are able to sneak by the guards."

"I had to close the original portal that I created for Carly," Magna said. "It was not safe to leave it open and would have drained too much of my energy to keep a protective spell in place. The other is a natural portal, but leads to a protected sea cave on the Isle of the Sea Serpent. It is the only passage between our worlds now."

"She has healed the things done while she was under the control of the creature," Kell reflected. "Word will spread of her deeds, and in time, she will be accepted not as a monster but as the Sea Witch who saved our world."

"I feel as if I can finally begin a new life without guilt," Magna said with a sigh, threading her fingers through Kane and Gabe's hands. "My parents would like to stay for a while. I hope you don't mind."

"That's fine by me. They can attend the wedding," Gabe stated.

"Wedding?" Magna repeated in a stunned voice.

"We decided that we weren't going to chance losing you again once you came back," Kane replied, shaking his head at Gabe. "We were going to ask you after dinner tonight."

Gabe grinned at Kell and Seline. "I hope you don't have a problem with having two sons-in-law, because we've already claimed your daughter," he informed them.

Kell shook his head, his lips twitching in amusement. "I always knew Magna was a handful. I am relieved to see she now will be well protected," he chuckled.

Seline laughed in delight. "Does this mean I will have twice as many grandchildren?" she asked with a hopeful smile.

Kane chuckled when he saw Gabe's expression. For once, the big guy was truly speechless. Magna's face was a rosy red. Lifting Magna's hand to his lips he answered for them all.

"Yes, I believe that is exactly what it means," Kane replied.

Magna's beautiful smile filled him with warmth. She could let herself have a life with them now. His Sea Witch had found her redemption – and it was in the form of the two men who would love her forever.

To be continued:
Ruth and the King of the Giants

Ruth Hallbrook pursed her lips as she hung up another flyer. If the frigging FBI wouldn't take finding her brother seriously, she would take matters into her own hands. Mike was a police officer for crying out loud! She would have thought the disappearance of a police officer would have made front page news, but it had been stuffed to the back of page three.

Sure, there had been a massive search a little over six months ago, but within weeks, it had stopped. Mike had called her and left some ambiguous message telling her that he was alright. She had been out of the country and hadn't received it until two weeks after he'd left it. Muttering under her breath, she pressed the staple gun to the information board at the Yachats State Park entrance.

Stepping back, she gazed at the laminated picture of Mike. She had returned to the park based on a crazy story a woman she'd met earlier at the hardware store had told her. It was too late to go down to the spot where Mike's car had been found. She scowled as she pocketed the stapler and grabbed the stack of papers with Mike's picture and her contact information. She figured she might as well post a few since she was here.

Returning to her car, she slid behind the wheel and stared down the curving road. She bit her lip and glanced at the time. It was getting late and the park would be closing soon. A sigh escaped her when she saw the park ranger step out of the booth and glance at her.

"Tomorrow," she muttered. "I'll come back and tear this place apart rock by rock if I have to, but I'm going to find you, baby brother, and when I do, I'm going to kick your sorry ass for making me worry!"

Find the full book at your favorite distributor with the link below!
books2read.com/Ruth-and-the-king-of-the-giants

Enjoy this adventure? There are more series to love!
Read on for a sneak peek.

A Warrior's Heart
A Marastin Dow Novella

Only the most ruthless Marastin Dow are allowed to live, and Evetta and Hanine have killed enough of their own to stay alive, but they desperately want a different life. When they meet two human brothers fighting for their lives, the sisters are in agreement: this alliance could be their only chance.

This novella is free: books2read.com/A-Warriors-Heart

Hunter's Claim
The Alliance Book 1

USA Today Bestseller!

When Earth received its first visitors from space, the planet was thrown into a panicked chaos. The Trivators came to bring Earth into the Alliance of Star Systems, but were forced to take control of Earth to prevent the humans from destroying it in their fear, and to protect them from the militant forces of other worlds. They aren't prepared for how the humans will affect the Trivators, though, starting with a family of three sisters....

Alone in a world gone mad with just her teenage sisters, Jesse Sampson has seen the savage side of human nature and found they are not much different from the aliens who conquered Earth, but she's kept what's left of her family alive, that's all that matters—until Jesse sees an alien who will suffer a horrible death if she does not free him from his human captors. Her own nature won't allow her leave him to his fate, and that decision changes everything.

Check out the full book here: books2read.com/Hunters-Claim

ADDITIONAL BOOKS

If you loved this story by me (S.E. Smith) please leave a review! You can discover additional books at: http://sesmithfl.com and http://sesmithya.com or find your favorite way to keep in touch here: https://sesmithfl.com/contact-me/ Be sure to sign up for my newsletter to hear about new releases!

Recommended Reading Order Lists:

http://sesmithfl.com/reading-list-by-events/

http://sesmithfl.com/reading-list-by-series/

The Series

Science Fiction / Romance

Dragon Lords of Valdier Series

It all started with a king who crashed on Earth, desperately hurt. He inadvertently discovered a species that would save his own.

Curizan Warrior Series

The Curizans have a secret, kept even from their closest allies, but even they are not immune to the draw of a little known species from an isolated planet called Earth.

Marastin Dow Warriors Series

The Marastin Dow are reviled and feared for their ruthlessness, but not all want to live a life of murder. Some wait for just the right time to escape....

Sarafin Warriors Series

A hilariously ridiculous human family who happen to be quite formidable... and a secret hidden on Earth. The origin of the Sarafin species is more than it seems. Those cat-shifting aliens won't know what hit them!

Dragonlings of Valdier Novellas

The Valdier, Sarafin, and Curizan Lords had children who just cannot stop getting into trouble! There is nothing as cute or funny as magical, shapeshifting kids, and nothing as heartwarming as family.

Cosmos' Gateway Series

Cosmos created a portal between his lab and the warriors of Prime. Discover new worlds, new species, and outrageous adventures as secrets are unravelled and bridges are crossed.

The Alliance Series

When Earth received its first visitors from space, the planet was thrown into a panicked chaos. The Trivators came to bring Earth into the Alliance of Star Systems, but now they must take control to prevent the humans from destroying themselves. No one was prepared for how the humans will affect the Trivators, though, starting with a family of three sisters....

Lords of Kassis Series

It began with a random abduction and a stowaway, and yet, somehow, the Kassisans knew the humans were coming long before now. The fate of more than one world hangs in the balance, and time is not always linear....

Zion Warriors Series

Time travel, epic heroics, and love beyond measure. Sci-fi adventures with heart and soul, laughter, and awe-inspiring discovery...

Paranormal / Fantasy / Romance

Magic, New Mexico Series

Within New Mexico is a small town named Magic, an… unusual town, to say the least. With no beginning and no end, spanning genres, authors, and universes, hilarity and drama combine to keep you on the edge of your seat!

Spirit Pass Series

There is a physical connection between two times. Follow the stories of those who travel back and forth. These westerns are as wild as they come!

Second Chance Series

Stand-alone worlds featuring a woman who remembers her own death. Fiery and mysterious, these books will steal your heart.

More Than Human Series

Long ago there was a war on Earth between shifters and humans. Humans lost, and today they know they will become extinct if something is not done....

The Fairy Tale Series

A twist on your favorite fairy tales!

A Seven Kingdoms Tale

Long ago, a strange entity came to the Seven Kingdoms to conquer and feed on their life force. It found a host, and she battled it within her body for centuries while destruction and devastation surrounded her. Our story begins when the end is near, and a portal is opened....

Epic Science Fiction / Action Adventure

Project Gliese 581G Series

An international team leave Earth to investigate a mysterious object in our solar system that was clearly made by someone, someone who isn't from Earth. Discover new worlds and conflicts in a sci-fi adventure sure to become your favorite!

New Adult / Young Adult

Breaking Free Series

A journey that will challenge everything she has ever believed about herself as danger reveals itself in sudden, heart-stopping moments.

The Dust Series

Fragments of a comet hit Earth, and Dust wakes to discover the world as he knew it is gone. It isn't the only thing that has changed, though, so has Dust...

ABOUT THE AUTHOR

S.E. Smith is an *internationally acclaimed, New York Times* **and USA TODAY Bestselling** author of science fiction, romance, fantasy, paranormal, and contemporary works for adults, young adults, and children. She enjoys writing a wide variety of genres that pull her readers into worlds that take them away.

Printed in Great Britain
by Amazon